Cougar Surrender

MARISA CHENERY

CONTENTS

COUGAR HEAT

After four years of banishment from his cougar shifter family group, Taylor finds himself called home to take his rightful place. On the trip to Anchorage, he runs into some unexpected trouble with long legs and a body to die for. Suddenly, the long drive doesn't seem so bad.

Abandoned at a truck stop diner by her now ex-friend, Aspen seeks the help of an unwitting hottie when a trucker makes unwanted advances. Good thing the hunk is willing to act as her boyfriend, and to plant a panty-melting kiss on her lips to drive the point home. As things heat up between them, she's determined to see how far they can take the attraction.

Having taken on the responsibility of heir apparent, Taylor settles into his family group. Though dating a human is frowned upon, Taylor refuses to lose Aspen. The pleasure he finds in her arms isn't something he's willing to turn his back on.

CHAPTER ONE

Taylor looked at the three men who sat with him at a table inside one of Juneau's coffee shops. He'd thought he'd never see their faces again. Not after being kicked out of his cougar shifter family group. He'd been banished, never to be welcomed home. Or, at least, that was what he'd been led to believe four years ago.

He looked at his younger brother, Blaise. There was only a year between them in age. "How did you know where to find me? And how did you get my cell phone number?"

Blaise shrugged. "You'd be amazed at what you can find on the Internet as long as you know how to go about it. Luckily, I have a friend who does."

Taylor shook his head. It figured his brother would have the means to track him down. Blaise always "knew" someone who could fix whatever problem he had. Taylor looked at Blaise. His brother hadn't changed over the years Taylor had been gone. They had the same tawny-blond hair, though Taylor's was shaggier, and Blaise's was on the long side, but more controlled. They also had the same light brown eyes that verged on gold, a mark of a cougar shifter.

He looked at the two other men at the table, his cousins, Grady and Jase. "You two decided to just tag along?"

Jase smiled and nodded. "Of course. We're here to give Blaise support, and to make sure you don't brush him off."

Grady nodded, as well.

Taylor took a sip of coffee, then sat back in his chair. "All right. Why did you come looking for me when you know you're supposed to act as if I no longer exist?"

Blaise met his gaze. "You're aren't banished anymore."

He snorted. "Really? I'm supposed to take your word for it? There's no overturning banishment."

"Maybe not in the past, but yours has been. It was Father who made that decision."

Taylor schooled his features not to show any of the emotions he felt. The mention of his father had all the old anger he'd thought he'd left far behind rising to the surface. As the head of their family group, his dad was the one who had made the ultimate decision to banish Taylor and send him on his way. All because Taylor had gotten into a fight with a werewolf who had attacked one of his human friends. It wasn't as if he'd set out to kill him while in cougar form, risking the close-guarded secret of what he was to the outside world.

As the oldest son, before he'd been kicked out of his family, he'd been in line to take his father's place once he died. "Why would he do that?" Taylor asked in a low voice.

"He's dying."

It took Taylor a few seconds to get over that bit of news and regain his composure before he spoke again. "I'm sorry to hear that. I hope you didn't come all this way just to tell me. You could have called or even sent a text."

Blaise scowled. "You really don't care that our father is

close to dying?"

"What do you expect? The man turned his back on me, not caring what happened as long as I stayed away."

"You know he had no other choice. You broke one of the laws of our kind. His leadership would have been brought into question if he hadn't done what had to be done."

"Yeah, well, that makes me feel so much better about it all. I can now overlook the fact he kicked me out in the middle of fucking winter with nowhere to live and no clue where I would end up. It wasn't as if he gave me any money to start a new life, either. With no job and used to earning my living working with the family, I wasn't prepared for anything."

"You don't look the worse for wear."

Taylor glared at his brother, his anger no longer at a low simmer. "You have no idea what I went through before I ended up where I am now. I thank my lucky stars that Meadow — the woman who gave me a job and a place to live — took me on to look after her place. Since my banishment, I count her as my only family."

"She no longer needs to be," Grady said. "You have to come home."

He turned his attention to his cousin. "The hell I do. I like the life I have. I don't have to answer to anyone but myself. I sure as shit don't have to worry about archaic laws that say we have to remain hidden from humans and werewolves."

"You have a responsibility to the family," Jase said.

Taylor shook his head. "Haven't you been listening? That ended when my father banished me. I'm no longer in line to take over."

Blaise sighed. "That's changed. Father wanted me to take his place, and I refused. You were always better suited for the position than I'll ever be. It didn't take much for me to convince Dad that you were still the one up for it."

He met his brother's gaze. "That's too bad. I don't want it anymore. So that means you'll have to take it, Blaise, or some other member of the family will have to."

Blaise slammed his fist on the table, drawing the stares of the humans around them. His brother took a deep breath, then said in a quiet tone, "This is not something you can just say no to. There is no one else. After Dad decided you were once more in line to take his place, no one else in the family would dare to step up."

Taylor cursed under his breath. Once the head of the family made a decree, it was final. That was why Taylor couldn't understand why his banishment had been overturned. It put him in a spot he didn't want to be. Blaise was right. Taylor couldn't tell them to fuck off and go on as if they'd never spoken to him. Now that he'd been found, others would come and take him to Anchorage where his family lived, by force if necessary.

Having lived in close proximity to the werewolf sentinels, the very first werewolves, Taylor preferred the wolves over the company of his kind. Edensaw, the alpha of the sentinels, didn't rule over his wolf brothers with an iron fist. He also didn't think humans needed to be kept in the dark about them at all costs. Christ, all the wolf brothers' mates had been human—or mortals, as they called them—before being turned.

A cougar shifter having a human as a mate was unheard of. Taylor had no idea what would happen if a male or female of his kind ended up with one. That human sure as hell wouldn't be welcomed with open arms like the Sentinels' mates.

His brother and cousins wore determined expressions. They weren't willing to let him walk away. He had a feeling they were more than ready to drag him to Anchorage, no matter how he felt about it.

"You're not going to walk away and leave me to live

my life the way I want," Taylor said as a statement rather than a question. He already knew the answer.

"We can't," Blaise replied. "Father wants you back home...before the end."

"He's that bad?"

His brother nodded. "Yes."

"How? He isn't close to his time."

They weren't as long-lived as modern-day werewolves who could reach the age of three thousand, but they lived longer than humans. A cougar shifter's life didn't end until he or she was close to two hundred years old. His father was only sixty-five.

"Caleb doesn't know. It's some kind of illness he's never seen before. It makes Father grow weaker almost by the day, and nothing Caleb does counteracts it. Father is wasting away before our eyes."

Caleb was another cousin and a doctor. Taylor scowled. An illness? Their kind never got sick. Ever. Human ailments like cancer and other diseases of that nature didn't affect them, either. "How can he be ill to the point of dying? It shouldn't be possible."

"We don't know. We just know he is and has been for over six months now. So, you'll come home with us?"

Taylor sighed. "You really haven't left me much choice."

Jase smiled as he placed his now empty coffee cup on the table. "Let's go to your place, pack up your stuff, and be on our way home. We should be able to catch a flight later this evening."

He held up his hand. "I never said I'd go with you right now. You three can fly to Anchorage. I'll drive."

"Why would you want to do that?" Grady asked. "It takes a little over twenty-one hours to drive from Juneau to Anchorage. That's if you don't include any rest breaks."

"I don't mind."

Blaise shook his head. "You might not, but we do."

Taylor sat up straighter. "What? Are you afraid I won't show up if you let me do this?"

"I can't say the thought hasn't crossed my mind."

"Well, you can stop thinking that way. I go back on my terms, which means all three of you will fly home and I'll arrive by myself. It's not as if I can up and leave where I live now on such short notice. Plus, I have my things to pack. I promise I'll be on the road sometime tomorrow. You either accept it or don't expect me at all."

His brother slowly nodded. "Fine. Have it your way. If it were me, I wouldn't want to make that long-ass drive."

"Then it's a good thing it isn't you," Taylor said as he pushed back his chair and stood. "I'll see you in Anchorage in a day or so."

He turned and walked out of the coffee shop without a backward glance at his brother and cousins. Taylor continued down the sidewalk to where he'd parked his pickup truck. He shook his head as he thought over the conversation he'd had with Blaise, Grady, and Jase. When he'd first been banished, he would have been more than happy to be welcomed back into his family group. Now, not so much. He was used to being on his own and liked it. Since he was content with the way his life was, of course someone had to come along and fuck it up for him.

* * * *

The next day, Taylor was on the road headed for Anchorage as promised. Leaving Meadow behind had not been a thrill ride for him. She hadn't taken the news of his departure very well. He was just glad she had her mate, Durlach, to lean on. She wouldn't be alone and, as part of the Sentinels' werewolf pack, she had more than enough family to look after her, which was one of the reasons he found himself able to walk away. Meadow was like a sister to him.

He'd spent the rest of the day after leaving his brother and cousins packing up his belongings and preparing for the long drive to Anchorage. While he'd done that, Taylor had found himself thinking of what he would be getting himself into.

At one time, he'd been prepared to eventually take his father's place as the head of their family group. He'd been groomed for it since he was old enough to remember. It was something he'd taken pride in and had strived to learn all he could from his father so one day he'd be just as capable. That included Taylor following all the outdated rules that came with the life he'd been born into.

He hadn't dated humans and definitely hadn't gone near any female werewolves. He'd stuck with his own kind, though none of the women he'd slept with had ended up being his mate. Unlike werewolves, a male cougar shifter couldn't tell if one of the opposite sex was his mate with a single sniff of her scent. It took more than that.

Each male, once he hit adolescence, was given a cougar-head pendant hung on a gold necklace that was made with a bit of magic embedded inside. If a female was meant to be his mate, the ruby eyes in the male cougar's pendant would glow. That occurred once the male had accepted the female as his, even if only he knew it subconsciously, which caused an increase in his testosterone level. It wasn't something that took place with a first meeting or even the first time the couple had sex. It sometimes took months before the eyes revealed the truth. Once it happened, it was the female's decision to accept the necklace as hers, which would create the mating bond, joining the mated pair's souls.

If the female didn't take the necklace after the eyes glowed, the male ended up walking a fine line. He'd be unable to eat or sleep, basically only able to think about having sex with his newfound mate to hopefully tie her

8

emotionally closer with each bout of lovemaking.

After being banished, Taylor had taken off his necklace. Being kicked out of his family meant he had no chance of finding a female cougar shifter who would want him. Plus, it was part of the old life he'd left behind. It now, once again, graced his neck. It would be expected of him.

Taylor had put more than a few miles between him and Juneau when he decided to take a break. He'd been driving for hours and his butt felt as if it was asleep. He pulled off the highway into the parking lot of a truck-stop diner. A cup of coffee was in order. He planned to drive for as long as he could, then spend the night in a motel. He was in no hurry to get to Anchorage.

He sat in a booth that was set against the large glass window, facing the parking lot. Taylor ordered a cup of coffee and a burger, knowing he wouldn't be stopping to eat again for quite some time.

He was just finishing his food when he happened to look outside. A woman walked across the lot, carrying a suitcase. Taylor couldn't help noticing how pretty she was. He took a sip of coffee as he took in her long, light brown hair that fell over her shoulders. Her body was slim. His gaze dropped to her shapely ass that was hugged by a pair of skinny jeans. Before his brother and cousins' visit, Taylor would have considered going after the woman to see if she'd be interested in a one-night stand. That wasn't an option today.

Taylor pulled his gaze from the window and drained the rest of his coffee before signaling to his waitress that he wanted his bill. He'd better get back on the road. He had a lot more miles to go before he called it a day and found a motel.

* * * *

Aspen angrily watched the back of her friend's car

disappear out of the diner's parking lot and merge with the traffic on the highway. Cindy, whom she'd thought was a really good friend, had just abandoned her in the middle of nowhere with no way of making it home.

They'd been in Skagway for the summer, working in the tourist trade. During the warm months, since its port was a popular stop for cruise ships, there were more jobs that needed filling during that time. It had been Cindy's idea for both of them to look for work in the borough. In between positions, Aspen had thought it was a great idea.

The job aspect had worked out, but the trip back to Anchorage left her in desperate straits. Her so-called friend had turned on Aspen. Because of a man. Cindy had met a guy who worked on a cruise ship. He'd come into port in the middle of the summer and started a whirlwind romance with her friend. They'd only been together for a couple of days before he'd had to leave, but he and Cindy had talked all the time on the Internet.

Then he'd returned to Skagway two days before Aspen and Cindy were due to head home to Anchorage. He hadn't wanted Cindy to go and had arranged for her to work on the same cruise ship he did.

Aspen had been happy for her friend and had been all prepared to travel to Anchorage alone by bus. Then, the night before she was to leave, Cindy and her boyfriend had a big fight. Cindy decided to go home, after all.

They'd been well on their way when Cindy had gotten a call from her boyfriend, who managed to make up with her and have her, once again, ready to take the job on the cruise ship.

Aspen had tried everything to get Cindy to at least drive her to the closest bus station but, oh no, Cindy hadn't wanted to take the time to do that. With no care as to what Aspen would do, her traitor of a friend had dropped her off at the truck-stop diner before heading back to Skagway and then drove away without a backward glance.

So there Aspen was, alone and abandoned in the middle of the highway with no way of getting to the bus station. She didn't think she'd even be able to get a taxi to come out for her.

She picked up her extra-large suitcase and turned around to face the diner. She needed to find a ride. Surely there was someone who wasn't an axe murderer inside and wouldn't mind dropping her off at the bus station. It was either that or hitchhike, which wasn't something she felt comfortable doing.

"Are you needing some help?"

Aspen looked in the direction of one of the semis parked off to the side. A man who appeared about ten years older than her stood at the back of it, smiling. It wasn't exactly a friendly smile. More like one that said she was a morsel he'd like to eat. Considering he had a pot belly and needed suspenders to keep up his pants, she wasn't flattered, by any means.

She did her best not to make eye contact and shook her head. "I'm good."

"Are you sure? I couldn't help noticing the girl you arrived with just left you. From the way she was driving, I'd say she ain't coming back."

"I'm perfectly okay. Thanks for asking."

Aspen turned in the direction of the diner again and started walking. She heard the sound of the man's footsteps a short distance behind her but forced herself not to look over her shoulder. She didn't want to encourage him.

She'd made it almost across the lot to the diner's entrance when the man closed the distance between them. "I think you're not being truthful," he said behind her.

She spun around, not liking how near he was to her. There was no mistaking the look of lust in his eyes. Aspen tried not to gag when he eyed her up and down and licked his fleshy lips.

"How would you know that?"

"Well, I heard the argument you had with your friend as she got your suitcase out of the trunk of her car. You both had your voices raised. If you want, I can drive you in my semi." He looked her up and down again. "I wouldn't mind the company."

She and Cindy had been having a heated conversation as her friend had kicked her out of her car, but there was no way Aspen was going to let this idiot know she was stranded. He more than gave her the creeps.

"Thanks, but no thanks. Despite what you thought you heard, I'm meeting my boyfriend here." Aspen looked around the parking lot until her gaze landed on a black pickup truck parked off on its own. "He's already here. He must be in the diner. I'll wait for him at his pickup."

Aspen turned in the direction of the truck and hoped like hell it wasn't a woman who owned it. To her, the pickup looked as if it belonged to a guy and that it was used as a working vehicle.

The man followed her. "Why aren't you going into the diner to meet him then?"

"I told him I'd be at his pickup when I arrived. Since I'm on time, he should be out in a minute or so."

At the passenger side of the truck, the he reached out and grabbed her arm, turning her to face him. "Come on, admit you're alone. There's no one waiting for you."

Aspen tried to break free of his hold, but he held her too tight. "Let go of me," she said in a loud voice, fear slowly rising to the surface.

"What the hell is going on here?"

She looked to her right. A drop-dead-gorgeous man was a short distance away, walking toward them. Aspen sent up a silent prayer that the hunk would play along before she said, "Hi, honey. I told you I wouldn't be late." She looked at the him holding her arm. "There's my boyfriend now."

12

She yanked out of his grasp and quickly walked to the hunk. Once she stood in front of him, Aspen went on her tiptoes and kissed him. She only thought to give him a quick peck on the mouth, but it turned into a lot more than that when the man put his arms around her waist and tugged Aspen against his chest. He proceeded to kiss her thoroughly, his tongue pushing between her lips and exploring her mouth.

It only lasted all of five seconds, but it was enough to have a jolt of desire shooting through her. Once the hunk ended the kiss, she could only stare at him as her heart beat rapidly against her ribs.

"Babe, tell me what's going on here," the he said in a deep voice that made her toes curl.

It took Aspen a few seconds to get her brain functioning enough to understand what he'd asked. "He thought I lied when I said I was meeting you here. He saw Cindy drop me off and figured she'd left me here against my will."

The hunk took her suitcase and put his free arm around her shoulders, turning her so she was tucked against his side. His body was hard with muscles.

"You were harassing my girlfriend?" he asked the man.

The guy shook his head. "It's just a misunderstanding. I thought only to offer her a ride. I didn't mean anything by it." He appeared to be scared shitless, which didn't surprise her since the hunk had to be around six-foot-two and was all solid muscle.

"Good, because if it was more than that, I'd have to set you straight." He looked at her. "Let's go. It's getting late, and we have a lot of miles to go before we can stop for the night."

Aspen let out a silent sigh of relief that he was willing to play along and nodded. He turned her toward the pickup and unlocked the passenger door for her. She got inside the cab and then shut herself in as he went around to the bed to put her suitcase there before getting into the driver's side.

As they drove out of the diner's parking lot and then merged with the highway traffic, Aspen looked out the cab's back window to see the man watched their departure. There was no question in her mind that he wouldn't have stopped harassing her if the hunk hadn't come along. Just another reason Cindy was no longer considered a friend.

CHAPTER TWO

Taylor glanced at the woman who sat next to him in the cab of his pickup. She was the same one who had caught his eye back at the diner. Up close, she was even prettier. He now knew her eyes were blue-gray and, at around five-foot-five, she fit perfectly under his arm.

He'd come out of the diner to see her being harassed near his vehicle by an asshole who couldn't keep his hands to himself. Taylor, of course, had to intervene. He'd even been willing to play his part as her "boyfriend" when she'd called him "honey," but he hadn't expected the kiss. Her lips pressed to his, he'd found himself unable to pass up getting a taste of her. At least she hadn't minded. Had, in fact, seemed to enjoy it, if he went by the scent of desire that had rolled off her.

"Ah...thanks for back there," she said as she looked at him. "I don't think that guy would have left me alone if not for you. I'm Aspen."

He shot her a quick smile before focusing back on the road. "Taylor. No problem. He'd gone too far. You don't have to worry. I'm not like that."

"Nice to meet you, Taylor. I have to say you don't give off the same creepy vibes he did. If you don't mind, can you drop me off at the bus station? Cindy, my friend, who is no longer one, *did* abandon me back at the diner."

"Sure, I can do that."

"Thanks. Sorry about that whole *you being my boyfriend* and the kiss. I didn't know what else to do to get rid of him."

Taylor chuckled. "Don't apologize, especially for the kiss. That's one thing I'll never complain about—being kissed by a pretty woman."

A glance showed her cheeks had taken on a nice shade of pink. "I can't say it was any hardship for me to do it."

"Where are you headed?"

"Anchorage. What about you?"

"The same place. I've been living in Juneau for the last few years, but all my family is in Anchorage. It's time I moved back."

Aspen nodded. "I was working all summer in Skagway. I'm ready to go home. I miss seeing my mom and dad."

"Any siblings?"

"An older sister. She's quite a bit older than me...eight years. I was a surprise for my parents."

"I have a younger brother. There's only a year between us."

Taylor took the exit off the highway and headed for the nearest bus station he knew. The trip wasn't long enough for him to learn all that much about Aspen, but with them living in the same city, it was an opportunity for him to ask her out. Even though she was human, he wanted to get to know her better. He doubted she was the kind of woman who would be interested in a one-night stand. He'd had enough of them to know when the opposite sex was only looking for a good time with no strings attached. Aspen didn't seem to be like that. They'd shared a kiss, and she'd apologized for it.

At the bus station, Taylor pulled into a parking space and shut off the engine. He turned in his seat to face Aspen. "I'll stay with you until you catch your bus."

She shook her head. "You don't have to do that. I don't want to hold you up. You have a long drive still before you reach Anchorage."

"I'm not ready to say goodbye to you yet. Plus, I'd feel better if I saw you safely on the bus." He smiled. "Maybe before you do you'll give me your phone number so I can call you and set up a date."

Aspen smiled, making her whole face light up. "I'd like that."

"Good. Now let's see about getting you a ticket."

Taylor got out of the truck and went to the back to collect her suitcase. He fell into step beside her as they walked to the station's main building. Once inside, he let Aspen take the lead. She headed straight for the wicket. There were only two people ahead of her.

Once it was her turn, Aspen asked for a ticket for the next available bus to Anchorage. It turned out she'd missed the last one of the day by about ten minutes. She'd have to wait until early the next morning. Seeing the crestfallen expression she wore, Taylor thanked the woman at the wicket and pulled Aspen off to the side.

"Before you buy your ticket, I want you to consider something first," he said.

"Okay."

"I know you really don't know me, but I can assure you, you'll be safe in my company. Why don't you ride to Anchorage with me? We're both going there. That way you won't have to spend the night in the bus station, which I'm not fond of. I'll even let you take a picture of me with your cell phone and you can send it to your parents so they'll know who you're with. Plus, I have some very good friends back in Juneau who I can call who would be happy to vouch for me not being a murderer or anything."

Aspen's gaze searched Taylor's face while she appeared to think over what he'd suggested. She asked, "You'd really let me take your picture?"

"Of course. If it will make you feel safer with me, then go right ahead."

"Okay." She took her cell phone from her purse and got him to smile before she took the picture. Instead of sending a text, Aspen put the cell away.

"Aren't you going to send it to your parents?"

She smiled. "No. I just wanted it so I can look at it later. I wasn't going to pass that up."

Taylor laughed. "I would have gladly let you take my picture, anyway. So, what's your answer? Do you want to make the trip to Anchorage with me?"

"Yes. If you had wanted to hurt me, you could have done that right after we left the diner. I don't think I'll be in any danger with you. Plus, you did save me from the jerk at the truck stop."

"Great. Let's get on the road again."

He guided Aspen out of the building and to the parking lot. That she'd agreed to stay with him pleased Taylor more than it should. With what was going on with his family group, he really had no business getting closer to a human female, but the thought of leaving her behind hadn't sat well with him. He was drawn to Aspen, whether it was a good thing or not.

Once again inside his truck and on the highway, he said, "You should at least let someone know about the change in your plans. What if your friend calls your parents looking for you and you're not there yet? I'm going to stop at a motel for the night. I'm not going to take the chance of falling asleep at the wheel."

"I guess you're right. Cindy and I had planned to drive right until late, then stop for the night. The delay at the diner and the bus station will have me not showing up on time. My parents would worry. I'm going to be living in the apartment above their garage."

Out of the corner of his eye, Taylor watched Aspen take her cell out of her purse again and quickly type out a text message. It wasn't too long before her phone *binged* with a reply. She sent two more texts before she put away her cell.

"Done," she said. "Just so you know, I told them you were someone I met in Skagway, and that you were nice enough to offer me a ride when Cindy bailed on me. My mom is a bit of a worrywart. If I'd told her how I actually met you, and that I accepted a ride, she'd be up all night, pacing."

"I can understand why she'd worry." Silence fell between them before Taylor started the conversation again. "So, where would you like to go out on our date?"

Aspen chuckled. "You move fast, don't you?"

"Well, I do have your undivided attention right now. I figured we can plan it all out on the drive."

"That's very proactive of you."

"Nothing wrong with being organized."

"I guess not. Since you're asking me out on a date, I'm figuring you didn't leave a girlfriend behind in Juneau."

"No. I haven't had one in a few years. I take it you don't have a boyfriend."

"I find it hard to believe a man as good-looking as you has stayed single for so long. Correct, I have no boyfriend. I was too busy working all summer. Plus, I hadn't planned to stay beyond that in Skagway. Unlike my former friend, I'm not into long-distance relationships. As far as I'm concerned, they rarely work out."

Taylor glanced at Aspen and let out a short laugh. "I'll have to take your word on that. I've never had one. It's a good thing we'll both be living in the same city."

"It does make it easier. If you don't mind me asking, why did you decide to make the move from Juneau to

Anchorage?"

"I don't mind. My father's very sick. He's in a bad enough way my family wants me to come home."

"Sorry to hear about your dad. Here I was holding you up."

"It's okay. Seriously. I'm not all that overjoyed to be making this trip, anyway. I had a falling out with my family four years ago. Yesterday was the first time I'd actually spoken to one of my relatives since then. If I'd had my way, I'd still be in Juneau. I had to say goodbye to some very good friends."

"Families can be a pain in the butt at times. I'm not very close with my sister. Her being so much older than me, she still likes to think of me as her bratty little sibling. Even though I'm twenty-seven, she can't treat me like an adult. It drives me crazy."

"I can see that would be annoying."

Now that their conversation was moving along smoothly, Taylor was pleased Aspen had no problem keeping it going. He found her to be good company. The miles and hours passed without him realizing it. If he'd been alone, he would have more than likely spent the time dreading his first meeting with his father.

It was full dark and well into the night before Taylor decided he'd had enough of driving. He turned off the highway and found the closest motel. He parked the truck in front of the manager's office.

He undid his seatbelt and turned to look at Aspen. "Are you okay with getting your own room?"

She gave him a sheepish look. "Would you mind sharing one with two beds? I'd feel more comfortable if I wasn't alone. I'll pay for half of it."

"Are you sure that's what you want to do? I thought you'd want privacy."

Aspen nodded. "After the incident at the truck stop, I'll feel safer."

If that was what she wanted, Taylor had no problem sharing a room with her. He didn't say anything but wondered if Aspen was worried that if they weren't staying together he'd leave her behind in the morning. She'd already had one person abandon her out in the middle of nowhere with no way of getting home.

"Then it's a room with two double beds. You can wait here. I'll go in and book it."

As Taylor got out of the pickup, he smiled to himself. So far, his trip home had turned out to be surprising in a good way. Having spent hours with Aspen, talking and getting to know her, he was more attracted to her than when he'd first seen her at the truck stop. Not only was she beautiful, she had a great personality. For the first time in his life, he was seriously considering having a relationship with a human female.

* * * *

Aspen looked at the door to the manager's office. It had only been a minute since Taylor had gone inside to book them a room. She was sure he'd be a few more yet.

She silently sighed at the prospect of spending the night with Taylor. He was totally gorgeous. Even though Aspen wasn't letting it show on the outside, on the inside, she was drooling all over him. She'd screamed with glee to herself when he'd asked her out on a date. Her luck had definitely turned for the better after meeting him. Not only was he a hunk, he was a great guy.

How could she resist him when he'd come to her rescue the way he had? There had been a few other people in the parking lot when the jerk had accosted her, but Taylor had been the only one to step up and chase him off for her. That put him in her good book.

Aspen's stomach growled, reminding her it had been a long time since she'd last eaten. She looked out the pickup's window. There was a café next to the motel. She didn't think Taylor would mind getting some food. The last time he'd had anything had to have been back at the diner. That had been hours ago.

She caught movement out of the corner of her eye and turned her head to watch Taylor stride to the driver's side, then get in. She smiled. "You booked the room okay?"

He started the truck. "Yeah. We're good to go." Taylor backed up, then drove the short distance to the parking spot in front of their room.

After getting out of the pickup, Taylor unlocked the room's door. Aspen stepped inside and looked around. It was nothing special. Just the typical motel room found anywhere. There were two double beds with a small table between them, which had a lamp, telephone, and digital clock sitting on it. The only other thing in the room was an old-model television. No LED flat screen there.

"It's not great, but it should do for the one night," Taylor said.

She turned to look at him and chuckled. "It's a motel, after all. I saw there was a café. I don't know about you, but I'm hungry. Feel like going there and getting something to eat?"

"Sure. I'll bring the bags in, then we can go."

Taylor turned and headed toward the door. Aspen nibbled her bottom lip as she gazed at his muscled ass. His jeans showed it off perfectly. Maybe they could get a head start on their date. He hadn't tried to touch her again, but she felt it was because he wanted her to feel comfortable around him. If she had her way, she'd be more than happy to be in his arms, maybe getting a kiss or two or three or ten.

He came back not even a minute later, carrying her large suitcase and one for him. Taylor put hers on the floor at the end of one of the beds. "I still have some boxes in the pickup, but I don't want to bring them in here. I'll cover them with a tarp."

Aspen nodded, and he walked out again. She went and stood in front of the single window. It was pretty dark out there, and the lighting in the lot left much to be desired. Taylor appeared not to have any problem seeing as he got inside the bed of the pickup and set to work covering what was inside. He bent over with his ass in her direction. Aspen wondered what he would do if she went out there and gave it a good squeeze.

Taylor straightened and turned toward her as if he'd sensed her watching him. His gaze met hers. Aspen sucked in a sharp breath. The way he looked at her made her heart beat faster and her blood heat. Even in the dim light, she couldn't miss how he seemed to eat her up with his gaze. It made her hungry, and not for food.

He jumped out of the bed of the truck and the spell was broken. Aspen quickly pulled herself together. Even though she wanted nothing more than for Taylor to kiss her again, she really needed to get some food into her.

Taylor stopped just inside the doorway. "All set."

Aspen nodded. She walked to one of the beds and grabbed her purse where she'd tossed it earlier. "Okay."

After locking the room door, Taylor and Aspen made the short walk to the café. Since it was well past what would be considered the dinner rush, if the place had one, only a few tables were taken. They were seated and then left alone to look over the menu.

It didn't take Aspen long to decide what she wanted. Surprisingly, everything looked delicious. Some of the items she wouldn't have thought to find at a place that was practically out in the middle of nowhere.

She looked up to find Taylor intently watching her. Once again, her body reacted to his stare. Aspen licked her lips, almost able to feel what it would be like to have his claiming hers. His gaze lowered to her mouth, desire showing starkly in his eyes.

A wave of arousal shot through her, her pussy clenching with need. She'd told Taylor she hadn't been with anyone all summer, but it had been longer than that. Even before leaving Anchorage to work in Skagway, she'd been single. Six months before that, she'd split with her long-term boyfriend. They'd been together for two years. The breakup had been mutual. The relationship hadn't been going anywhere, and both of them had known it.

Now, having Taylor look at her with such hunger, her long-neglected body reminded her how much time had actually passed since she'd had sex with a man. She needed to get out of her slump. One mostly caused by her. After her past relationship had ended, she hadn't been ready to be with someone new. With Taylor, that was no longer the case. She was more than willing to see how far things would go with him.

Aspen cleared her throat. "I'm ready to order. How about you?"

Taylor nodded. "I've decided. Just so you know, this is my treat."

"Then I guess we should consider this our first date?"

"If you like. I promise our next one will be in a better place than this."

"I'm not complaining. At least the company is good."

The waitress came and took their order. After that, much of the meal seemed to pass in a blur. She ate the food that was placed in front of her, but her attention was more on Taylor than it. Her thoughts kept straying to what could possibly happen once they returned to the motel room. Arousal still rode her, making her body ache to be filled.

It didn't help that Taylor gave her heated looks from time to time as they spoke between mouthfuls of food. Each sizzling glance sent her desire to higher levels. By the time she had finished eating, there was only one thought on her mind—how soon could she get her hands on

Taylor's hot body.

He paid the bill, then stood at her side to help her out of her chair. He kept her hand in his, their fingers linked, as he silently walked her out of the café. Excitement coursed through her with each step that brought them closer to the room they'd be sharing for the night.

CHAPTER THREE

Taylor was so aroused he was surprised he could walk straight. His cock was hard and pressed against the front of his jeans. Luckily, it was dark out and there wasn't anyone around as he and Aspen headed to their motel room. There was no mistaking the state he was in.

So far, he didn't think Aspen had noticed. If she had, it wouldn't have bothered him. Actually, he wanted her to. During the entire meal, he'd only been able to smell the scent of her need. Her arousal was an ever-present sign of how ready she was to accept him into her body. More than a few times he'd had to hold back a purr when the scent of her desire became almost too much.

He unlocked the room door and then pushed it open wide to let Aspen step through before him. He followed her and closed them inside. She turned on the lamp on the small table between the two beds as he went to the single window and pulled the curtains closed.

Taylor turned to face Aspen. She sat on the end of one

of the beds, watching him. He crossed the distance between them until he stood directly in front of her.

Her head fell back as she looked up at him. "So, which bed do you want or…would you like to share?"

Aspen's gaze drifted down his body and landed squarely on the bulge in his pants. Taylor heard the sharp indrawn breath she took at seeing how aroused he was. He did nothing to hide it from her, stayed exactly where he was.

"Are you sure that's what you want?" he asked in a voice gruff with desire. "Because if I share that bed with you, we'll be doing more than sleeping. I already find you tempting."

She nodded. "I knew what would happen when I offered. You're not the only one who feels tempted."

Taylor took Aspen's hand and tugged her to her feet. "If we do this, I can't promise you anything. I've never been one for being in a lasting relationship, but I do want to see you again."

"That's better than one night and I never see you afterward."

"I know for sure I can give you more than that."

He bent his head and claimed her lips. A breathy sigh left Aspen as he slanted his mouth over hers for a tighter fit, his tongue pushing inside to taste her. It ramped up his desire. Taylor put his arms around her waist and hauled her closer so their bodies touched from chest to knee. She wrapped her arms around his neck, her fingers sinking into the back of his hair.

Now used to finding his pleasure in human women's arms, Taylor was well practiced in the art of keeping his cat side hidden. Unlike his werewolf friends, he didn't have to worry about his eyes taking on a muted glow once he became very aroused. The only thing that would give him away was the loud cat-sounding purrs that built inside him. Instead of allowing them free, he groaned.

Aspen held him tighter and rubbed against him. The scent of her desire increased. Taylor dropped his hands from her waist to her ass and cupped it to grind along her pussy. She moaned into his mouth, the fingers in his hair tightening on the strands.

Their kiss became more erotic with each second that passed. Soon, it wasn't enough. Taylor had to taste her skin, take her more-than-a-handful breasts in his hands and suck on her nipples. He wanted to strip her naked and learn every inch of her with his tongue.

He broke contact with her mouth and tugged her shirt over her head and off. Taylor reached behind Aspen and unhooked her bra. She pushed the straps down her arms before tossing it aside. She took hold of the bottom of his long-sleeved t-shirt and removed it.

Aspen ran the tip of her finger across his cougar-head pendant. "It's beautiful."

"Thanks." Taylor dragged his gaze over what he'd revealed of her. "So are you."

He lifted her off her feet and claimed her lips once more. She wrapped her legs around his waist and held on to the tops of his shoulders. Her tongue met his as he pushed inside her mouth.

Taylor climbed onto the bed with Aspen still in his arms. He lowered her to the mattress, following her down to stretch out on top of her. He rocked his hips into the V of her spread thighs as he covered one of her breasts with his hand. He plucked at her taut nipple, causing it to tighten even more. She arched her back, pressing closer to his palm.

He left her mouth and shifted to lie at her side. Taylor pressed a smattering of kisses across the top of Aspen's chest before changing direction to take a nipple into his mouth. He sucked on it, then gently bit down. She moaned, her hips lifting restlessly.

Taylor switched to her other breast and trailed his

fingers down her flat stomach. At the top of her jeans, he pushed the button undone before pulling the zipper down. He parted the material and ran a caressing hand down the front of her panties. The satin was smooth under his fingertips.

With Aspen's help, he took off her pants. Taylor raised himself on a bent arm and looked down at her. Her body was gorgeous, slim and curvy in all the right places. His cock jerked inside his jeans as he thought of what he'd reveal once he removed her panties. She'd be wet for him. The scent of her arousal wafted around him.

Aspen turned on her side to face him. "I think you have on entirely too many clothes."

She made short work of the fastenings on his pants and pushed them down past his hips, leaving his boxer-briefs in place. He shoved his jeans the rest of the way off and kicked them over the side of the bed.

"Is that better?" he asked in a husky voice.

She ran her hand along his chest and down his abs to the top of his underwear. She slipped a finger under the waistband and ran it from side to side. "Almost. We're definitely getting there."

Aspen hooked and tugged the front of his boxer-briefs down, freeing his cock. She circled the head of it, gathering the pre-cum that leaked from the slit before she traced the length of his shaft. Taylor couldn't stop himself from thrusting his hips toward her, his erection jerking.

He soon groaned with pleasure as she took him fully in her hand and pumped up and down. She squeezed him tight, using long strokes. More pre-cum leaked out of the head of his cock as his excitement grew. At the rate she was working him, he wouldn't be able to stand this for long. He didn't need to lose control and come before they'd even started. Also, unlike his werewolf friends, cougar shifters couldn't maintain an erection for hours at a time. Just like human males, they needed recovery time.

Taylor gently pulled out of Aspen's grasp. He finished removing his underwear, then focused on her, pushing her onto her back. "Now you're the one who has more clothes on."

He slid her panties off her hips and down her legs, using caressing strokes as he went. Her skin was soft to the touch. Taylor ran his hand along the inside of her thigh, not stopping until he encountered the wet opening to her body. He brushed a finger along it before he slid inside. Her inner muscles clamped around the digit as he stroked in and out.

Aspen moaned, her hips lifting to meet each of his thrusts. He looked at her to find she had her eyes closed and her bottom lip between her teeth. She was an erotic vision. One he wouldn't soon forget.

Unable to hold back any longer from possessing her, Taylor pulled his finger out of her pussy and shifted so he lay between her spread legs. He pressed the head of his cock against her slick opening and slowly pushed forward. The sensation of her inner walls closing around his shaft had him fighting for control. It hadn't been all that long since he'd last been with a woman but, for some reason with Aspen, he swore it'd been years. The urge to take her hard and fast until he came deep inside her was almost overwhelming.

Instead, he continued to thrust slowly into her. Once he was seated to the hilt, he stilled, savoring the feel of her pussy wrapped around his cock. Taylor pulled back until he was almost all the way out, then pushed inside, Aspen taking all of him again. She felt so damn good. As he continued to pump, the sounds of pleasure she made hyped his arousal even more.

Aspen gripped his biceps and lifted her legs to either side of his hips. She squeezed her inner muscles as she matched him stroke for stroke. Taylor could no longer keep the slow and steady pace he'd set. He thrust faster, harder, his climax building at the base of his spine. He groaned, but with the pleasure rioting through his body, it came out half as a purr. His ability to keep his cat side hidden slipped. He usually had no problem doing that.

Taylor was almost at the point of no return when Aspen let out a keening moan. Her pussy rhythmically clutched and released the entire length of his cock. It had his climax roaring to meet her. He pumped his hips faster as his orgasm overtook him. He spilled deep inside her, giving her everything he had.

After it was over, Taylor collapsed on top of Aspen. She wrapped her arms around his back and held him tight. They breathed hard. He turned his head and kissed the side of her neck. One time wasn't going to be enough. Being with Aspen was the best sex he could ever remember having. He definitely wasn't prepared to let her go once they arrived in Anchorage.

* * * *

The sound of an unfamiliar alarm clock going off made Aspen jerk awake. She lifted her head and looked around, at first not remembering where she was. It wasn't until her gaze landed on the man who lay next to her that it all clicked into place.

She rubbed her eyes as Taylor reached over and shut off the alarm. She stared at his naked chest once he turned onto his back. She'd touched every inch of his body during the night, had learned all the planes and angles of it. They'd made love three times. Aspen would have gone for another round, but Taylor had said they'd better get some sleep since he wanted to get an early start on the road in the morning. He wanted to push through to Anchorage with no long rest stops.

Her gaze landed on the cougar-head pendant he wore around his neck. During their lovemaking, it had come to rest on her skin more than once, and she swore it warmed against her. Though, it was possible it only retained Taylor's body heat. The man was a living, breathing furnace.

Taylor turned his head and gave her a smile. "Morning. Did you sleep okay?"

After a yawn, she nodded. "As can be expected in a motel room. The bed isn't all that comfortable and waking up this early sucks."

He chuckled. "The ache in my back can attest to the uncomfortable mattress. I know it's not much later than dawn, but if we want to get to Anchorage before it's really late, we should leave shortly."

"I know, but my body is still complaining about it."

Taylor rolled toward her and gave her a kiss. "Well, you'll have to tell that sexy body of yours it can sleep later. We need to get up. You can have the shower first."

"Or, to save time, we can take one together."

A flash of desire showed in Taylor's eyes before he shook his head. "Not going to happen. If I get you in there, I'll be doing all the things I still want to do to your body. We'll have to save that for another time."

That was something for her to look forward to then. "It was worth a shot. I won't take too long since you want to get going."

Aspen threw back the covers and walked naked to the bathroom. She looked over her shoulder at Taylor before she went inside. He lay in the bed with his hands under his head, his gaze on her. Seeing how the sheets over his hips were tented, he appeared to like what he saw. She gave a wistful sigh before she closed herself in the smaller room.

Once she had the shower at the temperature she wanted, Aspen stepped inside the bathtub and under the warm spray. Spending the night with Taylor was something she'd never regret. He was a generous lover with a body she wouldn't ever get sick of exploring. He put her last boyfriend to shame. She smiled as she thought how, if it hadn't been for Cindy abandoning her, Aspen never would have met Taylor. Her ex-friend had done her a favor in a roundabout way. It still didn't make what Cindy had done any better, but Taylor made up for some of it.

Aspen washed her body, feeling how she ached in intimate places in a good way. It had been too long since she'd had sex, but the soreness would quickly go away. She and Taylor had already planned to see each other tomorrow night. Today would be shot with the long drive and getting settled at home.

She finished her shower and then dried off with the motel's poor excuse for a towel. It was barely big enough to keep her covered as she walked out of the bathroom and headed for her suitcase to get her toothbrush.

"You can have the shower," she told Taylor. "Is it okay if I brush my teeth while you're in there?"

"No problem. Just don't flush the toilet on me."

"I promise not to do that."

She lifted her suitcase onto the bed as Taylor pushed the covers off him and slipped from under the sheets. Gloriously naked, he was a work of art with all his hard muscles. As if he sensed her staring, he turned to face her and let her look her fill. The grin he wore was crooked.

Aspen was more than tempted to close the distance between them and run her hands all over him but, before she could move, the sound of a cell phone going off reached her ears.

Taylor grabbed his phone off the small table next to the bed. "Hello? Blaise, why are you calling me so early...? I should arrive sometime this evening... No, you don't need to call again to see where I am. I'll get there when I get there. I said I'd come home, and I won't go back on my word. Bye." He disconnected the call and put his cell back where it had been.

"Someone checking up on you?" Aspen asked.

"Yeah, my brother. He wanted to make sure I was on my way to Anchorage."

"There was a chance you wouldn't go?"

"Blaise thinks there is. As you know, I've been estranged from my family for years now."

That was all the explanation Aspen got. Taylor walked past her and into the bathroom. By the time she'd collected her toothbrush and toothpaste, he was already in the shower.

Obviously, Taylor didn't want to talk about his family. She had no problem with that. They were still in the get-to-know-you stage, and she didn't want to push too hard. It did make her wonder what had caused the estrangement between him and his relatives, though. She couldn't picture herself being in that situation. At times, she had her differences with hers, but it never got so bad they stopped talking and seeing one another.

Aspen brushed her teeth, then returned to the main room to dress. She'd just finished and was combing her damp hair when Taylor stepped out of the bathroom with a towel wrapped around his waist. It didn't do much to cover him, either.

In the reflection of the mirror on the wall she stood in front of, she watched the towel get tossed away before Taylor took some clothes out of his suitcase. Aspen wouldn't have minded if he'd stayed naked all day, but she doubted he would go for that. A girl could dream, though.

Once they'd collected all their things and Taylor had put their cases into the bed of his pickup, he had Aspen get into the cab while he went to the manager's office to pay their bill. She'd offered to fund her share, but he'd turned her down flat and wouldn't take the money even when she'd tried to hand it to him.

The rest of the drive to Anchorage turned out to be uneventful. Aspen and Taylor used the hours to talk, learning more about each other. He was great company, and she figured with anyone else it could have driven her batty after a while. The drive out to Skagway at the beginning of the summer with Cindy had been torturous. Her ex-friend had done nothing but talk about herself and what she planned to do with all the money she hoped to make.

It was dusk by the time they drove through Anchorage's city limits. They'd only stopped briefly at a roadside diner to pick up some takeout and use the washroom. With Aspen's help, Taylor had eaten while driving.

She gave him directions to her parents' house once they were in the city proper. The closer they came to her home, the more she felt she'd miss him. Even though they'd only been together a little over twenty-four hours, it seemed longer than that. She really didn't want to say goodbye to him, which was ridiculous since she'd be seeing him the next evening.

Aspen did her best to hide how she felt after they pulled into her parents' driveway and Taylor put the truck into Park. He got out with her and took her suitcase from the bed.

"Thanks," she said. "I guess I'll see you tomorrow."

Taylor nodded. "I'll either call or text you sometime in the afternoon to tell you what time I'll come pick you up. I'm not sure what plans my family has for me yet, but I promise not to cancel on you if at all possible."

Aspen smiled. "Good, because I would hate it if you did. I'm looking forward to seeing you again."

He placed her suitcase by their feet and then took her into his arms. His lips claimed hers in a heated kiss that had her wishing he didn't have to go. Her apartment above her parents' garage was just in front of them. It would have been so easy to invite him up and continue where their kiss would take them.

Too soon for her liking, Taylor lifted his head and smiled. "I look forward to seeing you tomorrow, as well." He dropped his arms from around her waist and stepped back. "I better get going. Talk to you later, Aspen."

She picked up her suitcase and walked to the side of the driveway as Taylor climbed into his truck. He backed out onto the street before he waved as he drove away. Aspen sighed. God, he was a hunk and, the way it stood right now, he was all hers. She'd had to have done something right to land him.

Aspen lugged her suitcase to the front door of her parents' house and then walked inside. "Mom? Dad? I'm back."

Her mother came down the stairs and met her in the entranceway with a big hug. "I see you made it home all right. Was that Taylor?"

She shook her head. "You were spying on me from upstairs in your bedroom, weren't you? Yes, that was him."

"I didn't plan to. I happened to be up there when I heard his pickup pull into the driveway. I didn't want to interrupt, so I waited for you to come inside. I do have to say, Taylor looks nice."

Aspen laughed. "You mean you thought he was good-looking."

"All right, that's true. So, will you be seeing him again?"

"Yes, tomorrow evening. He's moved back to Anchorage, as well."

"That's good. It would have been hard on you if he stayed in Skagway while you're living here."

"It would have. That was mostly the reason Taylor decided to come back with me. Where's Dad?"

"He's on an emergency call. He should be home in a

couple of hours."

Her dad was a plumber and worked for himself. Even though he had a couple of employees, he still insisted on handling any emergency calls on his own.

"Well, I should get settled in, then have something to eat. Taylor and I only ate lunch since he didn't want to stop very often."

"Come on then. I'll let you into the apartment. I saved you some food from dinner."

"I still have my keys, Mom."

"I know. I did air the place out today since it's been shut up all summer, but I'm sure it's stuffy in there again. I also cleaned the apartment and stocked the fridge for you."

"You didn't have to do that."

"I didn't mind. I'm happy to have you home again. I missed you."

"I missed you and Dad too."

CHAPTER FOUR

After driving his pickup onto the short road on his family's property that led to the house, Taylor rolled his shoulders, trying to release the tension there that suddenly set in. He wasn't looking forward to this homecoming. He'd been on his own so long he would have a hard time settling back into his old life.

Arriving at his parents' home, Taylor parked in front of the four-car garage. He looked at the two-story, six-bedroom brick house that was attached to it. The last time he'd been inside was when his father had banished him. He dreaded setting foot in it again. It didn't feel like his home anymore. His was a small one-bedroom apartment above the stables at Meadow and Durlach's place.

Taylor took a deep breath and got out of the truck. It wasn't as if he could sit out there all night. He left his belongings in the bed of the pickup and walked to the front door. He stood there for a few seconds, not sure what to do at first. Should he walk right in or ring the doorbell? He decided on the latter.

It didn't take long before Blaise answered the door. His brother scowled when his gaze landed on Taylor. "What the hell are you doing ringing the bell? You live here."

"I don't yet. Not until I've moved my stuff in."

"There are already some of your things here. Mom kept your room the way you left it."

That was surprising to Taylor. Banishment meant an individual was permanently erased from their family group. Nothing was supposed to be left around as a reminder of them.

"How did Mom manage that? I would have thought Dad wouldn't have allowed it."

Blaise grabbed Taylor by the arm and hauled him over the threshold before he shut the door. "He tried to have your things removed, but dear old Mom turned into a spitting, snarling wildcat. She wouldn't let anyone near your room. Dad had to admit defeat, or he would've lost his mate. She wasn't happy with him banishing you and, to date, she's never let him live it down."

"If I were you, I wouldn't let Mom hear you call her old."

As if on cue, Taylor's mother rushed into the large cathedral-ceiling foyer. She rushed toward him with tears in her eyes, then threw herself into his arms, clutching him tight.

"I'm so glad you're home," she said with a sniffle. She stepped back. "Let me look at you."

Taylor smiled, realizing how much he'd missed her. They'd always been close. "Mom, I'm fine."

She shook her head. "I know, but I want to see for myself. You look different. Tougher and stronger."

"I've spent the last few years doing manual labor rather than sitting behind a desk."

His mom wiped tears from her eyes. "You're going to tell me everything that has happened to you, but not right now. You should see your father."

Taylor dreaded that meeting. He'd hoped to avoid it as long as he could. "Shouldn't I unpack my truck first?"

His mom looped her arm through his and walked him toward the wide, curved stairway that led upstairs. "He was adamant he see you right after you arrived. He's not doing that well."

He walked up the steps with his mother still at his side. "Caleb can't help him?"

"He's confused by your father's illness, as are the rest of us. It shouldn't be like this."

Outside his parents' bedroom doors, his mom tapped on one, then opened both of them. She left Taylor's side and walked to the king-size bed. He slowly followed, his gaze not leaving the man who lay stretched out on it.

At first, he didn't think it was his father. The male had always been so imposing-looking. The one on the bed was far from it. His dad was pale and, judging from the gauntness of his face, appeared to have a lost a lot of weight. Too much of it.

Taylor stared at his father. The other male met his gaze but didn't say anything. Taylor wasn't going to be the first to break the ice. The relationship he'd had with his dad before the banishment hadn't been a loving one. He'd been treated as what he was — the oldest son who would one day take over the family business and step into the role as head of their family group. Instead of doing father-and-son things, he'd been instructed on the ways of running a multinational company.

"Taylor," his dad finally said in a weak voice.

"Dad."

"You came."

"Well, it wasn't as if I was given much choice, though I can't help but wonder why since I was banished." Taylor couldn't keep some of the hurt and anger that hadn't diminished over the years out of his words.

"Your family needs you."

"The day I was kicked out, I was told I no longer had any."

There was no remorse in his father's eyes as he continued to look at him. "By the laws of our kind, there wasn't anything else I could have done. When you fought that werewolf and killed him in your cougar form, you risked us all. Our secrecy is too hard-earned."

"Then, by those same laws, I shouldn't be here. Nor should I be considered the next in line for leading our family."

"There was no one else. Blaise wouldn't take the position."

"I do have cousins who could have."

Some of the domineering father Taylor remembered rose to the surface in his dad's eyes. "It has always been our line of the family who has taken that role for generations. It will remain so."

Taylor had to grind his teeth to stop himself from telling his father how he really felt about all this. His dad hadn't changed. He was still as highhanded as always, thinking their part of the family tree was better than the others'.

"What if I don't want it? Will I be sent away again?"

His father pushed himself up as his mother quickly put some pillows behind him. "You can't refuse. You've been groomed for it since the day you were old enough to understand what was expected of you." His dad had a coughing fit that racked his body, leaving him gasping and weak.

"I think that's enough for now," his mom said, stepping in when things became heated between him and his dad, as usual. "You two can continue this discussion later. Taylor needs to settle in, and you," she looked at her mate, "need to rest."

Taylor was more than happy to get the hell out of there, but before he could turn and walk away, his dad said,

"Your banishment has been overturned. You will fulfill your family obligations."

His temper heating, Taylor answered, "Whatever." Then turned and stalked out of the room.

He made it as far as the top of the stairs before his mother caught up with him. She grabbed his arm to stop his forward movement. "Try not to let him upset you. He's worried about what will happen if he..." She shook her head. "I can't say it, but you know what I mean."

Taylor looked down the hallway at the now-closed master bedroom doors. "Aren't you afraid he'll hear you telling me this?" All cougar shifters had sensitive hearing, along with sight and taste.

"He's asleep. Something he does more and more of lately."

He met his mom's gaze. "I don't know if I can do what he wants. I'm not the same person I was back then."

His mother gave him a sad look and caressed his cheek. "I know. I can tell. You will do it because I'm the one asking you now. If your father does...leave us, I'll need you. Only you know how to run the company as well as him."

"You mean used to know. It has been a few years since I've been involved in it."

"Your father has made arrangements to have you brought up to speed. Please, Taylor, do it for me. I don't want to lose you again."

He cursed to himself. If it had been anyone else, he would have no problem telling them no. His mom was the only one he couldn't refuse. She was already under enough stress with the thought of her mate dying. She didn't need him to add to it by walking away. No matter how much he wanted to.

Taylor tugged her into his arms. "Fine. You win. I'll stay and take on the damn position if it comes down to that. I'll start back at the company, though stuck behind a desk for hours at a time in the corporate world no longer holds any appeal."

His mother stepped out of his embrace and smiled. "Thank you. It means so much to me."

"I know, Mom. I should unload my truck." He'd only taken one step when she stopped him again.

"Oh, before I forget, your father has had it arranged for the entire family group to come together tomorrow night to be shown you have once more taken your place."

"Tomorrow night? Is it necessary to be so soon?"

"Your father will have to put in an appearance to make it all official. He's afraid he won't be strong enough if we hold it off any longer than that. Once it's done, no one will be able to dispute your claim."

"All right. I'm going to unload my pickup, then settle in."

"Okay. We can talk more later."

Taylor nodded, then continued on down the stairs. Now he had to call Aspen and tell her he had to cancel their date for tomorrow night. There was no way he could bring her to this family gathering. As a human, she'd stick out like a sore thumb. Questions would be raised as to why she was with him. If she were a cougar shifter, no one would bat an eye.

He headed outside to his truck. Already his father interfered with his life. Taylor would call Aspen and set up another date with her. He wouldn't cancel that one, no matter what his dad had planned for him. Taylor wasn't going to let Aspen go because she was human and wouldn't fit in with his family. He would make the relationship they'd started on the trip to Anchorage work, even if he had to step on some toes to do it.

After lugging the few boxes and extra-large suitcase out of the bed of his pickup and up to his room, Taylor closed himself inside it. He gazed around the space. Blaise was right. It was exactly the same as when he'd left, thinking he'd never return.

He walked to the large walk-in closet and found all the clothes he'd left behind undisturbed. Taylor shook his head at the number of suits that hung there. At one time, it'd been second nature for him to wear one. The thought of putting one on now made him feel uncomfortable. It wasn't a part of who he was.

It would have to be now that he'd agreed to step in and take his dad's place in the family company. It meant being cooped up in a high-rise office building doing mounds of paperwork and sitting in seemingly endless meetings. Taylor would much prefer working with horses and looking after a piece of property, the job he'd left behind in Juneau. At least his family home had a stable of its own, though much larger than the one he'd once worked in.

Not in the mood to unpack, Taylor sat on the king-size bed and pulled his cell phone out of his front jeans pocket. He might as well get the call to Aspen over and done with. He wasn't looking forward to it.

He brought up Aspen's number in his contacts list and touched the screen to send the call. She answered after the fourth ring.

"Hello?"

"Hi, Aspen. It's me, Taylor."

"I didn't expect to hear from you until tomorrow. Do you miss me already?" she asked with a laugh.

"I do." He really did. Just hearing her voice over the phone made some of the tension between his shoulder blades loosen. "Which makes this hard. I have to cancel our date tomorrow. There's a family obligation I can't get out of, nor have it switched for another time. I do want to see you again. Can we make it for two evenings from now?"

"Of course, and I completely understand. How's your dad?"

"Not good. If he wasn't so bad, I would have blown off

this thing tomorrow night."

"Don't worry about it. You do what you have to do, though I'll miss you."

Taylor smiled, even though Aspen couldn't see him. "And I you. I promise to make this up to you."

"Hmm, that isn't a bad thing, especially if you use your body to do it."

Taylor's cock twitched inside his jeans. "I can," he said, his voice gruff at the surge of arousal that shot through him as the thought of all the things he'd do to Aspen came out to play.

"After that, I can use you any way I want."

Aspen spoke in a sultry tone that had Taylor's dick coming to life. Memories of their night spent in the motel rose to the forefront of his mind. He had, in no way, gotten enough of her. He ached to take her to bed and keep her there, making love to her until she begged him to stop.

"I'd like that," he said, a purr creeping into his words.

His bedroom door banged open and Blaise walked into the room. "Don't mean to interrupt your phone sex, but I can't seem to help myself."

Taylor stared daggers at his brother. He kept his gaze on Blaise as he said to Aspen, "We'll have to continue this conversation when I see you. A pain in my ass just walked into my room."

Aspen laughed. "Your brother, I take it. No worries. Even though we aren't seeing each other tomorrow, you can still call me."

"I will. See you soon." Taylor disconnected the call and glared at Blaise. "Ever heard of such a thing as privacy?"

Blaise grinned. "No. Who's the girl? I wouldn't have thought you had time to start seeing someone in Anchorage already."

"None of your damn business."

"Where did you meet her? Have you known her for long? Are we, and most importantly me, going to be introduced to her soon?"

Same old Blaise—always the smartass. "I repeat, it's none of your damn business. I won't be introducing her to the family. Ever."

The amused expression Blaise wore slowly changed to one of confusion. "Why wouldn't you? I'm sure we know someone in her family group. There are only a couple more in Anchorage and the surrounding area."

Taylor rubbed his face with his hand. "Remember the saying curiosity killed the cat? You are a cat, so it doubly applies to you. You ask too many questions, but since you won't shut up until I at least answer one, she isn't part of one of those family groups you mentioned."

"She's not? Then which one is she part of? From the conversation I overheard you had with her, it sounded as if she was from around here."

He lost some of his patience. "Damn it, Blaise. She isn't part of any family group." As soon as Taylor said that last part, he knew he'd given away too much.

Blaise's eyes widened. "You have a date with a human." He said it as a statement rather than a question.

"For the third time, it's none of your damn business." Maybe if he said it enough, his brother would actually listen to him, but he doubted it.

"We don't date humans."

Taylor scowled. "Do you have any idea how pretentious that sounds? There's nothing wrong with humans. Being banished, I've slept with my fair share of human women. There aren't any cougar shifter family groups in Juneau. Besides, I wouldn't have wanted one of their females if there was one. I lived as a human as much as I possibly could."

"You do realize you'll be expected to find your mate now that you've returned and retaken your place in the family. Dad will have a fit if he finds out you're seeing a human female."

"Too bad for him. I'll continue to see Aspen for as long as I want. The days where he could dictate to me like that are over. As for finding a mate, I won't be going out of my way to search for one."

Blaise met his gaze. "You've really changed. I can't say it's for the worse. Don't worry, I won't be telling anyone about Aspen. I wouldn't mind meeting her sometime, though." His brother smiled. "Maybe she has a cute friend she can introduce me to."

"You'd actually take a human female out on a date?"

"It's something I've thought of for a while now. They aren't like our females who have the high expectation of being able to claim a male's necklace, having him as her mate."

It was true. The one thing a lot of females of their kind dreamed about was the male who would one day be theirs. Most were raised to believe they wouldn't be complete until they were mated, which Taylor always thought was ridiculous. It was too reminiscent of the humans during the 1950s when their women had to be housewives and mothers and did everything for their men.

"Then go ask a human female out," Taylor said. "If I had my way, I wouldn't say it's such a bad thing."

Blaise cleared his throat. "Once you're head of our family group, you can do just that."

That was true. Taking his father's place, Taylor could make as many changes as he wished. There were old laws that pertained to all cougar shifters in general, but each family group made their own that were followed only by them. He could change those as much as he wanted.

"Don't give me any ideas," he said.

His brother laughed. "You know me. I'm good for that."

Taylor couldn't agree more. "Was there anything you wanted in particular, or did you just come in here to bug the crap out of me?"

"Grady and Jase are coming over in an hour. We're going to take you out for some drinks. Kind of our own 'welcome back to the family' kind of thing. Don't say no. Mom knows and she said she'll allow us to manhandle you out of the house if it comes to that. One night to let loose before you have to take on all the serious responsible stuff."

Taylor smiled and shook his head. "I guess I've been ganged up on. It'll be good to go out with you guys again." He, Blaise, Grady, and Jase had always been close. Grady and Jase's mother was Taylor's mom's younger sister. Blaise and Taylor had grown up with Jase and Grady like brothers, rather than cousins.

Blaise gave a short nod. "Good. I'll leave you to get ready." He backed toward the bedroom doorway. "Remember, one hour."

"I won't forget."

His brother walked out of Taylor's bedroom and shut the door behind him.

Taylor shook his head. He'd slipped into old times with Blaise and his cousins as if the years hadn't gone by at all.

CHAPTER FIVE

"**H**ere's to having Taylor back in the family fold," Jase said as he raised his glass of beer, then took a big swig from it.

Taylor took a sip of his as Blaise and Grady did the same with theirs. "Thanks," he said.

They sat at a back table in the bar they'd frequented together before his banishment. It was actually owned by a cougar shifter who was part of another family group in Anchorage. Being tucked out of the way, it was a hangout spot for their kind where they didn't have to keep hidden what they were. It was only the odd human who found the place, and they were usually made to feel uncomfortable enough to leave after a drink or two.

Grady smiled. "To celebrate, we should get shitfaced drunk."

Taylor shook his head. "You can but count me out. I don't enjoy waking up hungover the next morning." Cougar shifters could get drunk on the same amount of alcohol as any human. Only werewolves needed to drink huge amounts of it to get in that condition.

"Whatever," his cousin said. "I plan to have a good time."

"You always do," Jase said with a laugh as he clapped his brother on the back.

"Don't look now," Blaise said, "but we're about to have company."

Taylor turned his gaze in the direction his brother looked, then cursed under his breath. The woman headed toward their table was the daughter of the owner of the bar. Nikki had made it no secret she wanted Taylor as her mate, but he hadn't been interested in her, and still wasn't. He'd seen her manipulate too many males to get what she thought she deserved. She was spoiled, thanks to her parents.

"Well, look who's back," Nikki said once she reached their table. She came to stand next to Taylor's chair and leaned close enough for her thigh to come in contact with him as she put her hand on the top of his shoulder.

He shrugged out from under her palm. "Hey, Nikki."

"I guess the rumors about your banishment weren't true," she continued. "If you had been, you wouldn't be with these guys."

What happened in one family group was usually kept from any others, though sometimes whispers leaked out from time to time. Most of those usually didn't amount to more than rumors.

Not getting any response, Nikki asked, "When did you get back to Anchorage?"

Taylor glanced up to find her giving a sultry look that did nothing for him. Aspen was the only woman he wanted right now. He turned his attention back to his brother and cousins, then answered, "Today."

"It's nice to see you've returned." She hooked the chain of his necklace with a finger and pulled the cougar-head pendant out from under his shirt. "And it's nice to see this around your neck." Nikki leaned down and said into his ear, "I look forward to taking it from you very soon." With another sultry look, she straightened, then walked toward the bar.

Once she was gone, Jase let out a low whistle. "Damn, she's going to be trouble."

"More like a pain in the ass," Taylor said. "It doesn't matter how many times I rebuff her, she keeps insinuating we're going to end up as mates."

"You're the big prize as far as Nikki is concerned," Blaise added. "While you were gone, she tried out a few other males who are pretty high up in their family groups. None of them turned out to be her mate, so she kicked them to the curb once it became apparent it wasn't going to happen."

Grady shook his head. "The timing is bad for you, Taylor. She got rid of the last one a few weeks ago. She's on the prowl now and you're her new prey."

"Well, she can keep her claws to herself. I'm taken."

"Yeah, we know. Blaise already told us about Aspen."

Taylor scowled at his brother. "I thought you said you wouldn't tell anyone about her?"

Blaise shrugged. "Jase and Grady aren't just anyone. Don't worry, they won't say anything. They feel the same way I do."

"I had no idea all of you would be willing to break free from the traditional way of thinking."

Jase snorted. "Do you know me? I do whatever I want as long as I don't call attention to myself."

Taylor chuckled. "That's true, but if you ever did take up with a human woman, and it was found out, would you be prepared for the fallout that would follow?"

"If you are, then so will we."

He looked at Blaise and Grady to see them nodding in agreement. "Well, I'm not going to go around stating the fact my girlfriend is human, and not because I'd be ashamed about it. I wouldn't want Aspen looked down upon by the others."

The rest of their time at the bar passed in friendly conversation as Taylor's brother and cousins caught him up on the happenings within their family group while he'd been banished. All the while, Nikki seemed to watch everything he did. She was going to be a thorn in his side every time he came there to have a drink. It made him think he'd have to find a new watering hole.

* * * *

Taylor woke up the morning after the family gathering his father had arranged to make it official that Taylor was no longer banished and had been accepted once more as the "heir." There had been some grumblings, but his father had soon put a stop to them. Even though his dad was weak, he remained very much the head of their family group. His authority wasn't questioned, nor did he tolerate it to be so. His word was law, after all.

The whole event had proved to Taylor he'd been away from his kind for far too long. With the older members of their family group, it was all about tradition and how one was supposed to portray himself. At one time, it had been the norm for him, but not now. Taylor realized how snooty and stuck-up they actually were. He'd lost count of how many snide remarks he'd heard about humans.

He pushed thoughts of the night before from his mind and got out of bed. This was his last day off before he jumped into the corporate world again. He planned to spend a great deal of it with Aspen. He'd missed her more than he thought he would. He craved to make love to her once more.

After a shower in his en suite, Taylor dressed in a clean pair of jeans and a long-sleeved T-shirt. He needed to phone Aspen but decided it would be better if he made the call outside. He didn't need Blaise interrupting like last time, nor did he need anyone overhearing and telling his father that Taylor had been talking to a woman.

He'd just stepped out of his room and into the hallway when his mother called his name. Taylor looked in the direction of his parents' bedroom to see her leaving it.

"Good morning, Mom."

She walked down the hall until she stood in front of him and gave him a hug. "Good morning. I was just coming to see if you were awake. Your father wants to see you."

"I was going to the stables. I haven't been out there since I returned."

"It'll have to wait. He wants to talk to you before Caleb arrives. It tires him out when your cousin comes to examine him. Your dad usually sleeps for a few hours afterward. Unless you want to wait around until he wakes up again."

No, he didn't. He wanted to see if Aspen would spend the afternoon and night with him. "All right, I'll talk to him now, only because I'm planning to go out this afternoon. Plus, don't expect me back for dinner. I'll be late coming home."

His mom smiled. "Do your plans happen to be with a female?"

"That, mother dear, I'm keeping to myself."

"Fine, I won't press. Once you're done with your father, come and eat something for breakfast before you go out to the stables. Knowing you, you'll be there for a while, especially since you've been working with horses the last few years."

Taylor had told his mom where he'd been living and working during his banishment. The only thing he'd kept from her was the fact the people he'd been close to were werewolves. Plus, the fact he'd told his friends about his being a cougar shifter.

"I promise," he said. After giving her a kiss on the cheek, he headed down the hallway to the master bedroom.

He knocked on the door that stood open, then stepped just inside the room. His dad sat propped up in bed with pillows behind his back. He waved Taylor closer.

"Come in and shut the door."

Once Taylor did as his father requested, he went and sat in the chair near the side of the king-size bed where his dad lay. "Mom said you wanted to talk to me."

"Yes. I want to discuss your future."

Taylor sat straighter, not sure he really wanted to have this conversation. "What about it? I've taken my rightful place again. There isn't anything more than that."

"I beg to differ. There's the matter of you finding a mate and producing an heir."

He ground his teeth to stop himself from telling his father to keep his nose out of his personal life. Instead, he said, "It'll happen when it happens. I'm only twenty-nine."

As if he hadn't heard what Taylor had said, his father continued. "I've made some phone calls and arranged for you to meet a couple of females of high standing in their family groups who are from around this area. The first one you'll take to that Mediterranean restaurant downtown. I've had my assistant make a reservation for seven. It's fine-dining, so you'll have to wear a suit. The female's name is — "

"No," Taylor said with a slight growl lacing the word.

His father scowled. "What do you mean 'no'?"

"I will not go out with any of these females."

"You will do as I say."

"Not when it comes to this, I won't. I'll find my own mate, without the help of you."

"These are females of good breeding."

"I don't give a shit. My mate could be from the lowest ranking in her family group and I would still accept her if she turned out to be the one meant for me. I will not take one as a wife just to make you happy, either."

It wasn't done very often, but it did happen. Since there weren't that many cougar shifters around, sometimes couples "married" and produced children. Each one of those unions was loveless, and the males generally cheated on the females, always in the search of their true mate. When they found her, the other female was abandoned along with any children.

"You will not disobey me," his father said, his breath laboring as his face grew red with anger.

Taylor's ire rose to the surface as well. "I'm not a child who can't think for himself. The days of you being allowed to run roughshod over me are done. I'm going to set some ground rules here and now and you're going to follow them, or I walk. It will be no hardship for me. I can go back to where I came from and be welcomed with open arms. I don't need you. Remember, it's you who needs me. So, first rule, you will stay the hell out of my personal life. I'll work in the family business and take on the duties of head of the family group if it comes to that, but everything else is my life to live."

This was the first time Taylor had ever stood up to his father. Even when he'd been about to be banished, he'd taken it, not doing anything to change his dad's mind. It was true what he'd said. Meadow, the werewolf sentinels, and their mates would be more than happy to have him return to Juneau. He'd always have a home there if he needed it. So, his father really couldn't do anything to hurt him if he sent him away again.

"How dare you." His father was taken over by a coughing fit, his face turning even redder as he fought to catch his breath.

"What's going on here?" asked the male who walked into the room and came to stand next to the chair Taylor sat in.

Taylor looked up at his cousin, Caleb. The doctor was the son of Taylor's father's younger brother. He was five years older than Taylor since Caleb's parents had been mated before his. Caleb's father had disappeared when Caleb was only a boy, leaving mate and son behind. No one spoke of his uncle or why he would have abandoned his family.

"We were having a discussion," Taylor said as he rose to his feet.

"Well, don't have any more like that. It isn't good for your father. He has to stay calm and relaxed. Being agitated won't help his condition."

Caleb took out a filled syringe from his bag and then injected his father with it. His dad's coughing eased, then he appeared to fall asleep, though his breathing remained labored.

"What is that you gave him?" Taylor asked.

"It's something I've been working on. It helps with the symptoms and takes away your father's pain."

"You still don't know what's causing this?"

"No, and nothing I've tried will cure it. This is something completely new for our kind." Caleb turned to face Taylor. "I have to examine your father. So, if you don't mind leaving, I'll get started. I have other patients to see."

Taylor didn't mind at all. His temper was still on boil. He nodded, then left the room. Even though he'd promised his mom he'd eat something for breakfast, after the conversation with his father, he no longer had an appetite. He had to get the hell out of the house. The walls felt as if they were closing in on him. His need to be with Aspen increased. At least with her, she wouldn't expect him to act according to old-fashioned traditions. He could be himself and not worry about her judging him.

He avoided the dining room where his mother would be having her breakfast. Taylor quietly slipped out the front door and hurried to his truck, which was still parked in the four-car garage. There had been no room for it inside.

After he unlocked the driver's door, he got inside and started the truck. He backed up onto the circular drive that looped to the front of the house, then headed down the quarter-mile lane that would take him to the main road.

Taylor didn't pull over to the shoulder until his family's home was out of sight. He put the pickup in Park, pulled out his cell phone, and called Aspen. A sense of calm settled over him at the sound of her voice when she answered.

"Hi, Aspen. It's Taylor. Are you busy right now?"

"Hey. I was just thinking about you and then you called. Actually, I'm not. I was looking through the want ads, trying to find a job."

"Would you mind if I came over to your place? I really need to see you."

"Sure. I'm in my apartment above my parents' garage, so don't knock at the house."

"Okay. See you in a little bit."

Taylor ended the call and then turned the truck back onto the road. During the drive to Aspen's place, he had enough time to cool his anger. He wasn't going to think about his father and would focus on the woman he wanted to have a relationship with. He'd stated his opinion about his dad's matchmaking, and that was that.

After he arrived at his destination, Taylor parked at the side of the road before he walked up the driveway to the garage. He took the short flight of stairs along the side of it, then knocked at the door. Once Aspen opened it, he gathered her close with one arm, pushed the door shut with the other as he walked them inside, and claimed her lips in a desperate kiss.

CHAPTER SIX

Aspen barely had enough time to register that Taylor stood in her doorway before he hauled her against his chest and kissed her as if he hadn't seen her for a year. She lifted her arms and put them around his neck as he walked her backward. She returned his embrace, getting more turned-on with each second that went by.

Taylor didn't stop kissing her as he continued to walk them to the center of her small living room, then stopped. He put his hands on the small of her back and pressed their hips closer together. Aspen moaned at the feel of the hard ridge of his erection settling against her stomach. Her pussy clenched as she remembered what it was like to make love to Taylor. She'd ached to have him again, had found herself daydreaming about it.

He pushed his hands up the back of her shirt and undid her bra. He left her mouth and placed kisses along the side of her neck. "I have to have you. Right now. I can't wait."

"You don't have to," she replied in a breathy voice. "I want you too."

Taylor made a noise that sounded like a cat's purr. If she'd been able to do that, she would have been purring right along with him. Her body had gone up in flames and she wanted to have his cock inside her. She'd missed him — a lot. From the way he held and kissed her, he must have missed her, as well.

He pulled away only long enough to drag her shirt up and over her head, taking her bra with it. She stripped him of his long-sleeved T-shirt, as well, relishing the feel of his warm skin against hers as he once more hugged her close.

Taylor bent Aspen over his arm and set his lips to the hollow of her throat, then worked his way down to the tops of her breasts. She gripped his shoulders to keep her balance, but soon didn't have to worry about that when he lifted her and took her to the floor with him. He stretched out half on and half off her as he continued to make a trail with his mouth toward one of her breasts. She sank her fingers into his tawny-blond hair and held him to her as he took a nipple inside his mouth.

Aspen gasped as pleasure swamped her. Taylor sucked at her breast, making her pussy clench and grow wet. As he switched to her other one, not only did he purr like a cat, he borderline growled like one too. It was the most erotic thing she'd ever heard.

She moaned, enjoying the feel of Taylor's mouth trailing along her skin in the downward path he'd taken. A warm sensation preceded him. Aspen lifted her head to see his cougar-head pendant brushed against her as he moved. Like the last time they'd been together, it seemed to have taken on a heat of its own.

Taylor's tongue dipped into her bellybutton, causing her stomach muscles to jump. He was decidedly taking too long to get to the good part. Aspen grabbed a fistful of his hair and gently tugged him back up her body until his lips were even with hers.

"Time to get this show on the road," she said in low

voice.

Not giving him any warning, she pushed against him and rolled him to his back. She landed on top of him. With a smile, she met his gaze as she undid his jeans and tugged them and his underwear down enough to spring his cock.

There it was. She'd been dreaming of it and of doing whatever she wanted to Taylor. Now was her chance to live the fantasies her mind had come up with. She straddled his thighs and fisted his shaft at the base. Aspen bent over and flicked the bead of pre-cum that had leaked from the slit with the tip of her tongue. That sexy cat's purr pushed out of him.

His cock jerked in her grip as she lowered her mouth over it, then took him inside. She was rewarded with another purr and cat-sounding growl. She slid him almost all the way out before she sucked him back as far as she could take him. She set a pace that had her head bobbing with the in-and-out motion.

Taylor grew harder, his harsh breathing filling the room. His hips lifted off the floor as he fucked her mouth. Wetness leaked into Aspen's panties as her arousal ramped up.

All too soon, Taylor gently pulled out from between her lips. "You've driven me crazy enough."

With a smile, Aspen nodded. She stripped his jeans and underwear the rest of the way off before she stood over him, her feet on either side of his legs. She undid her pants and pushed them down past her hips with a little wiggle. His gaze followed each of her movements. She managed to rid herself of the rest of her clothes without losing her balance. Bonus for her.

Now as naked as Taylor, she slowly went down on her knees. Aspen angled herself better, then took his cock inside her pussy. She pushed down by increments until he was seated to the hilt. He filled her completely, and he felt so damn good.

Aspen moved on top of him, taking him in steady strokes. Taylor thrust up into her as she pushed down on him. He slid so deep the head of his cock butted up against her cervix.

She looked down at his chest, her eyes caught by a flash of light. For a split second, it looked as if the ruby eyes in his cougar-head pendant glowed. Aspen figured it had to be a trick of the bright sunshine that filled the living room.

As she continued to ride Taylor, Aspen found her gaze drawn to his necklace again and again. For some unknown reason, she had the urge to take it from around his neck and put it on hers.

Taylor rubbed her clit with the tip of his finger, and Aspen forgot all about his necklace. She rode him harder and faster. Pleasure built inside her, coiling tighter, getting ready for the release she craved.

It didn't take long to achieve that goal. A keening moan pushed past her lips when her orgasm struck. Her pussy clutched and released his cock, which continued to plunge deep inside her.

Once the last wave of pleasure receded, Aspen found herself lifted off Taylor. He quickly positioned her on her hands and knees before he came up behind her. Taking hold of her hips, he thrust into her pussy. She pushed back to meet his rapid strokes. She was able to take him deeper this way. Since she'd already come, she hadn't been sure if she could climax again so quickly. Aspen soon found that wasn't the case.

Taylor reached around her and found her clit again. He continued to take her from behind as he stimulated the small bundle of nerves with the tip of his finger. His cock grew even harder.

Just as he thrust into her one final time, a second orgasm tore through her. She came along with him. His cock pulsed inside her pussy, filling her with his cum. Once it was over, he rolled them to their sides onto the floor with their bodies still joined.

"I have to say, that was the best hello I've ever gotten," Aspen said while she fought to catch her breath.

"I'm glad you liked it. It would seem I need to have you as soon as I see you."

Taylor's softening cock slipped free of her body. Aspen rolled toward him so she was on her other side. "I'm just as bad as you are. I was more than happy to follow along. I take it you're still willing to give this relationship thing a shot?"

He took her lips in a tender kiss before he met her gaze. "More than you can possibly know."

Aspen reached up and fingered Taylor's pendant. It remained warm to the touch. "You sounded a little ticked off when you called. Things not going well at home?"

"In some ways yes, and in others, no. I had an argument with my father. He's very ill, but he still acts as if he can dictate the way I live my life. I made it perfectly clear that wouldn't be happening."

She took the cougar-head pendant in her hand and rubbed her thumb over it, the urge to take it from Taylor once again present. "I'm sorry to hear about your dad, but I think you did the right thing by standing up to him. I'm lucky that neither of my parents are like that. The only person in my family who drives me nuts is my older sister, but I don't see her that often. She's married and has a couple of kids to keep her busy."

"Enough talk about family," Taylor said with a smile. "How about we move to your bedroom? It'll be a lot more comfortable than the hard floor. Plus, I don't think I'm quite finished with my hello yet."

Aspen looked down to see his cock was no longer soft. "I can see that. I think that's an excellent idea."

Before she could say anything else, Taylor gathered her into his arms and stood. He carried her to her bedroom and gently placed her on the center of her bed. He proceeded to make love to her slow and easy. He managed to wring two more orgasms out of her before he reached his own release.

Snuggled against Taylor's side, Aspen listened to his breathing even out as he fell asleep. She wasn't tired, but figured she'd let him have his rest. She'd get to wake him up with her lips and tongue. With nothing planned, they could spend the rest of the day in bed.

Aspen angled her head to look at Taylor's handsome face. They really hadn't known each other long, but the more time she spent with him, the more she felt as if they could really work. Being in his arms again, making love to him, the way she felt for him had grown stronger. She knew love at first sight was real. That's how it had been with her parents, but she never thought she'd ever experience it. With Taylor, she had a feeling she finally had.

For now, she'd keep that her little secret. Taylor didn't need her to dump that on him at this moment, especially if things weren't great with his father. She'd settle for letting him know she'd be there for him. Then when the time was right, she'd tell him how she felt. Hopefully, he'd feel the same way about her.

* * * *

Taylor and Aspen spent the majority of the day in bed. It wasn't until close to dinnertime that they finally came up for air. For Taylor, it was the first time he actually felt as if he couldn't bring himself to leave a woman. He was seriously considering staying the night, even though he had to be up early in the morning to start his first day at the office.

They'd gone out to get something to eat and were now back at Aspen's apartment. It reminded Taylor a lot of his old place in Juneau. They were on her couch, watching TV.

Aspen sat tucked under his arm, their feet up on her coffee table. It was nice, and something he could easily get used to. There, he wasn't the heir apparent. He was only Aspen's boyfriend.

During the day, he'd come to the realization Aspen meant a lot to him. He didn't think he'd be able to give her up a month from now, let alone a year or five years. Reaching that decision, Taylor had started thinking of ways to integrate her into the other aspect of his life — the cougar half and all it entailed. First off, he had to tell her what he was. At least having watched some of the sentinels go through that very same thing — telling their human mates they were immortal werewolves — he knew how to go about it the right way.

Aspen shifted out from under his arm and sat to straddle his lap. She rested her forearms on the tops of his shoulders, then kissed him. It started off as a soft brush of the lips, but soon heated to something more carnal. They tugged at each other's clothes until they were naked.

Taylor leaned his head against the back of the couch and watched Aspen take his cock inside her pussy. He purred, having given up a while ago on holding them back. Only with her did he lose all control.

He groaned, a cat's growl lacing the sound. "I love being inside you."

Aspen bit her bottom lip. "You feel pretty good yourself."

He took hold of her hips, lifting to meet her downward strokes, and pressing her tight against him. She ran her hands along his shoulders to his chest as she continued her up-and-down motion, his cock spearing into her. Her inner muscles squeezed around his length, increasing the pleasure he felt. It wasn't going to be long before he climaxed.

The pace Aspen set grew faster. She moaned, her motions becoming jerky. She sucked in a breath, then her pussy tightly gripped his cock, milking him with her orgasm. It was all Taylor needed to join her. He reached the point of no return in a rush and didn't hold back. He came, his dick pulsing as he gave her everything he had.

Aspen remained on his lap. His softening cock remained inside her. She ran a hand down one of his pecs, brushing along the chain of his necklace. "You know, every time we make love, I swear your pendant heats up. Now, I don't know if it's a trick of the light or what, but the cougar's ruby eyes look to be glowing. I have this almost overwhelming urge to take it from you and put it around my own neck."

Taylor stiffened. He looked down at his pendant. Aspen was right. The eyes glowed. His gaze shot to her face as the ramifications of what it meant sank in. He opened and closed his mouth a couple of times, unsure what to say. He found himself looking at Aspen in a whole new light. She was his mate. A human was his mate. With the surge in his hormones, all he could think about was making love to her over and over again until she took the pendant from him.

A knock came on the apartment door before a woman on the other side said through it, "Aspen, honey, would you and Taylor like to come to the house and have some pie? I made it this afternoon."

Aspen shot off his lap, swearing under her breath. She gathered his clothes and shoved them at him. "Mom, just give me a minute," she called. To Taylor she said quietly, "Go to the bathroom and get dressed."

He quickly did as she told him. A glance over his shoulder showed Aspen was pulling her clothes on in record time. Once he reached the bathroom, Taylor closed and locked the door behind him. His mind awhirl with what had happened, he fished his cell phone out of his jeans front pocket before he dropped them along with the rest of his clothing onto the floor.

Taylor found Blaise's number in his contacts list and

called him. He looked at his reflection in the mirror above the sink as he waited for his brother to pick up. The cougar's ruby eyes were still glowing.

"Pick up, pick up, pick up."

On the sixth ring, just before his cell would have gone to voice mail, Blaise answered. "Hey, Taylor."

"Where are you?"

"At the bar with Grady and Jase. Why?"

"Stay there. I really need to talk to you."

"Okay. What's the matter? You sound...different. Is it because of the argument you had with Dad? Caleb said he walked in on you and him having a disagreement about something."

"No, it doesn't have anything to do with that. I'll explain when I get to the bar."

"All right. We'll be here waiting for you."

Taylor disconnected the call, then pulled on his clothes. He kept his necklace under his shirt.

He opened the bathroom door and stepped out to find Aspen just closing the entrance door. She turned and smiled when she saw him.

"I told her we were too full from dinner and that we'd have pie another time. I also promised her I'd bring you to the house very soon. She wants to meet you."

"Good, because we're going out."

"We are?"

"Yes. Get your jacket."

While Aspen went to do that, Taylor put on his that he'd taken out of his truck earlier when they'd gone out to eat. Once she returned, he ushered her outside, down the stairs, and to his pickup.

"Are you going to tell me where we're going?" Aspen asked when they were on the road.

"To a bar. I need to talk to my brother about something and that's where he is. You'll also meet two of my cousins."

"You couldn't say it over the phone?"

"Nope. It's a serious matter, and I just remembered about it." Taylor glanced at Aspen. "Sorry."

"I don't mind. I only thought it was a bit sudden. Thanks for not getting upset about my mom interrupting. That's one problem with living above my parents' garage—she likes to stop by whenever she wants, which happens to be frequently."

Taylor smiled. "I understand. I'm not that close to my dad, but I am with my mom."

He parked on the street a half block away from the bar. Once they were out of the truck, Taylor took Aspen's hand while they walked. He turned down the short alley and went to the nondescript-looking door that was the bar's entrance.

Aspen looked at him. "There's a bar in there? Being so hidden away, I would think they wouldn't get much business."

"They do. They like to be discreet."

Taylor opened the door and then guided Aspen inside. He didn't get very far before Nikki confronted him. She glared at Aspen, glanced down at their joined hands, then gave him a hard look.

"Taylor," Nikki said. "What is this?"

"Nikki. This is my girlfriend, Aspen. I'm only here to talk to Blaise, then we'll leave."

A look of shock crossed Nikki's face before it changed to anger. "Girlfriend? How could you take up with a hu—"

"Back off, Nikki." Taylor cut Nikki off before she could get the word "human" out.

He brushed past Nikki, taking Aspen with him. Taylor spotted his brother and cousins at the same back table they'd sat at his first night in Anchorage. Once he reached it, he quickly made the introductions.

"It's nice meeting all of you," Aspen said. She looked at

Taylor. "I need to use the ladies' room since you didn't give me a chance to at my place."

He nodded, then pointed her in the direction of where the restrooms were. He watched Aspen until she disappeared into the washroom. He found Blaise, Grady, and Jase staring at him.

Blaise spoke first. "What were you thinking, bringing a human here? I don't have a problem with it, but that's not the case for everyone. I'm sure Nikki is as pleased as anything," he said sarcastically. "Aspen's scent is all over you and yours all over her."

Taylor pulled out a chair at the table and sat. "I think this will excuse me." He reached under his shirt and took out his pendant. In the dim lighting of the bar, there was no missing how the ruby eyes glowed.

Jase leaned forward. "You found your mate." Then a shocked expression formed on his face. "Aspen?"

"Yes, Aspen," Taylor said. "It just happened. She told me it's been warming against her while we sleep together. Plus, she has an almost overwhelming urge to take it from me and wear it herself."

Blaise whistled. "She's your mate."

Taylor nodded. "Have any of you ever heard of a cougar shifter having a human as a mate before?"

The three other men shook their heads. "I would have to say you're the first," Grady said. "Since she got your pendant glowing, there's nothing anyone can say about it. No one can dispute the magic in it."

That was true. Only a male's mate could set off the magic in the pendant. His father was going to blow his lid when he found out, but Taylor really didn't give a shit. Aspen was his. He'd already started to fall in love with her but hadn't picked up on what his feelings for her actually meant until now.

The sound of Aspen shouting his name in fear had Taylor shoving back his chair and running at no speed a human could ever achieve toward the restrooms. Blaise, Jase, and Grady quickly followed him.

CHAPTER SEVEN

Aspen walked out of one of the stalls in the ladies' room and went to the sink to wash her hands. The door opened, and Nikki walked in. Seeing the unpleasant look on the other woman's face, Aspen decided it would be best on her part to ignore her.

She finished at the sink and then dried her hands before she turned to head out of the restroom, but found her path blocked by Nikki. Aspen stepped to the side to go around her only to have Nikki move with her.

"What do you think you're doing, human, being with Taylor? We don't want your kind around here."

"Human?" Aspen asked, wondering if Nikki wasn't all there.

"Do yourself a favor and stay away from Taylor. He's mine. Stay the hell away from him."

Aspen instantly stood up for herself. It was obvious Nikki was jealous, but that didn't give her the right to try to intimidate her. She gave the other woman a hard look. "Since Taylor is with me, you have to see he never was yours in the first place. I won't be breaking up with him just because you're threatening me."

"Then I guess we'll have to see how much Taylor will want you once I get my claws into your face."

What happened next had Aspen's heart jumping into her throat. Nikki's body shimmered and blurred. An instant later, a very pissed-off cougar took her place. It snarled and growled as it bunched its back legs under it as if to spring. As it did, Aspen held her arms in front of her face and shouted Taylor's name as loud as she could.

The restroom door slammed open and Taylor, Blaise, Jase, and Grady ran in. Taylor caught the cougar around the middle before it reached Aspen and threw it into one of the open stalls. The large cat quickly recovered and shot out like a bullet.

Aspen found herself frozen to the spot while Taylor's body blurred and shimmered as Nikki's had, and a larger cougar stood where he'd been. The male cat blocked the female's charge, his large paw coming out and swiping her across the face, but that didn't stop her from attempting to get at Aspen again. It took the male grappling her to the floor, standing over her with his sharp teeth bared above her throat, to have her backing down.

The female cougar's form shifted to human and she was Nikki once more. "I'll leave your precious human alone for now, but don't ever bring her here again." She gained her footing and stomped out of the restroom.

The sound of harsh breathing filled Aspen's ears. It took her a few seconds to realize it was her making the noise. Her heart raced as the male cougar's body blurred and shimmered and Taylor was himself again. He turned and took a step toward her, but she stopped him by holding her hands out in front of her.

"Stop," she said. "How could you... What are... What the hell just happened here?"

"I can explain everything, but I don't think this is the

place to do it," Taylor said.

"Yeah, I'd get her out of here before Nikki flips her lid again," Blaise added.

Aspen looked at Taylor's brother and his two cousins. "All of you can change into cougars as well?"

Grady answered. "We're all cougar shifters."

"How?"

"We were born this way. Think of us as a different race who can do things a normal human can't."

"Different race?" she asked sarcastically. "I'd say it's more than that."

The sound of voices gathering outside the ladies' room had them all turning their heads toward the door. Taylor quickly took Aspen by the arm. "Time to go, and please don't fight me. I would never do anything to hurt you. The people out there, I'm not too sure about. Nikki and her family own this bar. I'm sure she just told everyone you're human."

Fear still pumping through her, Aspen figured she would be safer with Taylor and his family than the strangers outside the door. She allowed him to guide her out to the bar. There was a group of people there, all looking none too pleased to see her. Blaise, Grady, and Jase closed around her and Taylor, then all together, they left.

They parted company with Taylor's brother and cousins once they reached his pickup. After Taylor put her into the cab, he spoke a few words with the others, then got into the driver's side.

As they drove toward her apartment, some of Aspen's fear subsided. She felt numb, as if it were too much for her mind to accept. She made no move to touch Taylor, and he didn't try to touch her. Neither one of them said anything.

At her apartment, Aspen unlocked the door. Taylor didn't give her a chance to keep him out. He crowded behind her, then closed them inside. Needing some distance between them, she went and sat on the couch.

Taylor didn't give her much space as he came to stand in front of her.

"Are you going to give me a chance to explain?" he asked as he looked down at her.

"I guess."

He squatted and tried to take her hands in his, but Aspen pulled away before he touched her. Taylor sighed. "I'm not going to hurt you, so stop being afraid of me."

"Sorry, but seeing my boyfriend turn into a cougar does that to me."

"Look at me, Aspen. Really look at me. I'm still Taylor. I was a cougar shifter when I first met you. Not once have I done anything to harm you. You were even safe with me on the long drive to Anchorage."

She wrapped her arms around her middle. "I know. Were you ever going to tell me what you are?"

"Yes. I just hadn't figured out how I was going to do it. Then this happened." He pulled out his cougar-head pendant and angled it toward her.

The ruby eyes still glowed. "I don't understand."

"Every male is given one of these necklaces once they hit puberty. It's crafted with magic inside it. When he finds his mate, she will set off the magic it contains, and the eyes will glow. It's the female's choice to take the necklace from the male and put it around her neck. Only then will the mating bond form between them, joining their souls." He met her gaze. "You set mine off. It usually takes a little while after the couple meets but, if it's meant to be, it will happen."

"I'm your mate?"

"Yes. You can decide whether you'll accept my necklace or not."

"Once I do, we'll be mated? For life?"

"Correct. As far as I know, you're the only human to be a mate to a cougar shifter."

Aspen took a deep breath. That was a lot to take in. She

looked at Taylor and saw the man she had fallen for, but the cougar side still scared her. "Do I have to make the decision about being your mate right now?"

"No."

"Good, because I can't."

Taylor stood. "I think it's best I go and let you think through everything. I would never pressure you into doing something this life-changing, but I will say I love you. Now I know why my feelings for you were so strong right off the bat when I have never experienced it with any woman before you. Take as much time as you need. You have my cell number."

Aspen remained on the couch as Taylor gave her one last look, then walked out of the apartment. A minute later, she heard his pickup truck pulling away from the house. A part of her wanted to chase after him and tell him to come back, but she stayed on the couch. She had a lot of thinking to do.

* * * *

It was late the next morning when someone knocked on Aspen's apartment door. She opened it to find a woman who looked to be in her thirties standing on the other side.

"Can I help you?"

"If you're Aspen, you sure can."

"I am."

"Good. I'm Mara, Taylor's mom. Can I come in?"

It was then that Aspen saw the similarities in features. Mara had the same tawny-blonde hair and light brown eyes that verged on gold. She didn't look anywhere old enough to have a son Taylor's age.

Aspen took a step back. "I guess."

Mara walked through the doorway and looked around. "This is a great little place. I understand your parents live in the house."

"Thanks, and yes, they do."

"Enough of the pleasantries, I'm going to get straight to the point of my visit. It's about you and Taylor. He told me what happened yesterday. I had to pry it out of him, but he eventually opened up. I thought I'd come here and see how you were feeling about it all."

Aspen motioned Mara to follow her into the living room and they sat on the couch. "I don't know what to think. It's hard to accept the fact there are cougar shifters in the real world."

"I know. I blame that on the fact it was long ago decided we would keep our kind hidden from humans and werewolves."

"Werewolves?" Aspen asked, feeling her world tilt a little more. How many more mythical creatures were there that actually existed?

"Yes, they're real, as well, but as I was saying, we've kept what we are a secret. Because of that, Taylor was banished four years ago. He defended his human friend from a werewolf. They fought in animal form. Taylor ended up killing the werewolf in self-defense. Since he allowed others besides our kind see what he truly is, my mate, the head of our family group, decided to uphold the old law and banished him. I didn't agree with it. After hearing who my son has been friends with and living around while he was away, I think it's time we loosen the rules. I pried that out of him too."

"So, you're okay with a human being Taylor's mate?" Aspen had no idea what Mara referred to about Taylor's friends in Juneau.

"Of course. He's lived too long among humans. It makes sense. I can't say everyone in our family group will feel the same, but there isn't much they can do about it. You set off the magic in Taylor's pendant. Only a mate can do that. There will be no one else for him but you. I hope you don't mind me asking. Do you love my son?"

That was the one thing Aspen *could* settle on. She did love Taylor. Finding out he was able to shift into a cougar hadn't changed that. "Yes."

"Then tell him. Right now, he's probably in a fine mess. Once a male's pendant glows, he'll find himself...how should I put this? In a constant state of need for his female until she takes his necklace from him. He won't be able to eat or sleep until that happens."

Aspen swallowed. "I have to admit it has been on my mind too."

Mara laughed. "It's all part of the magic. Seriously, if you choose to accept Taylor as your mate, you will never have to worry about him straying. His love for you will never dim. You'll have a best friend and devoted lover, all rolled into one."

The thought of being able to have a relationship that close with Taylor had Aspen wanting to jump at it, but the whole cougar aspect scared her. "The only thing stopping me is the cougar part. What happened at the bar scared the crap out of me."

Mara frowned. "I heard about that from Blaise, Jase, and Grady, as well. I never did like that Nikki. Don't judge our kind by her. She'd be a bitch even if she wasn't a cougar shifter."

Hearing Mara swear, being as elegantly dressed as she was, had Aspen laughing. "I guess some people are like that no matter what they are."

"Exactly."

"Can you turn into a cougar for me? Maybe if I see you it will take some of my fear away."

"Of course. Just remember, I'm still the same person inside the cat. I'll be able to understand you, but I won't be able to respond."

As Mara stood, Aspen noticed the cougar-head pendant she wore around her neck. It was identical to Taylor's. Looking at it made Aspen want Taylor's even more.

Mara shifted to her cat form and stood patiently for Aspen to make the first move. Aspen screwed up her courage and sank to the floor in front of the large cat. She tentatively touched her head. Mara purred and gently placed her paw on Aspen's cheek. Looking into the gold eyes of the cat, she saw the intelligence that lurked behind them. As she continued to stroke the top of Mara's feline head, she found her fear disappearing. She felt as if she was in no danger. Only with Nikki had she felt it.

Aspen gave Mara one last scratch behind the ear, then sat on the couch once more. "Thank you. I'm not scared anymore. I know I have nothing to worry about from you."

Mara took on her human form. "You never will. I will say, since meeting you, I'd be more than happy to have you as a daughter."

For some reason, that made Aspen's eyes burn as tears threatened to rise to the surface. She usually wasn't the emotional sort. "I think I need to see Taylor."

"I'll take you to him. This is his first day back working in the family business, but I doubt he'll be able to concentrate enough to get anything done."

Aspen collected her purse and jacket, then followed Mara out to the dark gray luxury sports car parked in her parents' driveway. She didn't say anything until Taylor's mother pulled up in front of the tall office building that was owned by the biggest software company in Anchorage.

"This is your family business?"

Mara nodded. "Yes. Taylor's office is on the top floor. I'll call his secretary and let her know you're coming up so she won't stop you. Now, off you go."

Aspen got out of the car and then entered the building. No one stopped her as she got onto the elevator. The ride to the top floor had her feeling nervous. She wasn't second-guessing her decision. She wanted Taylor. His mother had set her fears to rest.

After the elevator doors slid open, Aspen stepped out into a large reception area. The woman behind the desk waved her toward the closed double solid-oak doors. Aspen swallowed her case of nerves and opened them, stepped through, then closed them again.

The first thing she noticed was the floor-to-ceiling windows on three sides of the office. The other was Taylor, who paced in front of the one opposite her. He wore a suit and tie. He looked handsome, but it seemed so out of character for him.

"Taylor," she said, thinking to make her presence known, but he was already turning toward her.

"Aspen. You're here." Taylor crossed the room, closing the distance between them.

"Yeah. Your mom came to my apartment and had a chat with me. She's the one who drove me over."

"When I told her where you lived, I never thought she'd go to your place."

"It's okay. She's really nice...and she helped me come to a decision."

"And?"

By way of answer, Aspen stepped even closer, reached up, and snagged the chain of his necklace with her finger. She pulled the pendant out from under his button-down shirt. She touched the glowing ruby eyes, then took hold of it and slipped it over Taylor's head. She turned it so the pendant would face the right way and put the chain around her neck.

The instant it came to rest against her chest, Aspen sucked in a breath. A sensation as if something snapping into place between her and Taylor surged through her. Looking at Taylor's expression, he must have felt the same thing.

"You took my necklace," he said quietly.

"I do love you, Taylor. I can't picture my life without

you in it."

With a cat's growl, he gathered her close and kissed her as if he couldn't get enough of her. Aspen returned his kisses with the same fervor. Her need to have him inside her bordered on desperation.

"Make love to me, my mate," she said between kisses.

Taylor purred. "I don't think I'll survive if I don't."

He picked her up off her feet, then carried her to the double doors, kissing her all the while. A flick of his wrist, and he locked them. Next, he went to his desk. A push of a button on a remote had curtains closing across the windows. After that, they ended up in a tangle on the floor. Their clothes went flying every which way. Taylor's suit was nice, but Aspen hated the fact it took too long to get him out of it.

Once they were naked, Taylor settled between her spread legs. The head of his cock brushed against her pussy, which was already wet. Not wanting to wait any longer, Aspen reached between them and guided his erection inside her. The feel of him sinking deep had her moaning and clutching his shoulders.

This wouldn't be a slow and gentle lovemaking. Taylor took her in hard and fast strokes. Aspen lifted her legs and wrapped them around his waist. She squeezed her inner muscles around his plunging cock. Her body coiled tighter, readying itself for the orgasm that inched closer to the surface.

"I love you, Aspen," Taylor said. "I'll make it so you never regret your decision."

She groaned. "You can start by making me come. Now."

"With pleasure."

Taylor lifted his upper body off her and balanced himself on his straightened arms. He thrust deeper, angling so his shaft rubbed her clit. Aspen tried to be quiet as her climax overtook her, but she couldn't stop the keening moan that pushed out of her. Taylor came with her, his cat growls joining the sounds she made.

After he collapsed on top of her, Aspen put her arms around his back and held him close. "I think we just gave your secretary something to be embarrassed about."

Taylor chuckled. "She's a cougar shifter too. She'll soon know you're my mate."

"Then maybe we should do it again. Now that we're mated, it has to mean this is the start of our honeymoon."

He rolled and took her with him so she ended up sprawled on top of him. "I have a feeling I won't be getting any work done today."

"I could always leave."

He took her face in his hands and kissed her until she breathed hard again. "Don't you dare. You'll stay right here. I'm far from done with you yet." Taylor's cock hardened inside her.

"Then let the honeymoon begin."

Lost in her mate's embrace, Aspen no longer cared what noises people would hear coming out of Taylor's office. All that mattered was that they were together.

The End

TO LOVE A COUGAR

While shopping for lingerie, Harley finds something she can't resist—sex on a stick in the men's section. Intrigued and turned-on, she sets a plan in motion. If she can get him to size a thong for her to purchase as a gag gift, perhaps he might be willing to do other things for her too. Wicked things. Curl-her-toes things.

Cougar shifter Blaise is hunting—for human women, that is. His effort pays off in spades when he finds himself in the changing room with the beauty who captivated him the moment he saw her.

Their attraction is immediate, and it isn't long before they're burning up the sheets. Harley soon finds herself embroiled in something she would never have imagined possible, with Blaise in the center of it. Despite what she may feel for him, it might not be enough to make her stay.

CHAPTER ONE

Blaise walked into the dining room for breakfast and found his mother, his brother, Taylor, and Taylor's mate, Aspen, already there, eating. Blaise took a seat on the opposite side of the table from Taylor and Aspen, then filled a plate with fluffy scrambled eggs, bacon, and a couple of slices of toast.

"Good thing I told Taylor to leave you some," Aspen said as she motioned to Blaise's filled plate with her fork. "Plus, it's a good thing you came down when you did. Taylor was about to eat your share."

"Then I guess I have you to thank for getting something to eat this morning." Blaise smiled at Aspen, then winked. "Are you sure you're mated to the right brother?"

Taylor let out a low cat growl. "Blaise, it was funny the first few times you asked Aspen that, but now it's getting on my nerves."

Blaise laughed. "I know. That's why I do it."

"God, you can be a pain in the ass."

"Now, boys," their mother said with a smile. "No

bickering at the table. Aspen and I would like to enjoy our food without listening to the two of you go at each other, even if it's only in fun."

Blaise chewed, then swallowed a big mouthful of eggs. "I promise to behave. Since it's Saturday, and Taylor doesn't have to go to work at the family corporation, what are the plans for the day?"

"Tonight, Aspen's parents are coming over for dinner so I expect you to be here," his mother said.

Unlike Blaise and the rest of his family, who were cougar shifters, Aspen was human. She was also the first to be a mate to one of their kind. Taylor and Aspen had only been mated a couple of months, and this was the first time her parents were coming over to their daughter's new home.

Even though as a rule cougar shifters made sure to keep their existence unknown from humans and werewolves, it'd been decided that Aspen's parents could be told the truth about them. Blaise's father, who was the head of their family group, had grudgingly agreed to it after his mate wouldn't take no for an answer. It wasn't the first time his mother had gotten her way on a major decision.

"Will Dad be coming down to eat with us?" Blaise asked.

His mother shook her head, a look of worry flitting across her face. "No. He's too weak to even manage that. In some ways it's better that he stays in our room."

His father was very ill, which shouldn't have been possible. Cougar shifters didn't get sick—ever. His dad had become ill eight months before and had been wasting away, getting sicker, with each month that passed. His cousin, Caleb, who was a doctor, couldn't do anything to make Blaise's father better, no matter what he tried.

Even though it wasn't spoken about much, everyone was worried his dad would eventually die from this mysterious illness. If he did, that would make Taylor the new head of their family group.

Blaise nodded. "Yeah, I can see that."

His father had made it no secret that he wasn't exactly pleased that Taylor, his firstborn and heir, had a human for a mate. Most of the older members of their family group thought humans were beneath them. The idea that one had been accepted into their ranks had outraged more than a few. Even though his father didn't exactly approve, he'd stood up for Taylor, but that didn't mean he'd go out of his way to be nice to Aspen's parents.

"It is better," Taylor said. "If Dad made any rude comments, I'd have to put him in his place. It wouldn't make for a nice evening."

Blaise chuckled to himself. Taylor no longer put up with any bullshit from their father. After being banished from their family group for four years over an incident with a werewolf that had revealed Taylor as a cougar shifter, his brother had come back a stronger man who thought for himself. Taylor hated all the archaic laws just as much as Blaise did. Whenever Taylor became the head of their family group, there would be a lot of changes happening that the older members would hate.

"I'll make sure I come back in plenty of time for supper," Blaise said.

"I thought you wanted to make plans with Taylor and Aspen?" his mom replied.

"Since they weren't very forthcoming with any, I'm figuring they'd rather spend the day together without me being the third wheel. In that case, I'm going to do a little hunting."

"Hunting?" His mother gave him a questioning look.

Taylor shook his head. "He means he's going to harass some poor human women until he can convince one of them to go out with him."

Their mom smiled. "Oh, good. I must say I like the idea of having another human female for a daughter." She gave

Aspen a smile. "I'm rather fond of the one I have now."

"Don't encourage him, Mom," Taylor said. "Human women everywhere will thank you if you didn't." Aspen chuckled at her mate's remark.

Blaise gave his brother an exaggerated scowl, playing the part of being insulted when that was the furthest thing from the truth. He'd missed having Taylor around to swap mock insults with and loved every minute of it now that he could.

"That hurt, brother mine," Blaise said.

"You'll get over it."

Their mother cleared her throat. "Before this goes any further, Blaise, are you going to visit your father before you go out?"

He nodded. "I planned on it. I figured I'd wait until Caleb is close to done examining him. I want to hear the results."

"Caleb should be here in a half hour or so." His mother emptied her coffee mug, then pushed back her chair. "I'll go keep your father company until your cousin gets here." She stood and walked out of the room.

"Now that it's only the three of us," Taylor said to Blaise, "as for tonight, you'd better behave."

"*Moi* not behave? I'm always on good behavior." He snickered at the look Taylor sent him that said he didn't agree with that at all.

Aspen chuckled. "What my mate is trying to say is, no shifting to cat form while my parents are here. They're not used to being around cougar shifters as I am now." She stopped Blaise before he could say anything. "Don't deny there's a chance you'd do just that. I've lost count of how many times you've surprised me in that form."

Blaise gave Aspen an innocent look. "I only did it so you wouldn't jump every time you see one of us shift."

"Sneaking up behind me late at night in a dark hallway didn't help with that at all, and you know it."

"So I got a little inventive." He'd stopped doing that once Taylor surprised Blaise by sneaking up on him and jumping his ass while in cougar form as well.

"Just try to act normal. Okay?" Aspen asked.

Taylor let out a bark of laughter. "Now you're asking for something that's impossible."

Blaise ignored his brother's comment, not hurt by it in the least, and finished the last of the food on his plate. He poured himself a cup of coffee, then stood and looked at Aspen. "I'll be good. I promise. Now I'm going up to my room with my coffee until Caleb gets here."

He left and headed upstairs. At the upper level, Blaise heard his mother's voice coming from the master bedroom. With his sensitive hearing, he listened as she told her mate what she planned to have served for dinner that evening, and how she hoped to become close friends with Aspen's parents.

That was his mother. She had the biggest heart. It helped her, considering the kind of mate she had. Even though his father loved her, there were times when he could get a little highhanded. His mother was more than capable of putting his father in his place. The only time she'd lost to him was when he'd banished Taylor. To this day she hadn't let her mate live that one down.

Blaise sat in his room for forty-five minutes before he went to see his father. He'd heard Caleb arrive as scheduled and figured he had to be just about finished with his examination.

He tapped on the closed double bedroom doors before he opened one and stepped just inside. Caleb put his stethoscope into his bag, then waved Blaise closer.

"I'm finished," his cousin said. "I've only to give him his shot."

His father struggled to push himself up higher on the pillows that were propped at his back. "Wait until after Blaise and I have had a chance to talk. Whatever is in that needle leaves me tired and even weaker."

Caleb nodded. "I have a little time to spare before I'm scheduled to arrive to see my next patient, but I'll stay here to make sure Blaise doesn't tire you out too much."

"I have no problem with that. Besides being my doctor, you're also my nephew. I enjoy your company."

Blaise waited until Caleb had moved out of the way to stand near the end of the bed before Blaise sat in the chair across from his father. Caleb was the son of Blaise's father's younger brother. His uncle had disappeared, leaving mate and son behind, when Caleb had been quite young. No one spoke of it much, and nothing had ever really been said as to why his uncle had left. His aunt hadn't taken the separation from her mate very well and had ended up taking her own life a year later. Caleb had been raised by an aunt in his mother's family group.

"How are you feeling today, Father?"

His dad shook his head. "Not much better than I was yesterday. Caleb says he's mixed a new concoction that should hopefully change that."

Blaise looked at his cousin to see him nod in agreement. He had no idea what was in the needles Caleb used. He'd explained it once, using scientific terms, and it'd gone straight over Blaise's head.

"Let's hope this is the one that will cure you. I'm going out for a while, but I'll be back for dinner."

His father snorted. "I'm sure your mother made sure you would be. I still can't understand why she had to invite those people over here. They're human."

The words "they're human" was said in a way that conveyed how distasteful his father found the idea of the visit. Blaise couldn't understand why his father couldn't get over the fact that his oldest had become mated to a human, and that she now was a member of their family group. It wasn't as if Aspen would be leaving.

"I guess she wants to be friendlier with her new

daughter's family," Blaise said. "I don't have any problem with them being around."

"Taylor is starting to rub off on you. You never used to think that way."

Actually, Blaise had. He'd just never voiced his opinion about humans around his father until Taylor had returned and become mated to Aspen. Blaise would be more than happy to have a human as his own.

From there they talked about mundane things until his father appeared to be tiring. Caleb stepped forward even before Blaise had a chance to say he would bring this visit to a close.

Blaise stood, then shifted out of the way for his cousin. Caleb pushed the sleeve up on his patient's pajama shirt, then injected whatever was in the syringe into his upper arm. Blaise couldn't help but notice how thin his father had become. Too thin. Once he was finished, Caleb straightened, then placed the cap on the end of the needle before putting it inside his bag.

It only took a matter of seconds before Blaise's father started coughing. He'd been prone to coughing fits, but usually he didn't have one right after Caleb injected him. His dad's face turned red as the racking cough made it hard for him to get a breath. Caleb didn't seem overly concerned by it, but that wasn't the case with Blaise, especially when his father pulled his hand away from his mouth and there was blood in his palm.

Blaise's gaze shot to Caleb's face. "What the hell is that? He's worse than before you gave him that shot."

His cousin shook his head. "This has to be another manifestation of the illness."

"Don't you think that's pretty sudden?"

His father's coughing fit finally subsided and he settled back into the pillows. His eyes closed, and he appeared to fall asleep. Blaise didn't like how pale he was or how labored his breathing. Blaise's gut clenched as Caleb wiped some blood away from Blaise's dad's lips with a tissue.

Becoming all professional doctor, Caleb said, "Sometimes a patient has to get worse before he gets better. I'll continue with this new serum I've come up with and monitor your father. If in a couple of days he doesn't show any sign of improvement, I'll switch back to the old one until I can mix up something new."

Blaise hated the fact his father had to be used as a guinea pig, but there was no other way. It wasn't as if they could take him to a hospital. Being a cougar shifter, if the regular doctors took blood, the results would come back showing the differences in their chemical makeup. Plus, his dad's illness being the one and only case in their kind, this was all new territory for Caleb.

Still worried over his father, Blaise said a quick goodbye to Caleb before leaving the room. He continued downstairs and then out the front door. He wasn't going to be the one to tell his mother about this new symptom. Caleb could do that.

Blaise drove to downtown Anchorage with no set destination in mind at first. He pushed thoughts of his father's condition to the back of his mind. He was on a hunt for the human female who could potentially be his mate.

He lifted his hand and stroked the gold cougar-head pendant he wore around his neck from a gold chain. All male cougar shifters were given one once they reached adolescence. It had a bit of magic embedded inside. To know a female was meant to be his mate, the male's cougar's ruby eyes would glow. It wasn't something that happened with a first meeting, or even the first time the couple had sex. It sometimes took months before the eyes revealed the truth. Once it happened, it was the female's decision to accept the necklace as hers, which would create the mating bond, joining the mated pair's souls.

If the female didn't take the necklace after the eyes

glowed, the male ended up walking a fine line. He'd be unable to eat or sleep, basically only able to think about having sex with his newfound mate to hopefully tie her emotionally closer with each bout of lovemaking. His condition would be caused by an increase in testosterone.

Blaise hoped he'd never get to that point once he found his mate, though the chances were good it could happen if she turned out to be human. She wouldn't have grown up knowing what a male's pedant meant to her, or that she was to claim it, and him, as her own. He was more than willing to take that chance. If it happened, it happened, and he'd deal with it when the time came.

Since it was too early to do the bar scene, Blaise decided the next best place to meet women was where they liked to go shopping—a mall. With that decision made, he headed for the Anchorage 5th Avenue Mall, which was right in the city's downtown core.

Once he arrived at his destination, Blaise parked his sports car in the parking garage and then headed into the mall. It being a Saturday, it was more than a little busy. He didn't mind. It meant there would be a better chance to meet potential women to ask out. Now he just had to determine where he wanted to begin his hunt.

Blaise just starting walking, going with the flow of people, hoping his gaze found a likely target. Much to his chagrin, going by those around him, a lot of the females were mothers with young kids, senior citizens, or teenagers. Not exactly what he was looking for.

His steps slowed once a women's lingerie store came into view. Now that was a place that could have a lot of potential. The only thing holding him back was whether or not he'd be considered a sicko for trying to pick up a woman there. Then again, when had anything like that ever stopped him?

He headed straight for the store and walked right inside. A quick look around and Blaise found he was the only male present. He noticed there was a small section of the store that was dedicated to men's underwear and sleepwear. He couldn't see a lot of guys actually deciding to come to a place like that to shop for those kinds of things for themselves. Unless the store thought the women would buy the items for their boyfriends or husbands.

Blaise walked farther into the world of women's intimates and spotted a raven-haired beauty standing in front of a display of panties. He'd always found himself attracted to women with dark hair since cougar shifters ranged from blond to light brown.

His prey chosen, Blaise stepped out of the middle of the walkway to observe her before he made his move. She wasn't far enough away for him not to be able to see the color of her eyes with his keen eyesight. They were a gorgeous blue, almost the color of sapphires. She flipped her long hair over her shoulder, appearing not that impressed with what she looked at.

She lifted her head and her gaze settled on him where he stood a short distance away. She put down the pair of panties she'd been looking at, then walked around the table before heading in his direction. Blaise stayed where he was to see what she'd do. He was more than willing to let her approach him first.

CHAPTER TWO

Harley couldn't tear her gaze off the hottie who stood in the middle of a women's lingerie store, and from the looks of it, alone. Up until now she'd been only browsing for herself, but a new idea come to mind that involved Mr. Handsome. It wasn't something she normally did, but she found this male specimen well worth the chance of having this backfire on her. For all she knew, he could have a girlfriend and she could just happen to be in one of the change rooms at the moment.

She walked up to him and said with a smile, "I was wondering if you could do me a huge favor."

He grinned back. "What would that be?"

Harley ran her gaze over him, loving the look of his long, tawny-blond hair that was more controlled than shaggy. His light brown eyes that were pretty darn close to gold held humor in them. She liked how tall he was. He had to be at least six feet two. At five feet seven herself, she liked men with a little height to them.

"Well," she said. "Would you be against trying on some

of the things in the men's section for me? My sister is getting married in a couple of weeks, and I'm having a bridal shower for her. I want to get something for her to give to her fiancé. He's close to the same size as you."

That was utter bullshit. Harley's older sister, Mel, was getting married in two weeks all right, but her fiancé, Sean, was barely five foot eight and was a skinny, nerdy computer programmer. Mel loved him with all her heart and soul, as Sean loved Mel.

"I guess I can do that," Mr. Gorgeous replied.

"Great."

Before he could change his mind, Harley grabbed his hand and pulled him toward the men's section. She bypassed the sleepwear and went straight for the underwear. She stopped at a table that had assorted thongs displayed. Harley selected a black nylon one with metallic gold hearts on it.

She turned toward him and held it out. "This one. What's your name?"

"It's Blaise." He looked at the thong and then back at her again. "You're sure this is the one you want me to try on?"

"I'm Harley, and yes. It's a bit of a gag gift as well, but I want to make sure it's not too…constricting. I want my sister's future hubby to be able to wear it at least for a little while without it interfering with his…ability, if you know what I mean."

Blaise burst out laughing. "I understand, but there's one small problem."

"What? Are you uncomfortable trying on a thong?"

"That's not it. You see, I'm the type of guy who prefers to go commando. I doubt the store would appreciate me trying on any underwear like that without at least buying it afterward."

Harley swallowed as her mouth went suddenly dry at the thought of Blaise being naked under the slightly formfitting jeans he wore. She shouldn't have looked, but she couldn't help herself. She dropped her gaze to his fly, checking out how large the bulge was behind it. It appeared to be a good size.

Not wanting to be caught gawking at his crotch, Harley quickly yanked her gaze back up to Blaise's face. "I'll buy it for you."

"Pardon?"

"You try it on, then I'll buy it for you."

"That would mean you'd have to buy two."

She shrugged. "So be it. I don't mind."

Blaise took the thong from her. He returned it to the spot where she'd gotten it, then selected the same one but without the hearts. "If I'm going to have to keep it, then I want one without the metallic gold. Not exactly my style."

"You'll do it then?"

"Yes. Who am I to turn down a beautiful woman?"

Blaise headed for the single changing area in the men's section. It was in the corner with only a heavy black drape to close it off from the rest of the store. He stepped into it and tugged the curtain around the rod until he was hidden from sight. Harley stayed just outside it. She listened to the rustle of clothing on the other side, then some seconds later he called her name.

"I'm right here," she said.

"Okay. As far as your concerns go, none of that is going to be a problem."

"All right, but can I see what it looks like on you?" It was pushing it, asking Blaise to model it for her, but if she were really lucky, he'd do just that. "You don't have to come out here. You can open the curtain a bit, and I can take a quick peek."

He did as she said, stuck his hand out and tugged her inside before he quickly shut the curtain again. Harley would have protested, knowing full well if they got caught they would be kicked out of the store, but seeing Blaise in nothing but the thong left her speechless. She couldn't stop herself from running her gaze over his body. His chest was well-padded with muscle that was cut, as were his six-pack abs. His legs were just as muscular.

She stopped at the front of the thong and licked her lips. Oh man, Blaise's body was definitely well-proportioned. There was no hiding the size of his cock in that poor excuse for men's underwear.

Harley quickly pulled her wits about her, then said, "The front looks really good. How about the back?"

Blaise turned away. Harley started at his wide back, which tapered to a narrow waist. A little lower and she stared at the finest butt she'd ever seen. It looked hard enough to bounce a quarter off it.

"Liking what you see?" he asked.

Harley tore her gaze off his butt and found him looking over his shoulder at her. "Yeah." That single word came out breathy.

He gave her a wicked grin. "I bet you want to give it a good smack. Go ahead. I dare you. I might even like it."

God help her, but she really did want to. Her fingers itched, that was how badly she wanted to learn that muscular ass with her hands. She could test its firmness with a few well-placed taps.

"Is everything all right in there?" a salesgirl asked.

Harley jumped, the spell of lust that had come over her breaking in an instant. "Yes, we're fine."

"Then I'm going to have to ask you to leave the changing area. We don't allow men and women in there together."

"I'm coming out now."

Harley gave Blaise one last wistful look before she slipped through the curtain, trying not to reveal too much of him to the salesgirl as she did so. She smiled at the other woman as she yanked the drape closed behind her.

The saleswoman gave Harley a knowing smile and

leaned in closer to say quietly so only the two of them could hear, "If I had one of those, I'd be right in there with him as well. The only problem is if my manager realized I knew about it and didn't say anything, I'd be in trouble. I do have to say, though, you're a lucky lady." She gave Harley a wink and walked away.

In less than a minute, Blaise yanked open the curtain and stepped out of the changing area. His gorgeous body once again clothed. For the first time, Harley noticed the gold cougar-head pendant he wore around his neck. Its ruby eyes flashed in the store's bright lights as he stepped closer.

"Do you need me to try on anything else?" Blaise asked, his deep voice rolling over her and making her shiver inside.

"No, I think I found my gag gift." She went to the table of thongs, picked up the same pair Blaise had tried on, only with the metallic gold hearts and a size smaller, then walked back to him. She held out her other hand. "I'll pay for that now."

Blaise handed over the thong he held. It was still warm from his body. Harley turned, then headed for the counter where the till was. He followed her. The same salesgirl who had spoken to her was behind it.

She smiled at Harley, her gaze flitting to Blaise briefly. "Did you find everything you wanted?"

Harley nodded. "Yes."

She paid for her purchases before she and Blaise headed for the store's entrance. He walked at her side and took her hand in his, linking their fingers. Harley looked at him.

Blaise bent his head closer to hers. "Well, since I belong to you, I'd better act like it."

Harley smiled. "Very true." She was surprised Blaise had heard what the saleswoman said to her. She'd barely spoken above a whisper, and he'd been in the changing area at the time.

They strode out into the mall, then walked a few stores down before Blaise pulled Harley to a stop off to the side out of the way of other shoppers. Still holding her hand, he turned to face her.

"You've seen me in nothing but underwear. Is there a chance I can see you like that as well?"

"I think so. Are you going to ask me out on a date first?"

"Of course. I have a family dinner to go to this evening, so how about tomorrow evening?"

"Or we could go to the food court here right now and grab something to eat. I'm not busy."

Blaise smiled. "Sure. It's nothing fancy, but it's the company I'm with who matters."

"Then it's a date."

He stepped to her side again and got them moving in the direction of the escalator. The mall had five levels and the food court was on the very top one. They were now on the third.

As they walked onto the first escalator, Harley looked at Blaise. This trip to the mall had turned out a lot better than she'd hoped when she'd set out for it, thinking to help pass the hours on a Saturday. She now had a date with a hot hunk, and she'd already seen him in nothing but a thong.

*

Blaise looked at Harley out of the corner of his eye as they rode the first escalator up to the food court level. He couldn't believe his luck. The first human female who caught his interest, and she'd accepted a date with him.

Much to his pleasure, he found it to be a lot less stressful than approaching a female of his kind. There was always the added pressure she'd place on him, hoping he would be her mate. Most were raised to think that was their biggest ambition in life, to set off the magic in a male's cougar-head pendant, and that they wouldn't be complete until they had.

Since Harley was human, she had no clue about his pendant. She could still set the magic off in it, as he'd learned from Aspen setting off Taylor's, but it wasn't something she'd be hoping for. No pressure for it to happen.

"So, do you always let strange women talk you into trying on underwear for them?" Harley asked with a smile.

Blaise shook his head and laughed as they stepped off the escalator and headed for the next one. "No. You're the first."

"I guess I should take that as a compliment then. What made me so special?"

He shrugged. "I can't say it was just one thing. You caught my eye so I was more than willing to play along. It seemed like the best way to get you to agree to go out with me."

Harley smiled. "I'll let you in on a little secret. I would have gone out with you anyway without you modeling for me. Since we're being so honest here, I didn't think up the gag gift idea until I saw you."

"What would you have done if I'd said no?"

"I haven't a clue."

"Then it's a good thing I didn't. I will pay you for the thong."

"No, you won't. Think it of compensation for making you go through all that." She winked. "Plus, maybe you'll feel as if you have to wear it for me again since I did buy it for you."

"That would mean a second date so I can't see that being a problem."

They finally arrived at the upper level where the food court was located. Since it was a little on the early side for lunch, they had a lot of tables to pick from. Blaise let go of Harley's hand and followed her as she wove her way through them until she settled on one sort of off by itself.

Once they were seated across from each other, Blaise looked at all the different places offering food. "What do you feel like eating?" he asked.

Harley looked around as well. "I'm thinking of getting a slice of pizza."

"Sounds good. I could go for one myself. Why don't you tell me what kind you want and I'll get it. While I do that you can stay here and save the table. My treat since this is supposed to be a date."

Harley chuckled. "I don't think we have to worry about that, but fine. I want a slice of pepperoni and a can of cola to go with it."

"Will do."

Blaise stood, then went to the pizza place. There ended up only being one person in line ahead of him. Once it was his turn, he ordered the slice Harley wanted and a meat lover's for himself. Tray in hand with food and drinks on it, he worked his way back to the table.

They ate for a bit before Blaise started up a conversation. "Do you spend a lot of Saturdays at the mall?"

Harley smiled. "More than I'd like to admit. It's not because I like to shop. Wandering around the mall gives me something to do to pass the time. How about you?"

"Very rarely do I come here. Today I thought I'd switch up my daily routine."

"If you can come to the mall and have this free time as part of your normal routine, it sounds as if you don't have a job."

Blaise smiled. "I don't, and it's not because I'm unemployed. My family has a very lucrative corporation that's in the business of computer software. I worked there for a while and have taken a bit of a leave of absence, with pay."

"What's it called?" Blaise said the name of his family's corporation, and Harley's eyes widened. "Holy shit. You must be stinking rich. Everyone knows that software company. My future brother-in-law has dreamed of working for you guys. He's a computer programmer."

"Then before our date ends, I'll give you a name and phone number he can call to be set up for an interview. He just has to tell the person in human resources I referred him, and he'll get a position."

"Just like that? You don't know Sean or his work background."

"He's going to be a part of your family, and after today, I hope you'll want to keep seeing me, so why wouldn't I want to help him out?"

"In that case, if he turns out to be shit rotten at the job, don't blame me."

Blaise laughed. "I won't. What do you do for a living?"

"I'm a medical technician at a lab. I run some of the tests on the various specimens that come in."

"Sounds very complicated."

"Not to me it isn't. I like working in the lab."

"I guess I know who to go to if I ever need a blood test."

Harley smiled. "I promise to be gentle with the needle."

"That's good to know."

They finished eating, then by mutual consent decided to leave the food court. It was well into lunchtime and more people had arrived, causing the noise level to increase. Plus, they no longer had that many empty tables around them.

Blaise captured Harley's hand in his and walked them out of the busy area. "Now what would you like to do on our date? I still have hours before that family dinner and I'm not ready to say goodbye to you yet."

"Well, we can either continue to wander around the mall or we can go to some other place that's a little more private."

"All right. Where do you suggest we go?"

"I'd offer my place, but I have a roommate who works steady midnight shifts. She's sleeping right now and tends to get really grumpy if I have anyone over while she is. She's a bit of a light sleeper."

"All my family live together, but our house is pretty large. Plus, if you like horses, we have a stable full of them. We can go for a ride."

"Actually, I do know how to ride. It's been years since I've last been on a horse. I'd love to see yours."

"Then it's a plan. Do you need to go home first?"

Harley shook her head. "No, I'm good to go."

"All right. You can follow me to my house."

She nodded, then stood. Blaise gathered what was left of their lunch onto the tray before he took it to the garbage and got rid of it. That done, he and Harley headed for the down escalator.

At the parking garage, it turned out they hadn't parked too far from one another. Blaise waited until Harley got into her compact car, then climbed into his sportier one. She followed him to the exit, and once they paid their fees, they were on their way.

As he drove, Blaise made sure to look in his rearview mirror from time to time to make sure Harley was still behind him. She had no problem keeping up, not that he was speeding, much.

He was pleased she'd agreed to come to his house. The longer he was around her the more he liked her. He wanted to see just how compatible they were. A crowded mall hadn't been the place where he wanted to test those waters.

Once they arrived at his family's home, Blaise directed Harley to park next to him in front of the four-car garage. He got out of his car, walked to the driver's side of hers, and waited for her to get out as well.

As they headed for the front door, Harley said, "Yup, your house is as big as I thought it would be."

"Is that a good or bad thing?"

"Definitely good." She handed him the bag from the woman's lingerie store. "Don't forget this. I took out the one for my sister's fiancé and stuck it in my glove box."

"I'll have to get this up to my bedroom before we head to the stables. If my mom or my brother, even his wife, sees me with this bag there will be questions asked."

"Ones you don't want to answer," Harley added with a chuckle.

"Exactly. I would feel a tad uncomfortable if I had to show my mother the thong you bought me."

"I guess so. I know my mom won't know where to look when my sister opens my gag gift at her shower. I'll get a good laugh out of it, though."

Of course as fate would have it, Blaise opened the front door, allowed Harley to walk in first before he did, and found his mom standing in the foyer. She had a jacket on, looking ready to go out somewhere.

Her gaze landed briefly on Harley before it settled on the pink bag he held. "Please don't tell me you've taken up wearing women's underthings."

"Mom!" Blaise said. "No. It just happens the store has a men's section as well."

"Oh, yes. I forgot they did. Are you going to introduce me?"

"This is Harley. Harley, this is my mother." He gave his mom a meaningful look. "Aren't you going somewhere?"

His mother shook her head. "I'd have to be pretty thick not to get that hint. Yes, I'm going out for a bit. Your father is resting, so don't disturb him."

Blaise scowled. "Again? He did that this morning after Caleb was done examining him. He usually doesn't sleep that much during the day."

"Caleb said to expect it because of the change in

medication he gave your father." A look of worry flitted across his mother's face before it quickly disappeared. She looked at Harley. "It's nice meeting you. I hope to see you again." With that said, she walked around them, then out the door.

"Your dad is sick?" Harley asked once they were alone.

"Yeah. My cousin, Caleb, is a doctor, but he can't figure out what's wrong with my father."

"Have you taken him to get another doctor's opinion?"

"No." Hoping to change the subject, Blaise held up the pink bag. "I'll just run this up to my room, then we can go to the stables."

He hurried across the foyer to the wide stairs that led to the upper floor. With Harley being in the medical field, she would think it strange they hadn't taken his dad to see another doctor if Caleb wasn't helping him get better. He couldn't exactly tell her the reason there was no one else. Not right now, anyway.

CHAPTER THREE

Harley watched Blaise take the stairs two at a time. She dropped her gaze to his ass, seeing how his jeans stretched tight across it with each step he took. Once he disappeared from sight at the top, she sighed to herself. The man had a killer bod.

She didn't have long to wait before Blaise came back down again. He smiled as he met her gaze. Along with his hot body, he was handsome as sin. Harley was pretty pleased with herself for taking that chance back at the mall. He'd turned out to be better potential boyfriend material than she'd first thought. If she could get her claws into him, she would hold on for all she was worth.

"Let's go," Blaise said once he reached her.

Harley nodded, then followed him through the front door. She zipped up the jacket she wore as he brought her around the side of the garage and onto a graveled lane. A short distance away there was another building that presumably was the stable. The large structure was all red wood and white trim. The paddocks near it were enclosed with white wood fencing.

Once they reached the building, Blaise led her through the large sliding door that stood open. Harley looked down the row of stalls. There were about ten of them and each one was occupied. As they walked farther inside, large equine heads appeared over the tops of the doors. The horses snorted in greeting as they walked by.

Blaise stopped at the end in front of a stall on the right and stroked the nose of a black one. "This is my horse. He's a gelding called George."

Harley burst out laughing. "You named your horse George?"

"I know it's a suck-ass name. It started out as a joke. I couldn't come up with one so my brother, Taylor, kept calling him George, thinking I'd get sick of hearing it and pick a better one. That didn't happen so the name stuck."

She ran her hand along the horse's cheek. "Despite his terrible name, he's beautiful."

Blaise walked to the stall beside George's. "This is the one you can ride. Her name is Star."

Harley could easily see why the bay mare was called that. She had a white star in the center of her forehead. "Hello, girl. Are you ready to go for a ride?" She scratched Star's nose.

"I'll get them saddled and then we can go."

Blaise got saddles and bridles, then put the horses' tack on while they were still inside their stalls. That task completed, he led Star out to Harley before taking George out of his. Once they were outside, they mounted. Even though it'd been a few years since she'd last been on a horse, Harley had no problem adjusting the stirrups or holding the reins properly.

Blaise kicked George into a walk, and Harley brought Star up beside him. They rode in silence until they left the stable behind them and were in a large stretch of open land. Fall had set in and turned the leaves around them to gold and red.

"All this belongs to your family?" she asked.

"Yes, as far as you can see and then some. How about we go a little faster? Since you've ridden before, you shouldn't have any problem handling Star in a canter."

Harley nodded as she set her heels into Star's sides, getting the mare from a walk to a trot and then into a canter. She settled into the rocking motion of the horse and kept pace with Blaise and George.

They rode like that for about five minutes before Blaise pulled George to a stop close to a tall birch tree that stood alone in the center of the grassy land. There was nobody else around but them. She took a deep breath, filling her lungs with fresh air. It was nice to get away from city life once in a while. This was the perfect place to do that.

Blaise edged his horse closer to hers. He reached across and cupped the back of her neck before he leaned forward while nudging her in the same direction. He took her mouth in a light kiss, brushing his lips across hers.

He pulled back and met her gaze. "I've wanted to do that since shortly after I met you."

"Do it again," she said, her voice on the breathy side.

Hunger rose inside his eyes. "Like this?"

Blaise took her lips once more. Only this time it wasn't a light brush. His mouth settled over hers, sealing it tight. His tongue came out and pushed inside, dueling with hers. Desire shot through her body, causing her nipples to grow taut and a throbbing ache to make itself known deep inside her pussy. The man was not only a hunk, he also knew how to kiss a woman.

Harley dropped her horse's reins and buried her fingers into Blaise's thick hair, returning his passionate kiss with as much enthusiasm as he gave her. She tried to pull him closer, but their legs were already trapped between the two horses. Blaise soon took care of that.

He caught her under her arms and hauled her over to

him, sitting her on his lap so she straddled his thighs, facing him. With not much room in the saddle, her pussy ended up pressed against the hard bulge in Blaise's jeans. Harley wrapped her arms around his neck and ground against his cock. She couldn't help herself. He felt so damn good. He held her tight around her waist, pushing her down onto him, adding to the delicious friction.

The meeting of their mouths deepened. Their movements caused George to walk in a circle. Harley absently heard Star following him. For all she cared her horse could have taken off back to the stable. She could only focus on how George's rolling gait rocked her and Blaise together.

Harley sucked on Blaise's tongue, and he purred like a big cat. She did it again and got the same response. Obviously, he liked that. A lot. She continued to grind against his hard cock. Wetness leaked into her panties. At the rate she was going she'd be able to get off just like that.

Blaise pulled away first, breathing hard as he stared into her eyes. "I'm getting too many ideas about what you and I can do on top my horse. They're all X-rated."

"Then you and I are on the same wavelength." The idea of actually having sex on horseback appealed more to her than it should.

"Don't encourage me," Blaise said as he looked at her with stark hunger in his eyes.

"So, you got me all hot and bothered for no reason?"

Blaise took a deep breath, then purred like a cat once more. "You definitely are that."

"I've never had a guy purr for me like that before. I have to admit it's a turn-on."

"Then I'll have to make sure I do it all the time."

Harley bit her lip and let out a quiet moan as George took a hard step down and jolted her and Blaise together. "I'm embarrassed to say how easy it would be for me to come like this. I guess I'm showing how long it's actually been since I last slept with a guy."

"You know, telling me that isn't exactly helping me get things settled down."

She pushed against him once more. "I can see that. If it was summer instead of fall, and we weren't so out in the open, I could help you with that."

Blaise groaned. "Now I wish I didn't have this family dinner."

"Well, even if you didn't, I couldn't have you over to my apartment. My roommate will be there. She doesn't work tonight. To say she's nosy is putting it mildly. The only reason I don't mind living with her is because she's usually working when I'm home. On the weekends is when we pretty much see each other."

"How would you feel about coming back here afterward and spending the night with me?"

Harley gave Blaise a questioning look. "What about your parents? Won't they say something about it?"

"No. My brother lives here with his wife. Plus, my room is more like an apartment than a bedroom."

She smiled. "After what I've seen so far of your house, I have to admit I'm more than a little curious to see your room. Maybe you'll model that thong for me again."

Blaise captured her lips in a heated kiss, causing the flames of her desire that had been at a simmer to come raging back to life. Harley once again found herself drowning in the sensations swamping her body. She ached to have his cock buried deep inside her pussy, pumping in and out until they came.

He lifted his head. "I guess that means you'll do it."

"Yes." That one word was all Harley was able to manage. Her brain was barely firing on two cylinders.

"Good. I think we should continue our ride. I'm already finding it hard enough not to continue what we started."

Blaise gathered George's reins at Harley's back, then steered the horse to Star, who stood patiently waiting.

Once they were at the mare's side, Blaise lifted her off his lap and settled her in Star's saddle.

Setting off once again, Harley tamped down the arousal that still simmered deep inside her. There was no question of her not turning Blaise down. She wanted him too much. It might make her look easy by sleeping with him after only having recently met him, but she really didn't care. Sometimes it was better to take what she wanted rather than to wait and have it slip through her fingers. Blaise was definitely something she wanted to hold on to with both hands and not let go.

* * * *

After their ride, Blaise walked Harley to her car and gave her a kiss that would have to last him until he saw her again later that night. He'd reluctantly ended it before she drove down the long lane that would take her to the main road. Once her car was no longer in sight, he'd turned and headed inside the house.

Since he'd spent most of the afternoon on a horse, Blaise decided a shower was in order before dinner. He hadn't made it halfway up the flight of stairs to the upper level when his mother walked into the foyer and called his name.

He turned, and said, "I was just about to take a shower. I doubt you want me smelling like horse while you're eating dinner."

His mom walked up the steps and stopped on the one below his. "No, I wouldn't. I wanted to see how your afternoon went with Harley."

"It went very well, thank you. To let you know, she's coming over again later tonight."

"You really like this human." She said it with a smile.

"Yes."

"Maybe she can be the one for you as Aspen was for

Taylor."

Blaise reached inside his jacket and pulled out his cougar-head pendant. "As you can see, nothing so far. Even if Harley doesn't set off the magic, I still want to see her. I enjoy being with her, and she has the same type of sense of humor I have." The incident at the mall came to mind and he had to hold back a chuckle.

"If that's the case, then she has to be meant for you, though having two of you around with that same kind of humor might just drive us all crazy."

He leaned down and kissed her cheek. "You'd love it and you know it."

"Of course I would. Taylor, though, not so much."

"He'd have to get over it, but don't jump ahead of yourself now. I haven't even known Harley for twenty-four hours yet. To forewarn you, when she does arrive, we're going to be locked in my bedroom so don't disturb us."

"I wouldn't do that. You're an adult male, no longer a child. There is one thing, though. Try not to be too loud. Some of us will want to sleep."

His mom winked then turned and headed down the stairs. Blaise shook his head as he continued up to his bedroom. That would have been something he would have said.

After closing himself inside his room, Blaise hung up his jacket in his walk-in closet, then went to the en suite. He stripped out of his clothes. To his sensitive nose, they mostly smelled like horse, but he was able to pick up Harley's scent as well. His cock grew hard as he remembered how it'd felt to have her in his arms, her jean-clad pussy grinding on his erection. She'd said she'd been close to coming that way. Well, it wouldn't have taken much more for him either.

* * * *

The evening meal with Aspen's parents went well. They were good company and had accepted the fact their new son-in-law was a cougar shifter. The one person out of Aspen's family who didn't know the truth about Taylor was Aspen's older sister. Even her parents had decided it was best for their oldest daughter not to know. Aspen and her sibling weren't very close to begin with.

His father, of course, remained in the master bedroom. There was no question of him not being able to manage coming downstairs even for a little while. It would have been a decidedly strained evening if it had been possible. Aspen's parents inquired about how he was feeling, and that was as far as the subject of his father had gone. They had to have known how his dad felt about humans being part of their family group. Knowing Taylor, he would have informed his in-laws of that.

Just as they finished eating, the sound of the front door opening, and two very familiar male voices reached Blaise's ears. After he looked at his mother to say he'd greet the newcomers, he pushed back his chair and stood. His name was called before he made it out to the foyer.

"I'm right here," Blaise said as he met with Jase and Grady.

The two brothers were more like his siblings rather than his cousins. They, Taylor, and he had basically grown up together. Their mother was the younger sister of Blaise's.

"Are you ready to go?" Jase asked.

"Go where?" Blaise answered.

"It Saturday night. We decided we'd check out that new bar. Remember?"

"Shit, I forgot. I'm not going to be able to make it."

"What do you mean?" Grady asked. "There can't be anything you'd rather be doing than going out for a drink. There could be some hot girls there."

Blaise smiled. "I already found a hot girl, thank you

very much. She's the reason I can't go out with you. She's coming over in a little while to spend the night with me. She isn't here right now is because Aspen's parents are over for dinner."

"Human or cougar shifter?" Jase asked.

"Human. Her name is Harley."

Jase looked at his brother. "Maybe we should stick around and check her out."

Blaise shook his head. "Oh no, you won't. I just met her this afternoon. I don't need you two scaring her away."

Grady smiled at Jase before he turned his gaze back on Blaise. "Sounds as if you really like her. Where exactly did you meet her?"

"At the mall downtown."

"Maybe we should give the mall a try, Jase. We could see if we can find our own human female hanging out there."

Just like Blaise, his cousins wanted to find human women to date rather than cougar shifters. They felt the same way about the opposite sex of their kind as Blaise did. With Taylor mated to a human, there wasn't much the other members of their family group could say to stop them.

"That's a plan," Blaise said. "You can go now. The mall might still be open."

"He's trying to get rid of us already," Jase said.

"I know," Grady replied. "Maybe he's worried one of us will steal Harley away from him. After all, we are better-looking than him."

"I have to agree with that," Jase said with a grin.

Blaise snorted. "Yeah right. Now get out of here."

"All right," Jase said. "We'll leave. We can torment you another time."

"Good. I wish you luck at the bar."

Jase and Grady made Blaise promise to go out with them again soon, then walked outside, discussing what other bar they would go to if the first one ended up not having any hot girls.

Blaise shut the door behind them with a shake of his head. He had to pity any human women who actually showed interest in his cousins. They weren't exactly womanizers, but they did appreciate beauty in the opposite sex.

Since the meal was over, Blaise returned to the dining room only long enough to excuse himself, then headed up to his room. Once there, he called Harley to let her know she was welcome to come over any time. She said she'd be there in a half hour.

Blaise ended the call and then turned on his television to pass the time until Harley arrived. He'd only just settled on the bed when he heard his father having a coughing fit. Since his mom was downstairs with company, Blaise decided he'd look in on his dad.

He didn't bother knocking on one of the master bedroom doors and walked in. His dad was still coughing and wheezing, trying to catch his breath. Blaise went to the bedside table and poured a glass of water from the bottle that sat there, then waited for the fit to subside.

It was over a few seconds later before he helped his dad take a drink. Blaise looked down at the tissue his father had held against his mouth while coughing. The sight of blood on it had his gut clenching. There was more than had been present that morning.

"I think you need to tell Caleb to switch your shots back to the old one. You're getting worse," Blaise said as he placed the glass on the table, then helped resettle his father against the pillows at his back.

"He said it would be like this."

"I don't care. You're coughing up blood, Dad. That's not a good thing."

"I'll let him give me one more injection of the new medicine. He told me to give it a chance before making the decision to discontinue using it."

"At this rate, another dose of it could have you right at death's door. Tell him no."

"Your cousin is doing the best he can. I'm willing to try anything he suggests."

"I'm going to tell you right now. If you continue to worsen with the new medication, I'll tell Caleb to switch it whether you agree to it or not. It might be time to face facts that Caleb has reached the limit of what he's capable of doing for you. It might also be the time we check with another family group's healer."

His father scowled. "No. They aren't trained doctors. I paid for Caleb to go to medical school when he showed interest in that field for the very reason we'd have one if a doctor was needed."

"Be that as it may, this illness could be beyond Caleb. You have to admit that. He might be a skilled doctor, but he's not one who does research into finding cures."

"I'll still allow Caleb to try the new medication one more time."

"That's it. If you're settled again, I'm going to leave you."

"Are Aspen's parents still here?"

"Yes, and they happen to be very nice people."

"I suppose they are, but I still find it hard to accept humans being aware of what we are."

"You need to learn to relax about that. There's nothing you can do about Taylor's mate being human. Personally, I'm glad Aspen turned out to be his. It's allowed me to date someone out of our kind."

His dad narrowed his eyes. "You would date a human? Even though there's a chance she could end up being your mate?"

Blaise smiled. "As of today, I am dating one."

He didn't wait for his father to say anything about that comment. Blaise left the master bedroom, knowing full well he'd ticked his dad off, not that he cared much for that particular tradition. It was time to get over his kind's stuck-up ways when it came to humans.

CHAPTER FOUR

Blaise hurried to the front door and opened it after the doorbell rang. He'd been in the kitchen, looking through the wine fridge to see what kinds were already chilled. Seeing Harley standing on the other side, he yanked her over the threshold and into his arms, claiming her lips as he walked them backward. He kicked the door shut behind them.

He lifted his head and smiled. "Hello again."

"Hello yourself," Harley said. "Did you miss me or something?"

"You could say that. Do you feel like having something to drink? We have wine and beer. We have harder stuff as well. Your choice."

"I'm not much of a beer drinker. I could go for a glass of white wine if you have some."

"All right. You can come and pick a bottle for us to have. We have more than one."

Blaise captured Harley's hand and walked her through the house to the kitchen. He stopped at the wine fridge and pulled the door open.

"Make your pick," he said.

Harley looked around the room and whistled in appreciation. "This would be a chef's dream kitchen." She turned her gaze to the wine fridge, which was the same size as the regular one and full of bottles. "That is a lot of wine."

"My parents are something of wine connoisseurs. They like to have a large variety on hand. As for the rest, we have a personal chef who cooks all our meals. Mom isn't exactly handy in the kitchen."

"Must be nice. I'd love to have one. I can cook, but I hate doing it, especially when it's just me who has to eat the food when I'm done."

"Then I'll have the chef whip us up something nice for breakfast tomorrow." Blaise noticed the backpack Harley had slung over one shoulder. "I see you brought a change of clothes, which means you haven't changed your mind about staying overnight."

She brushed a kiss across his lips. "No, I haven't." Harley looked inside the fridge and took out a bottle of white wine. "Let's have this one. It's about the only one I've tried before and know I like."

Blaise took the bottle from her. "I'll grab some wineglasses and a corkscrew, then we can go to my room."

He tucked the bottle under his arm, took out the glasses from the cupboard, and the corkscrew from a drawer before he guided Harley up the stairs to his bedroom. He put what he carried on one of his bedside tables then closed and locked the door.

Harley had placed her backpack on the floor near his dresser and looked around. "You weren't kidding when you said your bedroom was more like an apartment. This is almost as big as mine. You even have a small sitting room." She walked to the en suite and peered in. "Yup, your bathroom is the same size as my bedroom." She went to stand in front of him.

While Harley had been checking out his room, Blaise had poured each of them a glass of wine. He held one out to her. "We do like our space around here."

Harley took the glass and sipped from it. "This is as good as I remembered."

Blaise had some as well. It wasn't too sweet and not too dry. Just the way he liked his wine. He waited until Harley had another drink before he took her glass from her, and with his, placed them on the bedside table next to the bottle.

He turned back to her and ran the pad of his thumb along her plump bottom lip. She opened her mouth and took the tip of it inside, giving it a suck. The sexual tension between them flared to life in an instant. Blaise's cock hardened as he imagined it was that Harley sucked on.

He pulled his thumb away and bent to claim her mouth in a kiss that was all lips and tongue. She pressed closer, her hands dropping to his waist. Blaise pushed Harley's jacket off and then dropped it to the floor. With it no longer between them, her taut nipples brushed against him through the thin layers of their shirts.

Harley moaned into his mouth and shoved her hands up the front of his t-shirt. She skimmed her fingers along his sides to his chest, then caressed in the opposite direction to his stomach. He couldn't hold back a cat's purr as she continued lower and cupped his erection through his jeans. It jerked under her touch.

"Mmm, I have a hold of something I've been dying to get up close and personal with," Harley said against his mouth.

"I can say it's wanted that too."

"Then I'd better not disappoint it."

Blaise held perfectly still as Harley's lips left his mouth and she nipped his chin before dragging his shirt up and over his head. She tossed it aside, her gaze landing on his bared upper body.

"Normally, I don't like necklaces on a guy, but your cougar-head pendant suits you," she said, trailing a finger down the middle of his abs.

"I'm glad you like it," he answered, his voice husky as his arousal increased.

Harley's nimble fingers set to work on opening his jeans. With no difficulty, she opened the button and tugged down the zipper. She parted the material and shoved a hand inside, wrapping around his hard cock.

She looked down and moaned. "Still commando I see. I had thought to suggest you put that thong on, but now that I have what I'm craving in my hand, I think that can wait for another time."

He couldn't agree more. With her fingers stroking his shaft, there was no way he wanted her to stop so he could change into a thong.

"Yes, I can definitely wear it some other time."

Harley pressed a kiss to the center of his chest before she tugged his pants down low enough to spring his cock. She flicked the tip of her tongue over each of his nipples, stroking his length as she did so. Blaise sucked in a breath. He'd thought he'd be the seducer in this first encounter, but it would seem Harley had taken on that role.

Her roving mouth left his chest and headed in a downward path, her lips skimming across his stomach muscles, which he couldn't help but tighten as her tongue flicked out to taste his skin. Another loud purr pushed out of him.

Blaise looked down. Harley slowly went onto her knees in front of him. She thrust her free hand into the back of his jeans and gripped his ass. She fisted his cock at the base and lapped the very tip with her tongue. He locked his knees to keep himself upright.

She gave him a couple more good licks before she opened her mouth and took him inside. She greedily sucked, stroking what she couldn't take with her hand. She moved her head forward and back as she slid him in and out, keeping the delicious pressure around his length. He rocked his hips, matching the pace she set.

All too soon Blaise had to stop her or risk coming in her mouth. It would end things a lot faster than he intended. Harley was still fully clothed, and he wanted the chance to explore her body as she'd done his before either of them found their release.

He eased away, then brought her to her feet with a gentle hand around her arm. Blaise removed her top. He stared at the sheer bra she wore, easily able to see the dusky-rose of her nipples. He covered her breasts with his hands and stroked his thumbs across the tight peaks before he set to work on removing her jeans.

Once Harley stood only in her matching bra and panties, Blaise took in what he'd revealed. Her body was curvy in all the right places. He couldn't wait to get his lips and tongue all over her, learning every inch of skin.

He met her gaze and held it as he undid the front clasp of her bra then took it off. Blaise lifted her and carried her the very short distance to his king-sized bed. He placed her on the mattress and climbed up next to her, stretching out onto his side. Her chest rapidly rose and fell with each quick breath she took. The scent of her arousal filled his nose, increasing his need for her.

Blaise bent his head and licked the hollow of Harley's throat before he kissed his way down to her breasts, which had been enticing him to suck on them. He cupped one and swirled his tongue around the nipple. She arched her back in invitation, a throaty moan leaving her. He took the peak into his mouth and sucked as he plucked at the opposite one with his thumb and index finger.

He left her breast and continued downward, placing feather-light kisses across her ribs to her bellybutton. He dipped his tongue inside it, then shifted even lower. Blaise used his teeth to drag her panties down. Once they snagged on her hips, he hooked a finger in them and pulled them the rest of the way off.

Blaise reached between Harley's legs and ran a finger along her pussy, collecting her juices. He brought it to his mouth and licked it clean, the flavor of her making him purr. His cock ached to be inside her, but the scent of her arousal enticed him to taste even more.

He settled between her spread thighs, his shoulders pressing them farther apart, and tongued her pussy. She let out a whimpered moan, her fingers sinking into his hair as she held him to her. He licked and sucked, returning the pleasure she'd given him when she'd taken his cock into her mouth.

"No more," Harley said on a gasp. "I want you inside me, your cock filling me. Now."

"Are you sure you're ready for me?"

She tugged on his hair. "Yes. God, yes."

Blaise shucked his jeans before he crawled up Harley's body, settling his hips between her legs, the head of his cock against her slick opening. "Then you can have me."

He pushed forward until her pussy closed around the head of his shaft. He pulled slightly back, then pushed a little farther inside. He kept up the forward-and-retreat movement until he'd worked his full length into her.

Blaise lifted his upper body onto his bent arms and set a steady pace, his hips thrusting between Harley's spread thighs. Her pussy fit his cock like a glove. Her inner muscles squeezed around his shaft, increasing the delicious sensations he felt. He purred, unable to hold them at bay, telling her in the way of his kind how much he enjoyed being inside her.

Harley raised her legs to either side of his hips as she lifted hers to match each of his strokes. She held on to his biceps, her fingers digging into his muscles. Breathy moans left her. He looked down to see she had her eyes closed, the pleasure she felt written on her face.

He quickened his pace, his cock growing harder. His release edged ever closer, building at the base of his spine. Blaise angled his thrusts higher so his shaft rubbed against Harley's clit as he pushed inside her pussy. She panted, her hands tightening even more around his arms.

"Just like that. Don't stop," Harley said. "Oh, so close."

"Come. I'll be right there with you."

Her inner muscles fluttered around his cock, then clutched and released it as she climaxed. He pumped his hips faster, his point of no return rushing up to meet him. He let loose with a cat growl, falling into an intense orgasm. His shaft pulsed deep inside her, filling her with his cum.

Once it was over, Blaise collapsed on top of Harley, making sure to take some of his weight on his arms so he didn't crush her with his larger size. He gently kissed her, his cock still buried inside.

"I don't know about you," he said, "but I want to do that again."

Harley smiled. "Most definitely. We can go for round two as soon as you're up for it."

Blaise rolled off her and sat up. "In that case, let's have more wine while we wait. No point in wasting the bottle."

He reached over to the nightstand for their drinks as Harley pushed herself into a sitting position. Blaise ran his gaze over her naked body. Making love to her one time wasn't nearly enough. He was pretty sure his recovery time wouldn't last any longer than it took for them to finish their glasses of wine.

* * * *

Blaise woke up with a start, not sure what had awakened him. He looked down at Harley who was fast asleep against his side, her head pillowed on his chest. A quick look at the clock showed it was late in the morning, pushing noon. He wasn't surprised to find it so. They'd been up most of the night making love. The last bout had ended close to dawn.

The sound of his mother shouting his name and Taylor's had Blaise sitting bolt upright. There was no mistaking the fear in her voice by the way she called them. He jumped out of bed and grabbed his discarded jeans, then tugged them on as he headed for his bedroom door, hopping on one foot and the other as he stuck his feet into each leg.

"What's the matter?" Harley asked, sitting up and looking at him in surprise.

"I don't know, but my mom is calling for my brother and me. I think something is wrong."

Blaise threw open his bedroom door and ran down the hall toward the master bedroom as Taylor reached the top of the stairs. Blaise entered the room first. It didn't take him long to take in the scene that took place at the bed. His mom stood at the side of it, crying, looking unsure what to do as his father appeared to be having a seizure.

"What's going on?" Taylor demanded as he came to stand next to Blaise, who had reached their mother.

"I think Dad is having a seizure," Blaise answered. To his mother, he asked, "Did this just start?"

She nodded. "Yes."

"Was Caleb here already?" She nodded again as she wrung her hands. "Did he give him another shot of the new medication?"

"Yes."

"Damn it, I told Dad to not let Caleb give it to him. I had a feeling something like this would happen."

"What are you saying?" Taylor asked.

"I think this new medication of Caleb's isn't helping Dad at all. It's making him worse."

"We can discuss this later," his mother said, her voice

nearing a hysterical level. "What should we do about your father?"

"Exactly what you're doing now," Harley said as she pushed her way past Blaise to stand by his father's side. "When someone is having a seizure, you leave them alone until it's over. Just make sure there isn't anything around them that they could hurt themselves on."

"Are you sure?" his mom asked tearfully.

"Yes. I'm a medical lab technician and have some CPR training. Did he just start seizing?"

"Yes," his mother replied. "How much longer will this last?"

"A seizure can last for up to five minutes, but I don't think he will. It appears to be slowing down."

Blaise looked at his father to see Harley was right. His father's jerky movements were slowing. Once they stopped completely, she instructed them to place his dad on his left side with his head also at the side just in case he vomited, which thankfully he didn't. It took a few minutes before his dad answered his mother when she said his name.

"I'm glad you were here," Blaise said to Harley. "None of us would have known what to do."

"Seizures can be scary things for anyone. Do you really think your dad is having an adverse reaction to the medication?"

"Yes."

Blaise paused once he noticed his dad had fallen asleep and he had his mother's and Taylor's undivided attention as well. He'd been thinking about something since Caleb started the new medication. Something that didn't put his cousin in a good light.

"You already mentioned that, but by the look on your face, I have a feeling you have other thoughts about it as well," his mom said.

He nodded. "Don't you think it's a bit too coincidental

that the new medication Caleb administered causes worse symptoms shortly after he's injected Dad? Today it was a seizure. Yesterday he started coughing up blood. Caleb's real lack of concern about the latter has me questioning if he cares if Dad gets better."

Taylor sighed. "I have to agree with Blaise, Mom. The idea had crept into my mind too."

"Wait a minute," Harley said. "Your dad is coughing up blood and his doctor isn't worried about it? That has warning bells going off for me."

"What do you suggest we do, Harley?" his mom asked.

"First off, I'd get him to see another doctor. I'd seriously consider taking him to an emergency room."

Blaise, Taylor, and their mother looked at each other before Blaise spoke. "That's really not an option, Harley."

"Why?"

"Just leave it at that. Take our word for it, we can't. Is there something else you think we should do?"

Harley stared at him for a few seconds, then sighed. "All right. The next thing I'd do is get his blood work done. The tests can tell you any number of things."

"Once again, it's not something we can do. Too many people would know."

She looked at all three of them with her brows drawn together. "Okay. How about this? I'd be willing to come here and draw some of your dad's blood. Since you want the utmost privacy, there's a way for me to run the tests myself without it going through the regular system of paperwork at the lab. I could come take the blood before I go into work tomorrow morning and have the results for you at the end of the day."

Taylor looked at their mother. "What do you think? It's your decision."

His mother nodded. "We'll do it. There really isn't any other way." She turned her attention on Harley. "Are you sure you can do it without getting yourself in trouble? I wouldn't want you to lose your job over it."

Harley smiled. "No one will know. I'll be careful. I can go today and get the things I'll need to draw the blood. I have keys to the lab since there are times when a doctor needs to have a test done at the last minute and I have to stay late to finish it."

"Would you mind sleeping over tonight again?" Blaise asked. "That way you'll be able to take the blood before Caleb gets here for his morning examination of my father. I think it's wise we keep what you're doing from him until we get the results."

Taylor quickly agreed. "I think that would be best. You don't mind, Harley, do you?" He winked at her. "Having to sleep with my brother and all that. I know it's such a hardship."

Harley laughed. "Of course I won't mind." She stepped closer to Blaise and put her arm around his waist. "It's hardly a hardship. I'll have to go to my apartment and pick up another change of clothes."

"I can take you," Blaise said. "I can drive you to the lab to pick up the supplies you need."

"That's not necessary. I did drive myself here so I have my car. It'll go faster if I go by myself."

"When will you leave?"

"Can I take a shower, then eat first?"

"Of course," his mom answered for him. "Lunch will be ready soon. If you have a shower now, you'll make it in time."

"All right, I'll do that," Harley said with a smile before she walked out of the room.

Once Blaise heard his bedroom door shut, he said, "I think I'll get ready for lunch, if you'll be okay with me leaving, Mom."

She waved him to go. "Your dad is sleeping now, and it isn't as if you aren't still in the house if something else happens." She glanced at his cougar-head pendant. "No glowing eyes yet I see. I'll be keeping my fingers crossed Harley does set off the magic inside it. I like her."

Blaise kissed his mother cheek. "It's still early days, Mom. I'll see you downstairs in a little while."

He left his brother and mother, then headed to his own bedroom. Inside, he closed the door and locked it. The shower ran in the en suite. With a smile, he shucked his jeans, then walked toward it.

CHAPTER FIVE

Harley closed her eyes and ducked her head under the showerhead to wet her hair. She stood there longer than was needed, enjoying the warm water beating against her body. Blaise's shower was a work of luxury with marble tile, glass surround doors, and body sprays running vertically underneath the head. It was more like a spa shower than a regular one. If she owned it, she could easily see herself running up a huge water bill by taking long showers every day.

Her mind wandered to Blaise and his family as she grabbed the bottle of shampoo she'd brought from home and squeezed some into her palm. They all seemed very nice. The only person she had to see yet was Taylor's wife, Aspen, but Blaise had told her about his sister-in-law.

Taylor and Blaise looked a lot alike, right down to the same tawny-blond hair and light brown eyes that were almost gold in color. Actually, their parents had those features as well.

Harley ducked her head under the water again, rinsing

out the shampoo. Thinking of Blaise had her thoughts straying to the night before, how she enjoyed being in his arms, taking his body into hers. No, staying another night with him would be no hardship for her.

As if her thoughts had lured him to her, Harley opened her eyes at the feel of two large hands caressing her breasts and found Blaise standing in front of her. She ran her gaze over his naked body, stopping on his cock, which was fully engorged. Her pussy grew instantly wet, a throbbing ache building with her need to have him inside her.

"Decided to join me in the shower, huh? We'll be late for lunch, you know," she said with a smile as she skimmed her hands from his wide shoulders to the center of his chest where his pendant lay.

She ran her fingers across the cougar head, the gold feeling warm under them. It wasn't the first time it'd felt that way when she'd touched it. During the night, as they made love, every time the pendant came in contact with her skin, she swore it heated against her. She found herself drawn to it, the urge to touch it one that was hard to ignore.

"We'll make it fast," Blaise said with a sexy grin. "Before my mom called, I'd hoped to wake you up by making love to you."

"I guess we can have a quickie." Harley stroked the cougar-head pendant again before she lifted her face and met Blaise's lips halfway with her own.

Passion blazed between them in an instant. Blaise wrapped his arms around her waist, pulling her flush against him. The water streamed down their bodies, making them slippery. Harley moaned at the slick feel.

Blaise left her mouth and sucked on her skin at the side of her neck. "I don't think I'll ever get enough of you," he said in a husky voice. "I crave your touch, need it as much as I need the air to breathe."

Harley shivered at his words despite the fact warm

water pelted her back. In that moment, she realized she was falling for Blaise. It'd started sometime during the night. His taking her over and over again had her wishing she could stay in his arms forever. Normally, it took her a little while to have strong emotions for a man. She lusted for them in the beginning, but only a few had her feeling as she did for Blaise. Even then it wasn't as strong as what she felt for the man who held her so intimately.

"God, I need you too."

To show Blaise she was more than ready to be claimed by him, Harley lifted a leg, placed it around his hip, took hold of his straining erection, and led it to her pussy. He made that purring sound that cranked her arousal up even more. He slowly thrust into her, feeding her his cock a little bit at a time, until he was seated to the hilt. He filled her completely.

In a show of strength, Blaise picked her off her feet, guided her other leg around his hip, then cupping her bottom, lifted her on and off his shaft. Harley put her arms around his neck and held on. She tightened her inner muscles around his plunging cock. He controlled everything else.

Blaise nuzzled the side of her neck before he nipped it, his pendant brushing against her breast. Harley felt the heat of it sliding along her skin, adding to her pleasure. His pace quickened as his shaft grew even harder. It stroked in and out of her pussy, stretching her, rubbing in all the right places.

Her body coiled tighter, readying itself to come. The sound of their loud breathing echoed off the tiled walls. There was no holding back her orgasm. It slammed into her, sweeping her away on a wave of intense pleasure. She cried out Blaise's name, a whimpered moan soon following. As her inner muscles spasmed around his thrusting cock, he let out a deep groan, coming right along with her. He held her tightly to him, emptying himself inside her.

He slowly let her legs down and rested his forehead against hers as he fought to catch his breath. She breathed just as quickly. She skimmed a hand along his chest until she reached his pendant, then hooked her fingers around it.

"Even though that was quick," she said, "it was pretty intense."

Blaise chuckled. "I have to agree. It just keeps getting better and better."

That was the truth. At the rate they were going, she wasn't sure another man would ever live up to Blaise's standards. He said he craved her touch, well, she had a feeling she was becoming addicted to his.

Once they came down from their pleasure high, they quickly finished showering. By mutual consent, they let each other wash their own bodies. If they'd done otherwise, they wouldn't have left the shower without going for another round.

They toweled dry and then headed into the bedroom to dress. Harley took her clean clothes out of her backpack. She'd pulled on the ones from the day before, sans bra and panties, before going to Blaise's parents' bedroom to see what was going on. She packed the dirty things to take home with her.

Once they were dressed, Blaise took her by the hand and walked her out of his bedroom and into the hallway. They silently headed down the stairs. The smell of something delicious hit Harley's nose after they reached the lower level. Her stomach growled in response.

"Hungry?" Blaise asked with a smile.

"Very. I think I've worked up an appetite."

"Then I'd better get some food into you."

They walked into the dining room to find his family already there eating, except for his father. Harley was introduced to Aspen. She took an instant liking to the other woman. From the way Aspen and Taylor acted with each other, Harley could tell they were deeply in love. She noticed Aspen wore an identical cougar-head pendant like Blaise, as did his mother. She guessed maybe it was something the men in the family did, gave their wives their necklaces once they were together. Harley thought it was cute.

She furtively gave Blaise's pendant a glance, imagining what it would look like around her neck. Maybe if things lasted between them he'd give it to her. Harley shook her head at her silly thoughts. It was just a necklace, not as significant as say an engagement ring. She wasn't expecting one of those any time soon.

Lunch turned out to be really good. There was freshly made bread, lobster bisque, and a spring mix salad dressed with a raspberry vinaigrette. There was no mistaking it as a chef-made meal with the way it was plated, and the garnishes sprinkled around to add color. Harley dug into the food, relishing every mouthful. The only time she got to eat like this was if she went out to a fancy restaurant, which didn't happen very often.

"I can see you like the food," Blaise said as he leaned closer where he sat beside her. "You haven't lifted your head since you started eating."

Harley felt her cheeks grow red. She realized what he'd said was true. She had been kind of wrapped up in enjoying it. "Sorry," she said softly.

"You have nothing to be sorry for," Blaise's mom said. "Blaise is just being Blaise. He sometimes likes to make people the butt of his jokes. If he says something stupid like that, you have my permission to give a smack."

"Now that's not very nice, Mom," Blaise said with exaggerated indignation.

"You mean like this?" Harley asked as she reached behind Blaise and gave him a smack to the back of his head.

The surprised look Blaise turned her way had Harley laughing, along with everyone else at the table. "You hit me," he said.

Between chuckles, she replied, "Well, your mom did say I could."

"I think you better watch out for that one," Taylor said. "She'll give as good as she gets."

The rest of the meal passed in good-natured banter. Once Harley was finished eating, she reluctantly pushed back her chair and stood. "Thanks for the great meal. I should do those errands before it gets too late."

"I'll walk you out," Blaise said as he stood as well.

After getting her jacket and backpack from Blaise's room, they returned to the main floor. He swept her up into a kiss that took her breath away, then let her go. Harley really didn't want to leave now.

Blaise opened the door and then walked outside with her. "You'll come back as soon as you get what you need, right?"

"Yes, I promise. I should only be an hour or so."

"Good." At her car, Blaise kissed her again.

Harley climbed into her vehicle and then waved to Blaise once she started up the long lane to the road. Leaving him, she came to the conclusion it was already too late. She was in love with him. Now the big question was if he felt the same way about her.

* * * *

Blaise decided not to go back into the house. Watching Harley leave had put him on edge. He hadn't been lying when he'd said he'd miss her. During their night spent together, he'd grown closer to her. Plus, sleeping with her and not having her wanting to check out his pendant to see if the ruby eyes glowed right afterward endeared her more to him.

Needing to expend a little excess energy, Blaise headed for the back of the house where he could easily get to the open stretch of land. He shifted to his cougar form, then took off at a run. He'd just hit the grassy area when another cougar came up beside him. It was Taylor. They ran until they reached the opposite end of the field before they stopped and took on their human forms once again.

"It's a nice day for a run," Taylor said.

"Yeah, it is." The sun shone brightly, and even though it was fall, it wasn't too chilly, not that they'd have felt the cold through their thick pelts.

"You really like Harley, don't you?"

"Yes. I now know why you prefer human women. No pressure."

"You mean *a* human woman, as in the singular. Aspen is the only one for me."

"I know. I meant before you met her."

"Being banished from the family group did give me a better perspective on life. I'm thankful one of our females didn't set off my pendant. I don't think I would have been able to stand it."

"Which is why you have a human for a mate. Speaking of your banishment, have you spoken to your werewolf buddies yet?"

Taylor had lived and worked for a werewolf. Meadow had been human until she became the mate of one of the werewolf sentinels, who turned her. Meadow and Taylor had become so close Taylor thought of her as a sister. When he'd left Juneau, where Meadow lived, he'd done so without telling her where he was going or why, not sure what to expect when he arrived in Anchorage. Banishment was usually meant for life. Only their father's illness had made it possible for Taylor to come back to the family group. He'd been the heir apparent to take their father's place. Since Blaise had outright refused to take his brother's place after he'd been kicked out, their dad had decided no one else but Taylor could do the job so he overturned it.

His brother nodded. "Yeah, I called Meadow a couple of days ago."

"How did that go?"

Taylor chuckled. "Good. I explained everything to her. Once she got done giving me crap for feeling as if I couldn't talk to her about it, she said she wants me to bring Aspen to Juneau for a visit or Meadow and her mate, Durlach, will come here. She made it perfectly clear she was going to remain a part of my life."

"So you told her about Dad." Blaise said it as a statement.

"Yes. Meadow offered a couple options if he starts to go downhill fast. She said she'd get Durlach to bite Dad and see if he would gain immortality like them or she'd talk to Ryder, the sentinels' shaman, about seeing Dad and trying to cure him with a magic spell."

The sentinels were the only werewolves who were able to turn a human or mortal, as they called them. The six original sentinels were the very first werewolves, who were from the ice age. Their shaman back then had used a spell to create them. They had different aspects about them that modern-day werewolves, their descendants, didn't have. Like being able to turn humans and werewolves alike, making them hybrids, and being immortal.

Blaise met Taylor's gaze. "The first one, I know for a fact Dad wouldn't tolerate. He'd be a mix of werewolf and cougar, and who knows if that would even be possible. Plus, if he became immortal, then Mom would have to be turned as well since she would want the same lifespan as him. The shaman on the other hand, I wouldn't turn him away."

Taylor nodded. "I already told Meadow I'd be giving Ryder a call if it came to it. She was going to pass on that message to him." His brother paused before he spoke again. "So, you've been having doubts about Caleb as well?"

"Yes, I have. I didn't really until the other day. Before that, I was starting to question if he was going to be able to help Dad. Now I'm wondering if he's purposely making him sick."

"Even though Caleb is our cousin, we aren't as close nor know him as well as we do Jase and Grady. He was raised in his mother's family group after our uncle disappeared and his mother died. We'd have to know for sure he's deliberately causing Dad harm before we accuse him of it. For one thing, Dad wouldn't believe us. He's always tried to look out for Caleb when he could."

"Even paying to send him to medical school. I know we'd have to have proof. Hopefully, the blood tests Harley does will show something."

"We don't know for sure, but you realize there's more than a good chance she'll see the differences in our blood compared to a human's."

"I know that. I'll deal with it if it comes down to that."

"How?"

"I'll tell her exactly what I am, what we are."

"Be prepared for her not to accept it."

"I will. She hasn't set off the magic in my pendant. There's a chance she never will. I'll let her go if she can't handle the truth. I'm pretty sure she'll keep the secret of our existence as well. If she told anyone, I doubt they'd believe her, and she'll know that. She's not stupid."

"If she does set off the magic? What will you do then if she still doesn't want to be with you?"

Blaise shrugged. "I have no damn idea. I'll have to hope she'll come around as Aspen did for you."

Taylor smiled. "That had a lot to do with the fact Mom went to talk to her and explained everything about us."

"Then I guess I'll have to ask Mom to do the same thing for me."

His brother clapped him on the shoulder. "We'll have to wait and see if it comes to that. In the meantime, let's hope Harley does find something to help Dad, be it giving proof Caleb is doing something fishy or a solid answer as to what Dad's illness is. I'm going to head back to the house. I told Aspen I would talk to you, then we're going for a horseback ride."

Taylor changed to his cougar form once more, then take off at a run toward the house. Blaise shifted as well but headed in the opposite direction. He still had some time to kill before Harley arrived.

He thought over all the things he'd discussed with Taylor. Now that his brother voiced his own concerns about Caleb, Blaise was thinking more and more that not everything was on the up and up with his cousin. If the blood tests did end up showing something was very wrong, he wondered how Caleb would be dealt with. Trying to harm a family group leader was not something that could be overlooked.

Blaise's thoughts strayed to what if Harley did end up setting off the magic in his pendant. He wouldn't dislike the idea of her being his mate. He was more worried about the fact she was human and wouldn't be able to accept him being a cougar shifter. Once the cougar's ruby eyes glowed, he wouldn't be able to think about anything but trying to persuade her to take his necklace from him and put it around her neck, thus causing a bond to form between them, claiming him as hers. By persuading, he meant sex. He'd be in a state of arousal almost constantly, unable to eat or sleep. Harley rejecting him wouldn't make it go away, either. It would make it worse. The idea had Blaise feeling leery about all of it.

He slowed his loping run, figuring he'd gone far enough. Blaise turned around and headed back the way he'd come. As he'd told Taylor, he would deal with all that when the time came, if it happened. There was no guarantee.

CHAPTER SIX

"What's going on, and why is this person I don't know standing in my bedroom?" Blaise's dad asked as his gaze landed on his mate, Taylor, Blaise, and Harley in turn.

"This is Harley." His mom nodded in Harley's direction. "She's Blaise's girlfriend. She also happens to be a medical lab technician. She's going to draw some of your blood."

"Why?"

Blaise knew what had to be going on in his dad's head that he couldn't voice out loud. He would want to know why Harley, a human, was going to take his blood. He probably wasn't too thrilled to hear she was Blaise's girlfriend either.

"We," his mother said, "have decided this is one thing Caleb should have done for you. Harley knows the results must be kept from those she works with, and at the risk of losing her job, has offered to run blood tests herself to keep them out of the lab's system."

His dad frowned. "If you think it's so necessary, why don't you discuss it with Caleb first?"

Taylor stepped into the conversation. "I'm going to be very blunt here. We're not telling Caleb anything about it right now, and we want you to do the same. We have our suspicions he might be behind you not getting better. We feel he could be doing you harm rather than good."

His father turned his gaze on Blaise. Even though his dad's body was weak, his eyes were as sharp as ever. "You agree with what Taylor said."

Blaise nodded. "Yes. Actually, it was I who first brought Caleb's actions into question. This new medicine he's giving you causes you to become sicker shortly after the injection. Caleb doesn't seem to care. Mom called him yesterday and told him about the seizure you had and asked him to switch back to the old medication. He refused, Dad. He basically told Mom she didn't know anything, and he, as a doctor, was the only one qualified to make that decision."

His father's lips thinned as he glanced at his mate, who nodded. He turned his attention back on Blaise. "I had no idea. Your mother never told me. Caleb has no right to talk to her in that manner." He paused, as if thinking over what he'd been told. "I can't say these new symptoms haven't bothered me. If you truly feel Caleb is behind it, then I'll agree to the blood tests so long as Harley is the only one who sees the results. If we're going to accuse Caleb of wrongful doing, we need proof before we can confront him."

"That's what Taylor and I agreed on," Blaise said. "Harley is the only one who might be able to do that with the results."

"You obviously trust her."

Blaise glanced at Harley and smiled. "I do."

"All right then," his dad said with a nod. "Let's do this before Caleb arrives."

"One other thing," Taylor replied. "I'll be here when my cousin arrives. I'm not going to allow him to give you another injection. To avoid him becoming suspicious, you and I are going to have a pretend argument in front of him about it, Dad, but the outcome will be I'll win. Harley should have the results at the end of the day." Taylor looked at her. "Correct?"

Harley stepped closer to the bed. "Yes. They'll be for my eyes only. I don't know why you need the secrecy, but I will abide by it. As soon as I draw the blood, I'll head for the lab and then get the tests going while I work on other ones. I'll bring the findings here at the end of my shift."

His dad gave another short nod, then tugged up the sleeve of his pajama shirt. Harley kneeled on the floor, then took out the supplies she needed to draw the blood from the small bag she carried. Blaise watched her set to work, her movements efficient and fast. It was all done in less than a minute.

She stood, placed the glass vials of blood, along with the items she'd used, back into the bag and smiled. "All done. I'd better go."

"I'll walk you out," Blaise said.

His mother stopped them before they could leave. "Harley, plan to stay for dinner."

"I will," she replied. "I look forward to it. Thanks."

Blaise and Harley left the others in the master bedroom and headed to the main level. At the door, Harley picked up her backpack, which she'd brought down earlier, and slung it over her shoulder. She turned to face him and went on tiptoe to kiss him. He resisted yanking her close and kissing her breathless.

"I'm going to miss you while you're at work," he said once he released her mouth.

"And I you." She smiled. "I'll be back. At the rate I'm going, I'll be living here soon."

"You're more than welcome to share my room with

me."

"You'd better watch it. I might take you up on that offer, especially since this place comes with a personal chef."

He pretended to look hurt. "You wound me. That's the only thing that would make you want to move in?"

"Okay, not the only thing. I'd have to say getting you comes in at a close second."

Blaise turned Harley around and smacked her on the ass. "Get out of here before I take you back upstairs to show you why I should be number one."

She laughed. "See you later. If I have time, I'll try to text you."

Blaise closed the door behind Harley after she walked outside. He headed back upstairs to his room to wait for Caleb to arrive. He didn't think he wanted to miss out on seeing his dad's and Taylor's acting skills. Though pretending to argue wouldn't be very hard for them since they tended to do that frequently anyway.

It wasn't very long before Blaise heard the sound of Caleb's footsteps coming down the hallway toward the master bedroom. Blaise opened his room's door and then poked his head out to see his cousin disappearing through the open double doors at the end of the hall. It was showtime.

Blaise left his bedroom and headed for his parents'. By the time he'd reached it, Taylor and their father were already starting the "argument." Blaise stood at the doorway and watched them put on a good show for Caleb's benefit.

His dad appeared to take Caleb's side when Caleb strongly urged Taylor to change his mind about the injection. His cousin tried to reassure Taylor by stating the new side effects from the medication weren't going to do any harm, and that he'd expected them to happen. Blaise didn't let it show on the outside, but on the inside, he seethed. Plus, more warning bells were going off inside his head. What kind of doctor would use a medication knowing his patient would go through such extreme side effects? Not a good one, in Blaise's opinion.

The "argument" was over shortly after it began, with Taylor ending up the winner as he'd planned. Caleb didn't look at all pleased with the outcome. If anything, he looked angry, even though he appeared to be trying to hide it. After a cursory examination of his patient, he stormed past Blaise and then headed downstairs. The front door slammed shut a few seconds after that.

Blaise walked to the bed. "Was it me or did Caleb seem angry?"

"Oh, he was pissed," Taylor said. "Even though he tried to quickly get it under wraps, I was closer to him and smelled it in his scent for the split second it lasted."

Their father sighed. "I think you were right. Caleb is hiding something. Either it's his inability to help me and he doesn't want to admit defeat or he's purposely doing me harm."

Blaise breathed a silent sigh of relief that his dad was now on the same page with them. It would have been more difficult if he'd stuck up for Caleb. Taylor and Blaise could have had a real fight on their hands.

* * * *

Harley didn't waste any time getting the blood tests started once she arrived at the lab. The way its system was set up, it wasn't hard for her to slip the vials in without anyone being the wiser. Being higher up on the ladder, she had more leeway with doing things than others, which helped the process.

As those tests ran, Harley worked on the others she had to do for the day. She enjoyed working in the lab, but today she found her thoughts straying to Blaise from time to time, and watching the clock, counting how many hours there were until she could leave. She did manage to get a text sent to him during her lunch break, which he replied to. She'd had to make sure no one could see her phone since he'd texted what he planned to do to her once he had her locked inside his bedroom after they'd eaten dinner with his family. Her whole body had heated with arousal when she'd read what he'd sent.

She now had an hour before it was quitting time, and the first results of Blaise's father's blood tests were ready. Harley looked at the printouts, ready to spot anything that would suggest what the illness was or if something else was going on.

The first thing that brought her up short wasn't what she'd been prepared to find. It was an irregularity in the blood itself. Harley switched to the second test she'd run and found the same finding. Not used to seeing that result, and not knowing what it stood for, she had to look it up.

What it turned out to be had her shaking her head. The irregularity was cougar hemoglobin, which was impossible, but the third test's printout showed the same thing. If she hadn't taken the blood herself, she would have thought someone had mixed big cat blood with the human one.

As she scanned the rest of the page, she put the irregularity aside. What the results showed was definitely more concerning. Blaise had been right. His cousin had set out to harm Blaise's father. There were not one but two strong poisons in his system. How he'd survived for so long was a miracle. A normal person would have died shortly after it was introduced. In the back of her mind, Harley had to wonder if it had to do with the cougar blood. She quickly pushed that thought away. She'd talk to Blaise about it after his dad was fixed up. Even though the poisons were deadly, there were medications that counteracted them, and quickly.

Harley couldn't get her hands on the antidotes yet, but she knew a doctor who could give her what she needed. He wouldn't ask questions. He was a research doctor who Harley had worked for right out of school. He would trust she would need the medication without having to know the reason. All it would take would be for her to talk to him and he'd call in the prescription to a drugstore for her to pick up.

She made her call, having the result she wanted. The only thing he asked was for her to keep him informed if all didn't work out as she'd planned. Harley had quickly promised she would, then gave him the address to the drugstore not too far from the lab, not wanting to use the one right next door.

Harley left work and headed for the drugstore. There she was able to pick up the prescription, along with a small package of syringes, without having to wait. Her doctor friend had made sure the pharmacy filled it as a rush prescription.

During the drive to Blaise's place, Harley found herself flicking her gaze to the blood test result printouts, which sat on the passenger seat with the white pharmacy bag. She now couldn't get the thought of cougar hemoglobin being mixed with Blaise's father's blood out of her mind. There was no way it could have been added later. She'd taken the sample herself, and no one had touched the vials but her. It didn't make sense.

She turned onto the long lane that led to Blaise's house. Once she arrived, Harley parked in front of the four-car garage. She gathered up the things from the passenger seat and then got out. She knocked on the front door once she reached it.

Blaise answered. He smiled before he pulled her inside and into his arms. He kissed her hungrily, showing how much he'd missed her, before he released her. It took a second for Harley to gather her wits about her once again.

"You have the results?" Blaise asked as he glanced down at what she carried.

"Yes. I think you should get everyone up to your parents' room so I can tell you all at the same time."

He met her gaze, then gave a short nod. "All right. Wait right here. I'll get them."

Blaise walked to the living room. Once he disappeared, Harley heard him tell his family she'd arrived and that she wanted to talk to them all upstairs with his father. They were a silent group as they stepped out into the foyer.

Taylor took the lead up the stairs with Aspen as his mother, then Harley and Blaise, followed. Inside the master bedroom, they stood around the bed. Blaise's dad pushed himself up higher on his pillows once his gaze landed on Harley.

"I take it you have the results," he said to her.

Harley nodded. She held up the printouts. "It's not good."

"You found out what illness he has?" Blaise's mother quickly asked.

"It's not that. It's not an illness." Harley looked at Blaise. "You were right. Caleb is doing your father harm. He has to have known it." She turned her gaze on her boyfriend's dad. "I found two strong poisons in your blood. I don't know how you're still alive. The amounts would have killed anyone else."

"Poison," he replied. "It wasn't medicine Caleb was injecting me with."

"No. He was administering the poison that way. That's the only thing I could come up with. I understand you've been sick for over half a year. He probably managed to somehow get the first doses of poison into you through your food or something you drink. Then once you became sick enough that you needed more care, that's when he started with the shots."

Blaise's father glanced at his wife with a grim

expression. "It wasn't through my food. It was through something I drank. Caleb gave me a bottle of ten-year-old scotch in way of showing appreciation of all I'd done to help him become a doctor. He hadn't given me anything before. He knows I'm the only person in the house who likes scotch. It has to be that. Now that I think about it, I started to become ill shortly after I had a few drinks of it."

Harley nodded. "The poison is the type that doesn't leave a person's system. It just built up with each drink you had until you thought you were really sick."

"Is there something we can do to counteract the poison?" Blaise's mom asked.

Harley held up the white pharmacy bag she carried. "I have it right here. I know a doctor who was able to write me a prescription for it. He's a good friend of mine and didn't ask any questions. He knows I wouldn't do anything stupid with it. I have to give you two shots. One dose of each should be enough, but if you don't improve in a couple of days, he told me to give you another."

Blaise's father held out his arm. "Do it. I'm sure one dose will be enough."

She dumped the medicine and syringes onto the bed before she prepared the first injection with the amount her doctor friend had prescribed. Once she administered it, she readied the second.

Harley had just stuck the needle into Blaise's father's shoulder when she heard, "What's going on here? What's she giving to my patient? I came back to check on him since I couldn't give him his medication, and this is what I find?"

She quickly pushed the plunger home, emptying the syringe. Harley barely managed to take out the needle before she was roughly pushed aside. This was obviously Caleb.

"She was undoing what you did," Blaise said.

Anger clouded Caleb's face. "What do you mean by

that exactly?" he demanded.

"Harley is a medical lab technician. We allowed her to run some blood tests on my father's blood. She found the poison you've been giving to him. We know what you've been doing."

It all happened so suddenly Harley had no chance of getting away. Caleb grabbed her around the throat, then spun her so her back was against his front. He growled like a big cat, his fingers tightening until she could barely breathe. She reached up and tried to tear his hand away, but he was stronger than she.

"If not for this meddling bitch, none of you would have known," Caleb said in a voice laced with another growl. "I never would have thought you'd have allowed a human to do any kind of test on him. Who would have known our glorious leader of our family group would have taken the risk of letting one learn the secret of what we are. You've surprised me."

"Let her go," Blaise said, his upper lip lifting in a snarl. "You've been found out. It's time to face up to what you've done."

Caleb laughed with no humor. "I think not. Your human girlfriend is my ticket out of here. None of you will try anything as long as I have her." He slowly backed away from the bed and the others.

"Why, Caleb?" Blaise's father asked, stopping Caleb. "After all I've done for you."

"All you did for me? Like taking my parents away so I could grow up with an aunt who hated me and mistreated me whenever she got the chance? I used you, took whatever I could get out of you. Don't try to deny what you did. Tell them. Tell your precious family what you did to my father. My aunt knew because my mother told her before she took her own life."

"I didn't do anything. Your father, my brother, made the decision to abandon you and your mother himself."

"That's a lie. He never would have left my mom on his own. You knew he wanted to take your place as leader of our family group. You gave him the choice of losing his life for trying to force you out or banishment. He chose the latter."

"Is that what your mother told your aunt? If it is, then it's a lie. Your mother had…problems…when it came to perceiving the world around her."

"Shut up," Caleb said with a snarl as he tightened his grip even more on Harley's throat, causing her to whimper with fear.

Blaise's father held out his hand. "Stop, Caleb. I'll tell you the truth. Your mother was never my brother's mate."

"Bullshit. She wore his pendant. I remember her wearing it."

"It wasn't his. She had a human jeweler make a copy of one. There was no mating bond between your parents. When your mother became pregnant with you, my brother tried to make it work, even though she wasn't his mate. He strayed as a lot of males do when they stay in a relationship with a female who isn't meant to be his. He found his mate. Your mother didn't take it well. She plotted to kill your father's new mate, and almost succeeded.

"My brother deemed she would always be at risk as long as he stayed in Anchorage. Not wanting your mother to learn where he ran to, he left one night and never came back. It was years later he finally contacted me. Your mother was already dead, but my brother had made another life for himself and his mate. He thought you were better off being raised by your aunt."

Caleb growled. "It's still because of you I lost my family. As our leader, you could have kept him from running. You could have ordered him back."

"I wouldn't have done that. It was my brother's choice to make, not mine."

Caleb took a step back, then another and another, dragging Harley along with him. She didn't understand half of what had been said. Talk of family groups, mates, and mating bonds weren't a part of her world.

Fear rode her as Caleb continued to inch closer to the bedroom door. Her gaze latched on to Blaise. She pleaded desperately with her eyes for him to do something to save her. He followed, keeping enough distance between them so as not to have his cousin feel threatened. Taylor followed as well, and so did their mother. Aspen stayed in the room with their father.

They made it down the stairs and to the foyer. Caleb kept his hand locked around her throat and an arm around her waist. He removed that one only long enough to open the door before he held her against him once more. He took a step outside, dragging her right along with him.

"Time to show you, little human, what a cougar shifter can do to your kind," he growled into her ear.

Caleb shoved her away. The rest happened in a matter of seconds. His body blurred, then shimmered and a cougar took his place. The big cat went to pounce on her, but Blaise stepped between them, shifting to a cougar as well and blocked the other. Caleb spun in midair before taking off at a run toward the back of the property.

Harley let out a whimper and crab-walked away from the remaining cougar. Her fear took her over, her vision swam as she tried to scramble out of reach, but her legs refused to work, leaving her unable to get to her feet and run away.

The cougar that was Blaise would have chased after Caleb, but Taylor stepped in front of him. "I'll go after Caleb. You have Harley to worry about." Blaise's brother turned into a cougar as well and took off at a run in the direction his cousin had gone.

Blaise turned to face her and took a few steps in her direction. Harley grabbed a handful of stones from the drive and threw them at him, hitting him in the side and head. "Stay away from me," she cried. "Just stay away."

CHAPTER SEVEN

laise hardly felt the stones hit him, he was so focused on Harley. Her first introduction to his world was not the best, by any stretch of the imagination. No one had expected Caleb to return to the house. He normally came to do his examinations only in the mornings. Obviously, them not allowing him to inject his patient hadn't sat well with Caleb. He'd more than likely come back to try to convince them to change their minds or somehow sneak the shot in when no one was looking.

He reached for the magic inside him and shifted to his human form. As a cougar, there was no way he could verbally communicate with Harley. Right now, she needed explanations, if she was in any state to listen to them.

"Harley," Blaise said softly as he took a step toward her. "It's all right. No one here is going to hurt you. You have nothing to be afraid of."

She whimpered and managed to surge to her feet. Harley shook her head. "Stay away from me. I don't want you near me."

"You're safe with me. With my family. Taylor has gone after Caleb. We won't let him near you again."

"No. I can't do this." Harley quickly sidestepped around Blaise. "You're not normal. I found cougar hemoglobin in your father's blood. I was going to question you about it, but now I know why it was there. You're cougar shifters? That's what Caleb called himself."

"We are. We've been living among humans for a very long time without any of you knowing. There aren't that many of us. You might think we're not normal, but we're just a different species."

"One that can change into a big cat whenever you want, and obviously fight off a poison that would have killed a human in a day."

"That does have a lot to do with my dad still being alive. We don't ever get sick, that's why his illness didn't make any sense to us. We live longer than humans. We can see up to two hundred years before death takes us. My father is sixty-five. My mom is only a year younger."

Harley backed up more. "They don't look that old. I thought they were in their thirties, which didn't make sense because you're twenty-eight, or at least that's what you told me."

"I really am twenty-eight."

"I can't deal with this."

She turned and took off at a run toward her car that was parked in front of the garage. Seeing her trying to leave, a wave of stark need washed through him. He couldn't let her go. He had to convince her to stay with him. He'd show her how good they were together, make love to her until she accepted him for what he was. He loved her and couldn't let her go. He *loved* her.

Blaise caught up with Harley as she reached the driver's side door and tried to yank it open. He used his body to pin her against it, his erection pressing along her bottom. She cried out, her breath sawing in and out of her.

"Harley, please stay with me," he said as he nuzzled the back of her neck. "I love you. I don't want to lose you. We can work this out. Aspen is human. She was afraid like you when she first found out about Taylor, but she took his pedant from him and became his mate."

Harley surprised him by throwing back her head and cracking him on the chin as she viciously jabbed her elbow into his stomach. Blaise took a step back as he grunted in pain. That was all she'd needed to wrench open the car door, clamber into the driver's seat, then lock herself inside. She fumbled with her keys and eventually stuck them into the ignition and managed to get the engine turned over.

Blaise pounded on the window. "Harley, I want to make you understand. You can't leave."

"Move, Blaise," she yelled through the glass. "Or I'll run you over."

He quickly jumped out of the way as Harley backed the car up almost on him. She gunned it as she sped down the lane to the main road. Blaise watched her go, the overwhelming need to be with her increasing.

He ran his hands through his hair and bent over, taking deep breaths as he tried to calm himself down. This kind of behavior wasn't normal for him. It was then he caught a flash of red in his gaze. He looked down at his pendant and saw the cougar's ruby eyes glowed. Harley had set the magic off inside it. She was his mate, and she'd just rejected him.

Now he understood the throbbing arousal that coursed through him. Seeing her fear of him, and realizing he couldn't lose her, that he loved her, she'd set off the magic inside the pendant. That in turn caused a spike in his testosterone level. Her not accepting him made his body react in the only way it knew how to convince her he was the one for her—with sex.

"Blaise," Taylor called as he came up behind him. "The

bastard got away. He must have thought something was up. His car isn't parked here so he had to have left it somewhere else in case he felt he needed to make a run for it. We'll find him, though. Where's Harley?"

Blaise straightened. "She left me."

"Well, at least she didn't set off your pendant. You won't have to go through what I did while you try to win her back."

Blaise turned around and faced his brother. With the coming twilight, there was no mistaking the glowing ruby eyes of his cougar-head pendant. "She did."

Taylor's gaze flicked to Blaise's necklace before he looked at him with pity showing on his face. "Shit. She's your mate."

"Tell me something I don't already know," he said with a growl.

"You have it bad. Come inside. We'd best tell Mom and Dad. We'll put our heads together and see what we can come up with to help you get Harley back. I don't think you have to worry about Dad being upset with the idea of her as your mate. She did save his life, after all. Without her, we never would have known what Caleb was doing."

Blaise followed Taylor into the house, even though every fiber in his being called out for him to chase Harley down. He prayed like hell she would come to realize they were better off together than apart.

* * * *

It'd been almost a week since Harley had found out about Blaise being a cougar shifter. She hadn't been able to bring herself to talk to or see him, even though he'd constantly called and left messages on her cell over the course of the days. He'd even sent long text messages, explaining everything about his kind. All the things he probably would have said in person if she'd allowed him to come near her.

Her initial fear of what he was had long since dimmed. What remained was a kind of numbness. Harley went about her normal daily routine, going to work, coming home to her apartment, and eating only because her body needed the food. When she slept, most of the time her dreams were filled with Blaise, of when they'd been together and how good it'd been to be in his arms.

By the end of her work week, Harley had to admit she felt as if a part of her was missing, and that it was Blaise who was that piece. She'd already come to the conclusion she loved him before finding out what he was, but now she realized her feelings for him hadn't changed. She could get over the fact he was able to shift into a cougar.

She'd let so much time pass since that fateful day, she was afraid to make the first step to let him back into her life. The text messages and phone calls had stopped the day before. What if Blaise had decided to give up on her? What if he no longer wanted to be with her because she couldn't accept what he was? She only had herself to blame. She was the one who'd run from him, was the one who held him away.

Harley jumped at the sound of her cell phone ringing. She picked it up off the coffee table, her heart thumping at the thought it could be Blaise. The display showed it was someone buzzing from downstairs in the lobby.

"Hello?" she answered.

"Harley? Good, you're home. It's Taylor."

"Is Blaise with you?"

"No, it's just me."

Harley's heart dropped, but she pushed it away. "What can I do for you, Taylor?"

"I need you to come home with me. Blaise isn't doing well."

She sat straighter on the couch. A number of things flew through her mind. Had Caleb done something to Blaise?

Had he injured himself?

"What's the matter with him?"

"I think it best you see for yourself. Will you come downstairs?"

"I'll be down in a minute."

Harley disconnected the call. Fear made her rush around the apartment as she grabbed her purse, then put on her sneakers. She was out the door and at the elevator in a matter of minutes.

In the lobby, Taylor was in the vestibule, waiting for her. She pushed open the first glass door to where he stood. "How bad is he?"

"Bad. Thanks for deciding to come. I'm parked in the visitors parking, but if you prefer, you can always follow me in your car."

"No, it's okay. I'll go with you." Seeing Taylor again made Harley realize how much she'd missed Blaise.

Once they were on the road, Taylor glanced at her. "How are you doing? You're not nervous to be around me, are you? I'm harmless."

"I know. I didn't answer Blaise's calls or his texts, explaining everything about cougar shifters, but I did get them. I read all the messages."

"So, you've decided we aren't so scary, after all?"

"I guess so. I never felt as if I had to have anything to fear from Blaise before I knew."

"Then why haven't you let him see you?"

She shook her head. "I don't know. I held him off for so long, I was afraid to take the step to let him back into my life."

"I'm glad I came today."

They spent the rest of the drive in silence. As Taylor stopped the car in front of the garage, all that had happened the last time Harley had been there came rushing into her mind.

"Did you end up catching Caleb?" she asked as she and

Taylor walked to the front door.

"No. He got away. We're still looking for him. My cousin, Jase, has taken on the job of hunting Caleb down. He'll be found. Don't worry about that."

Inside the house, Taylor guided her up the stairs. Once they reached the top, he led her to Blaise's closed bedroom door.

"Blaise is in there," Taylor said. "Go right in."

Harley was about to ask him why he wasn't going to come in with her, but by the time she'd turned her head to look at him, Taylor was gone. She figured he had to have used the preternatural speed all cougar shifters had. Blaise had told her in his texts that they were faster than humans.

She focused on the closed door, took a deep breath and opened it. Harley had expected to find Blaise in bed. Instead she found him walking out of the en suite, naked, his hair damp as if he'd just gotten out of the shower. He came to a sudden standstill once he spotted her.

"Harley?"

"Hi. Ah, Taylor came to my place to get me. He said you were in bad shape and that I needed to come here to see you. I thought something terrible had happened to you."

"The only thing bad that happened to me was you leaving. You have no idea how much I've missed you."

Harley ran her gaze over him. There was no mistaking how haggard Blaise looked or the fact he appeared to have lost some weight. "I missed you too."

Blaise crossed the distance between them in a few long strides. As he walked toward her, Harley noticed the ruby eyes on his cougar-head pendant glowed. She had the sudden urge to touch it, to slip the chain from his neck and put it around her own.

Once he stood in front of her, she said, "You look a little the worse for wear." Her heart beat faster from him being so near, and it wasn't with fear. Her body remembered what it was like to have him thrusting deeply inside her.

He gave her a small smile. "That's your fault."

"It is?"

"Yes. You see, there was one thing I didn't tell you about cougar shifters in my texts." He pointed to his pendant. "I didn't tell you about this. Every male cougar shifter is given one once he reaches adolescence. It has magic inside it. When the male meets the female meant to be his mate, and he's come to accept her into his heart, she sets it off. The cougar's ruby eyes glow. Once it does, the female gets the decision to claim the male as her own."

Harley licked her suddenly dry lips, knowing what Blaise was telling her. She was his mate. "How does she do that?"

"It's simple. She has to take his pendant from him and place it around her own neck. After that, the mating bond forms between them and their souls join. From then on, there will never, ever be anyone else for them."

"If the female doesn't take the pendant?"

"The male looks like crap because he can't sleep, can't eat, all he thinks about is her and the need to have her as his own. To make love to her until she takes what belongs to her and her alone."

Arousal slammed into Harley's body, making her breath catch. She focused on Blaise's pendant. It drew her. She wanted it. There would be no denying the urge that swept through her.

With fingers that shook, Harley reached up and took hold of the cougar-head pendant. She wrapped her fingers around it, then lifted, slipping the chain over Blaise's head. Once it was free, she pulled it over her own until it came to rest between her breasts. The instant it did so, she felt something snap between her and Blaise, like an invisible string that connected them.

"Did you feel that?" she asked.

"You're damn right I did. Now I'm going to show you

that you've made the best decision of your life."

Blaise lifted her off her feet and raised her until her mouth was even with his. He kissed her hungrily, feeding from her lips as if he'd die without tasting them. Harley returned the kiss with as much fervor, the need to have him inside her just about overwhelming everything else.

"I love you," she said. "Please take me. I can't wait any longer."

"I love you too. I'm glad one of us is naked. We can get to the good part faster."

He let her down onto her feet and proceeded to strip off her clothes, showing her exactly how fast a cougar shifter could move when he wanted to. Harley found herself naked and placed on the bed between one breath and the next. She gloried in the feel of Blaise coming down on top of her skin-to-skin.

His hard cock brushed against her pussy. She reached between them and fisted him, stroking his length. Blaise purred as she knew he would. She led the head of his shaft to her slick opening and rubbed it in her wetness, circling her clit with it.

Blaise groaned. "If you don't stop that, I'm going to come. It's been too long since I last had you."

"We can't have that."

Harley led his cock inside her pussy then lifted her hips to take more of him. Blaise thrust against her, filling her completely with one stroke. He set a fast pace of in and out. She wrapped her legs around his waist and held on to his arms, her build up to her climax growing each time he sheathed himself to the hilt. His shaft grew even harder, the purrs she loved so much constantly rumbled out of him.

Blaise had to thrust a half dozen more times before Harley's orgasm slammed into her, stealing her breath. She let out a keening moan as her inner muscles clutched and released his plunging cock, milking him into his own release. He held on to her hips, holding her tightly to him, as he filled her with his cum.

Once the pleasurable sensations faded, Blaise collapsed on top of her, taking most of his weight on his bent arms. He kissed her tenderly.

"I love you, Harley. I wouldn't want anyone else as my mate."

She smiled at him. "I'm sorry I made you go through that. I had no idea."

"I know. I thought it best not to put any more pressure on you. You already had enough with just coming to grips with me being a cougar shifter."

"It's in the past now. I'm yours, and you are mine. Since we're mated, and technically this would be considered the start of our honeymoon, I have a request."

"That would be?"

"Get that thong out I bought you. I want to see you in it again."

Blaise chuckled. "Already making demands, but this one I don't mind fulfilling."

He crawled off the bed and then went to his dresser. He held up the thong once he turned around. Harley had not only gotten to see him wear it once more, she also got to remove it with her teeth. She then showed Blaise how enjoyable she found that.

The End

A COUGAR'S DESIRE

On the hunt for the man who'd tried to kill his uncle, cougar shifter Jase runs into a little spitfire who throws him for a loop. She doesn't fall at his feet. As his prey escapes, he realizes Katarina is a different sort of prey he refuses to lose sight of.

Katarina is a loser magnet. Having resigned herself to never finding Mr. Right, she reluctantly agrees to go out with Jase. He's sexy as all get-out and just the sort to hit it and run. But this man with the smoldering eyes and made-for-sin body passes all her tests, and she finds herself letting him in.

As one night of passion leads to so much more, Jase's prey comes back to claim what he left behind, and Katarina finds herself stuck in the middle.

CHAPTER ONE

Jase knocked on the front door of the nondescript bungalow in Anchorage where his cousin, Blaise, had sent him to hopefully get some good information as to where Caleb could be. Caleb was a physician and cousin to Blaise and his older brother, Taylor, and on the run. He'd been treating Blaise and Taylor's father for an "illness" that had turned out to be Caleb poisoning him. Jase had taken on the job of hunting him down to face his uncle, who was the head of their cougar shifter family group.

He knocked again, louder than the time before. Blaise had promised Jase his friend would be at home and expecting him. Finally, he heard movement on the other side of the door.

It swung open, and a large man filled the doorway. He had to be at least six foot seven, topping Jase's own height by six inches. His body was heavily padded with muscle, which Jase hadn't been expecting since Blaise had called this guy a computer geek. He was a cougar shifter but from another local family group.

"Are you Jase?" the man asked, peering at him closely.

"Yeah. And you must be Dacian."

Dacian took a step back. "Come on inside. Blaise told me what you were looking for. You brought some kind of computer device, right?"

Jase walked into the house and waited for Dacian to shut the door before he answered. He held up the tablet he carried. "Will this do?"

The other man nodded. "You'll just need Internet access."

"I have mobile Internet on it."

"Good. Come on back to my office, and I'll get you what you need."

Jase followed Dacian down the hallway to the back of the house, where an office was located. There was a large solid-wood desk with not one but three flat-screen monitors sitting on it. Each one was twenty-two inches in size. There was also a laptop on the very end. It was a computer geek's heaven.

Dacian walked around the desk, then sat. He held out his hand for Jase's tablet, which Jase gave to him. Jase took a seat in the chair on the other side of the workstation. The larger man's fingers flew over the keyboard, which had been hidden away on a sliding shelf under the desktop.

After a few seconds, Dacian said while he continued to type, "Blaise already gave me Caleb's cell phone number. This program I'm going to give you will track the signal each time he uses it. It's not up to the minute, but it won't be so far from it that you won't have a chance to catch him before he runs if you move quickly enough. I do have to say he's an idiot for not ditching his cell. That's the easiest way to track someone. Hopefully, he makes it easy on you to bring him to face the head of your family group."

"Well, his stupidity just works out in my favor. I'm surprised Blaise told you everything Caleb did to cause him to be on the run." Most family groups kept the goings-on from others.

Dacian smiled. "Blaise knows he can trust me not to talk. Just as I trust him to keep my business private. We have an understanding."

Jase figured they did. For one thing, Dacian looked like one tough son of a bitch who wouldn't mind using his fists, or claws, to show his displeasure if someone crossed him. The man was huge for a cougar shifter. It was the werewolves who normally grew as big as that.

"I bet," he said as Dacian plugged Jase's tablet into his computer. His fingers flew over the keyboard once more.

After he finished, Dacian handed Jase his tablet. "You're all set. Just run the program when you want to see the last time and from where Caleb used his cell phone. Usually, I charge for this, but I owed Blaise one, so this is on the house."

"Thanks." Jase stood. "I guess I now know who to go to if I need anything like this again."

Drave gained his feet, then walked around his desk to Jase. "I'm your man. Blaise told me how you and your brother, Grady, like to hit the human bars and check the women out, and how now that Blaise is mated, he doesn't join. I wouldn't mind going out with you two sometime."

Jase nodded. "Why not? You sure you want to take the flak from your family group if you end up going out with a human woman?"

As far as Jase knew, Taylor had been the very first of their kind to have a human for a mate. A lot of the older, more traditional cougar shifters looked down their noses at humans, thinking they were beneath them. He didn't think that way, nor did his brother, Grady. It wasn't as if Taylor had set out to look for one to mate.

All male cougar shifters were given a gold cougar-head pendant once they hit adolescence. Each one was made with a little bit of magic embedded inside. Only a male's mate would set it off, causing the cat's ruby eyes to glow.

It was then the female's choice to take his pendant from him and put it around her neck, thus causing the mating bond to form between them. If she didn't, the male ended up a mess, unable to eat or sleep. He would only be able to think about one thing—sex. He would want to use it to bring his would-be mate closer, to force her to see he was the one for her and to convince her to take his necklace.

Dacian chuckled. "I don't give two shits what my family group would think. I do whatever I want. I'm what you would consider the black sheep. They leave me alone, and I return the favor. It makes everyone happy."

Jase wasn't going to go there. Plus, it was none of his business. "In that case, I have your number and I'll be giving you a call soon."

"All right. I look forward to it."

The big man walked Jase to the door after they shook hands. Once outside, he headed for his sports car parked in the driveway. Now that he had a tool to help him, he would begin his hunt. Hopefully, Caleb was as dumb as Dacian had said and would use his cell in the next little while.

* * * *

It took a few hours, but his prey finally used his cell, showing how well the computer program Dacian had given him worked. Caleb's location was downtown in a part of the city where low-income properties could be found. It made sense he would be there, because it wasn't an area the doctor would have been caught dead in before going on the run. Even though Caleb wasn't that old and set in his ways like many of the family elders, he still felt humans were below cougar shifter standards. Not wanting his prey to give him the slip, Jase wasted no time driving to the designated spot the computer program had found.

Jase parked his car about a half block away from the

location. Since Caleb would recognize it, he didn't want him seeing it before Jase had a chance to get close. He walked down the street, looking at the property numbers until he arrived at the address Dacian's program had come up with.

The apartment building looked to have seen better days. It was old and showed its age. It had a maximum of four floors and didn't even have a secured entrance, so anyone could walk in off the street. It posed a bit of a problem—Jase had no idea what floor Caleb would be on. The program didn't exactly give him an apartment number, just the main address.

He blew out a breath as he looked up at the building. The only thing he could do was search each floor until he found Caleb's scent. It would take more time, and the chance of his prey giving him the slip was high, but Jase couldn't come up with any other way to do it.

With a silent curse, Jase walked up the four steps that led to the main entrance. Inside, he started with the basement level. Not catching Caleb's scent there, he moved on to the next floor.

Having finished the third and still no trace of his prey, Jase wondered if Caleb had already given him the slip. That would totally suck if that ended up being the case and he'd wasted all that time for nothing.

On the fourth and final floor, Jase managed to pick up an old scent trail. It was hard to detect, but it was there. He followed it down the hallway, almost to the very end. He stood between the two doors that were on either side of him. The trail led to both. Which one was the correct one was the question.

Jase did a game of eeny meeny miney moe to pick the first one to try. After one was selected, he stepped closer to the door, then sniffed around it to see if he could detect a stronger trail. If he did, it would be a sure sign Caleb was inside that apartment.

With hands on the wooden surface and his eyes shut, Jase was taken by surprise when it was yanked open. He didn't catch himself in time to stop from falling face-first in a heap across the threshold. Something hard pressed into the center of his back and kept him from trying to gain his feet.

"Don't move."

The female voice came from above where he lay. Jase slowly turned his head until he focused on a pair of feet directly in front of him. They were clad in white sports socks and were much smaller than his.

The thing on his back jabbed him harder. "I said don't move. I'm not afraid to use this baseball bat on your head if I have to."

So that was what it was. "I'm not going to do anything to warrant you to do that. If you'll remove the bat, I'll get up and be on my way."

"Not so fast. Why were you trying to break into my apartment?"

"I wasn't."

"The hell you weren't. I saw you through the peephole. It looked as if you were trying to do something to the door."

The woman, who sounded young, was human. There was no way he could explain he was only trying to pick up a scent trail of another cougar shifter. She'd think he was lying and more than likely use that bat of hers on his head like a ball as threatened.

"I promise you I wasn't trying to break in. I'm looking for someone. I thought this was his apartment. I think he lives across the hall."

"If that's so, why didn't you knock like a normal person?"

"I wanted to surprise him. Maybe you know him. His name is Caleb."

The woman was silent for a few seconds before she

slowly pulled the bat away. "I know him. He moved in across the hall the other day."

Jase carefully stood, not making any sudden movements. He didn't trust that the bat wouldn't still be aimed at his head. He lifted his gaze to the woman who was in front of him. He sucked in a quiet breath as he took in her face, which was gorgeous. She had shoulder-length brown hair and eyes that were a light green. She was a small thing. He guessed she had to stand around only five foot three. He towered over her.

"Then I'll knock on his door." He slowly backed up, keeping an eye on the bat she held at her side.

"I'll watch you to make sure you do that."

Jase spun around to hide the smile he couldn't hold back. He doubted she'd take it the right way. He couldn't help it, though. She looked so cute acting so tough. Actually, if he didn't have to chase after Caleb, he would have tried asking her out. She was the first human woman he found himself really attracted to.

Instead of knocking, Jase tried turning the doorknob, which ended up being locked. A sudden crash from inside the apartment had him taking a step back before kicking the door in. He heard the woman behind him shout something as he ran through the doorway.

It took him only a matter of seconds to find the window in the living room open, along with the screen. The curtain in front of it hung outside as if someone hadn't taken the time to pull it away before going through the space.

Jase hurried over and looked down. There was no fire escape. It was a straight drop to the alley below, which was empty. A jump like that wouldn't do anything to a cougar shifter. Caleb must have heard Jase and the woman and escaped when Jase had tried the door. As he continued to look out the open window, he felt a now familiar sensation of something hard poking into the center of his back.

"I thought you were a friend of Caleb. Why did you kick in his apartment door?"

"I do know him, but I never said I was his friend." Jase turned to face her. "He's obviously gone. If you could tell me which apartment is the superintendent's, I'll pay for the damage I did to the door."

She pegged him with a hard stare. "That would be me. I don't think I've ever heard of a thief actually wanting to pay to fix what he's damaged before."

"I told you. I'm not a thief." When she poked him in the stomach with the bat, he realized she might not let him just walk away without some kind of explanation. "Look, my name is Jase. I'm looking for Caleb because he isn't a very nice man. He tried to kill my uncle. I want to bring him to face the consequences of his crime."

"Are you a cop?"

"No. I happened to get a lead on Caleb's whereabouts and thought to see if I could corner him myself. Since I told you my name, will you tell me yours?"

She seemed to think it over, then said, "Katarina. If Caleb did what you said he did, shouldn't you have tipped the cops off as to where he was? They have to be looking for him too if he tried to kill your uncle."

Something else Jase couldn't really explain. There were no human police involved, and there never would be. It was a matter his family group would handle. His uncle would be the one to decide Caleb's fate.

"I didn't want to take the chance of them showing up too late, but it would seem I did anyway. You can lower your bat. You don't have to worry about me jumping you." He smiled. "Unless you want me to, that is."

Katarina narrowed her eyes. "You wouldn't be trying to hit on me to get out of paying for the door, would you?"

"Absolutely not." Jase took a step closer. "In fact, I really would like to take you out on a date."

"You want to ask me out? Why?"

Jase was a little taken aback by Katarina's question. "Because I find you really attractive," he said slowly.

"So in other words, you'd like to fuck me, and you figured you'd better take me on a date first before you try to worm your way into my bed."

For the first time in his life, Jase found himself dumbfounded by a woman. Katarina was beautiful, but from what she'd said, he had a feeling she didn't have too many good experiences with men or dating.

He shook his head. "No, that wasn't the reason I asked you out." She arched a brow to say she didn't believe him. "Okay, it wasn't the *only* reason. I'll admit I'm very attracted to you, even though you threatened to bash my brains in with that bat."

Katarina gave a very unladylike snort, then motioned him to follow her as she turned away. They walked across the hall and into her apartment. Jase was pleased when she propped the bat in the corner next to the entranceway.

"About the door," she said as she came to stand in front of him. "I have to call someone in to fix it, so I won't know how much it'll cost until later. Give me your phone number, and I'll let you know once the job is done."

"I can do that. If Caleb comes back, I'd like it if you could let me know. You never gave me an answer about a date."

"I thought I gave you one."

"No, you didn't. Not really."

Katarina rolled her eyes. "I'll spell it out for you. I'm not interested in a one-night stand or anything casual. To be brutally honest, good-looking guys like you tend to have a wandering eye. I don't put up with that crap. So if any of those things apply to you, I'm not interested."

Wow, she was a tough nut to crack. She was going to make him work for it, and Jase was more than willing. She was the complete opposite of the females of his kind, who lived for the day when they set off the magic in a male's pendant. It really turned him on.

Jase took a step closer and gave Katarina the sexiest grin he could. "Why don't you say yes and see for yourself that they don't apply to me. Plus, I like the fact you think I'm good-looking. I'll take you wherever you want to go. You can plan the whole date."

"If I say yes, I'll drive myself. I want to be able to leave when I feel it isn't going to work out, which will more than likely happen."

"I have no problem with that." Talk about a vote of confidence.

"Fine," Katarina said as if it pained her. "I'll go out with you tomorrow evening. You can pay me for the door then. I should be able to get someone in today since it'll be an emergency call."

Jase gave Katarina his cell phone number, then left after he had her promise to call him tomorrow during the day to let him know where and when to meet her that evening. As he left the apartment building, he figured he hadn't completely wasted his time. Caleb may have given him the slip, but Jase had a date with a human woman who would more than likely keep him on his toes.

* * * *

Katarina turned the locks on her door after she closed it behind Jase. She looked out the peephole until he'd walked out of range. She turned and headed into her living room. After sitting on the couch, she placed the piece of paper she'd written Jase's number on the coffee table. She picked up her cell, then made the call to the guy who did the handyman-type work around the building.

Once she hung up, she found her gaze drawn to the paper. Katarina couldn't believe she'd agreed to go out on a date with Jase. She'd kind of given up on finding Mr. Right about a year ago. Usually, she seemed to attract the losers. She was a veritable magnet for bad boys, self-centered assholes, and men who were only after one thing. At twenty-seven, she was already jaded when it came to the opposite sex. In a lot of ways, she felt as if she'd be better off staying single.

An image of Jase rose inside her mind. He was a hunk—there was no question about that. All that remained to be seen was whether or not he ended up being as bad as the rest of the men she'd gone out with. The very small part of her that still held on to the hope of finding the one man who would be perfect for her prayed he'd be different.

Katarina sat back and smiled. At least she'd get to see how he passed her first test, which would be what they did on their date tomorrow evening. She'd come up with something he'd either be able to handle or would send him running.

CHAPTER TWO

After he returned to his car, Jase tried the computer program once more to see if Caleb had used his cell while Jase had been with Katarina. To his disappointment, his prey hadn't. With nothing left to do, he started his vehicle and then drove to Blaise's place. His cousin would be expecting to hear how Jase's meeting with Dacian had gone.

A mental picture of Katarina — threatening him with her bat — made Jase chuckle. For her lack of stature, she came across as one tough woman. He figured her being the superintendent of the apartment building, and given the area she lived, she would have to be.

At his cousin's family's house, Jase parked in front of the four-car garage before he knocked once on the front door, then let himself in. He called Blaise's name, who answered from the living room.

Jase walked into that room to find Aunt Mara, Uncle Nate, Blaise, his mate, Harley, his other cousin, Taylor, and his mate, Aspen, there. He looked at his uncle. It'd only been a few days since Harley, who was a lab technician, had found the poisons in Nate's bloodwork, but the leader of their family group had greatly improved. No longer did he have the debilitating symptoms of his "illness." He was still a bit weak and too thin, but that wouldn't last long. Being a cougar shifter would make his recovery swift. They healed a lot faster than humans. If Nate had been one, he would have died from the poisons long ago.

Blaise greeted him first. "Hey, Jase. How did things go with Dacian?"

Jase crossed the room, then sat in the empty armchair. "Good. He gave me a program that tracks Caleb each time he uses his cell phone. It isn't up to the minute, but it's close enough."

"Did you find him?" his uncle asked.

He shook his head. "I came close, though. I did find where he was hiding. He rented an apartment in a low-income building in a not-so-great part of Anchorage. He must have heard me talking to the superintendent, who lives across the hall. I ended up kicking in his door, but he'd jumped out the window and gotten away. So far, he hasn't used his cell phone again."

"You'll catch him eventually," Nate said. "He obviously is staying in the city for some reason. I would have thought he would be long gone by now."

To be honest, so had Jase. He'd been all prepared to catch a plane to wherever Caleb ended up. So far, his prey had done two dumb things—using a traceable cell phone and staying in Anchorage, where he would be hunted the most.

"I guess Caleb won't be returning there anytime soon," Taylor said.

"He could. I didn't get a chance to look through the apartment since the super was with me and not pleased that I'd kicked in the door, but it appeared as if Caleb left a lot of things behind."

"He might just walk away from it all," Blaise added. "We now know where he's been staying."

"I've asked Katarina to let me know if Caleb returns before I can track him with the program."

"Katarina?" his aunt asked.

"She's the superintendent of the building." Jase decided to get everything out in the open in case things did work out between him and Katarina. "Before you can ask, because I know you will, I'm taking her out on a date tomorrow evening."

"I take it she's human," his uncle said.

"Yes." Jase looked Nate straight in the eyes when he'd said it, almost daring him to say something negative, but he didn't, much to Jase's surprise.

"If she ends up setting off the magic in your pendant, she'll be just as welcomed into our family group as Aspen and Harley have been."

Everyone in the room appeared to be as shocked as Jase was by that statement. At one time, Uncle Nate was very vocal about the fact he thought humans were beneath cougar shifters. He really hadn't been all that thrilled when Taylor had become mated to Aspen.

Nate looked at each of them before his gaze settled on Harley. "I no longer think the way I did in the past. If it wasn't for Harley, I could very well be dead right now. I owe her my life." He looked at Jase. "I'll stand by any male who has a human female as his mate. Taylor is right. It's time to make changes to the laws and mores we follow."

Jase turned his gaze on Taylor to find his cousin staring at his father with his mouth hanging open, a look of incredulity on his face. Never in a million years had any of them expected Nate to say it was time for such a major change in their family group. They thought it wouldn't come to be until Nate had passed away or stepped down as group leader and Taylor had taken his place.

Aspen chuckled as she put a finger under her mate's

chin and pushed his mouth closed. "You'll be catching flies soon if you're not careful."

Taylor shook his head. "I can't believe it. I didn't think…" He shook his head again.

His uncle smiled at his oldest son. "I know you didn't. From what Caleb did to me, and the fact my sons have forged their own paths in life, I've been able to see the error of my ways. We have to move with the times or be left behind."

Mara, who sat next to Nate, turned his head toward her and laid one hell of a kiss on him. Both in their sixties, they were far from old by cougar shifter standards, which allowed a lifespan of around two hundred. So this display of affection wasn't out of place for people their age. When Nate had been so sick, Mara wouldn't have been so enthusiastic with her kiss, but now that he was recovering, it seemed that was no longer the case.

Nate pulled away first, then surged to his feet. He reached down and took his mate's hand before he pulled her to stand next to him. With his gaze still on Mara, he said, "I have to discuss something with Mara upstairs. Right now."

His uncle hurried out of the living room, taking Jase's aunt with him. The sound of Mara giggling reached his ears once they disappeared from sight. It wasn't too long before a door on the upper level closed.

Jase burst out laughing. "I guess someone is definitely feeling better."

Blaise groaned. "I'm not sure if I'm going to like this new Dad. Having to see displays of affection like that, which end up with them going upstairs to have sex, might scar me for life."

"Poor baby," Harley said with a laugh. "Isn't that a bit of the pot calling the kettle black? Since I moved in here with you a couple of days ago, I think we've done the same thing more than once."

"Try four times," Taylor said.

"You were counting?" Aspen asked, a smile playing on her lips.

"No, not really. It's kind of hard to ignore when it happens right in front of me, though."

Jase interrupted before that topic could go any further. "I guess I'm going to see what Grady is up to. At least I don't have to worry about my brother being distracted by a mate since he doesn't have one."

"I'll walk you out," Blaise said and stood when Jase did.

At the front door, his cousin asked, "So, what did you think of Dacian?"

"You told me he was a computer geek, but you neglected to tell me he sure as hell doesn't look like one. The guy is the biggest cougar shifter I've ever seen."

Blaise laughed. "I know he doesn't look the part, but he's a whiz when it comes to anything to do with computers. He might come across as intimidating, but once you get to know him, he's a great guy. I'd trust him with anything."

"He said you mentioned to him that Grady and I like to go to human bars to look at the women. Dacian wants to go with us sometime."

"It might only be Grady now that you've met Katarina," Blaise said with a grin.

Jase shook his head. "I only have a date with her. You have no idea how hard it was to get her to agree to even that."

"Wow, that's a first. I don't think there's been a woman you haven't been able to charm enough to get her to agree to sleep with you. Did it hurt your ego?" His cousin laughed.

"Har, har. Laugh it up. No, it didn't hurt my ego. I was more afraid she'd use the baseball bat she threatened to take to my head."

That just made Blaise laugh even harder. Once he got

himself under some control, he asked, "Why did she do that?"

Jase sighed. "It might have had to do with the fact she thought I was trying to break into her apartment."

That set Blaise off once more. "What did you do to make her think that?"

"I didn't know which apartment was Caleb's at first, okay? I was trying to pick up his scent trail. Forget it. I'm leaving. I'll call if I manage to corner Caleb somewhere."

Blaise waved him off. Jase walked outside, then closed the door on his cousin's laughter. He was pretty sure he'd go through the same thing with his brother, Grady, when Jase told him the same story.

* * * *

Katarina sat in her car in the parking lot of the Alaska Zoo. It was the first activity she'd planned for her and Jase's date. She'd changed it from starting in the evening to the middle of the afternoon. She hadn't known if he would be okay with it, but he'd quickly reassured her the time change wasn't a problem.

She got out of her vehicle and then locked it. Since Jase didn't know what she drove, and she didn't know what he did, Katarina figured it would be better if she was more easily seen. Pushing closer to late fall, the days were definitely cooling off. She zipped up her jacket before she shoved her hands into the pockets.

The parking lot wasn't overly full since it was later in the day and the zoo closed at five. Katarina watched each car that turned off the road and into it. At exactly three o'clock, the time she'd wanted Jase to meet her, a flashy black sports car appeared at the entrance.

At first, she didn't think it was Jase. For some reason, she'd assumed he would drive a car like hers — not new and definitely not expensive. Katarina soon realized it was indeed him when the vehicle drove toward where she stood and then parked in the empty space next to her. There was no mistaking him as the driver.

Jase got out before he walked around to where she waited. "Hi, Katarina. I made it just in time."

"Yeah, you did."

Much to her dismay, Jase was even better-looking than she'd remembered. She didn't have high hopes that this date would end up going well. The last really good-looking guy she'd dated had had a wandering eye that soon led to his hands doing the same.

"Are you ready to go into the zoo?" Jase asked.

"Sure."

As they walked side by side to the entrance, he said, "I was a bit surprised when you decided on coming here. I thought you would have picked something else."

She peered at him. "What would that be? The regular dinner and a movie or going out to a bar?"

"No. I had a feeling you were going to pick something different. I was all prepared to do whatever you decided on, even if it happened to be making me jump out of a plane. I would have pissed my pants on the way down and would have had to excuse myself to change once I hit the ground, but I would have done it."

Katarina couldn't hold back a smile as she thought of Jase screaming like a girl as he jumped out of a plane. She chuckled. "Why would you think I'd choose that? No one could pay me enough money to skydive."

He smiled. "Well, you did come across as a tough woman yesterday. I got the impression you might have a daredevil side too."

"Nope, I don't. I'd more than likely be pissing my pants right along with you."

Jase laughed, the sound of it causing Katarina to smile bigger. At least he appeared to have a sense of humor, something she liked in a guy. Once they reached the entrance to the zoo, he paid for their admissions. With maps in hand, they started their tour.

As they headed for the first attraction, which was where the river otters and harbor seals were, a group of kids came running toward them. Given as how they were carrying party favor bags, Katarina guessed they'd been part of a birthday party there.

The kids didn't seem to slow down once they reached her and Jase. He put his arm around her shoulders and pulled her against his side before he stepped out of the way. The small group ran past, laughing and yelling at each other. Four adults chased after them, calling for them to slow down.

The heat from Jase's body soaked through Katarina's jacket and into her. Being this close, she easily smelled the aftershave he'd used. It was spicy and all male. Pressed against him, she couldn't mistake how hard his body was. Hers reacted to his nearness as her nipples grew taut. She hated to admit how much she liked the fact she fit perfectly under his arm, or how small he made her feel.

Jase got them walking again but kept his hold on her. He matched his strides to her shorter ones so she didn't have to feel as if she had to run to keep up. Katarina should have pulled away, but she liked having him against her.

He looked at her. "Is there any animal in particular you want to see?"

She nodded. "Actually, there are a couple. I like watching the tigers and snow leopards. The big cats are my favorite."

"I have to say I'm partial to them as well."

"Is that why you have a cougar-head pendant? I noticed it yesterday."

Jase pulled it out of the front of his jacket. "I guess you could say I feel more for the cougars than any other large cat."

"Too bad they don't have any here."

"The tigers and snow leopards are just as nice."

They walked in silence for a bit until they reached the first set of animals. As they went from one attraction to the next, Katarina found her gaze drawn to Jase's pendant from time to time. The cougar's ruby eyes would flash in the sun when it hit them just right.

It took Katarina and Jase about twenty minutes to reach the tigers. They had a large open grassed area to roam. At first, she couldn't see any, but one came running to the edge of the enclosure, then snarled once he reached the fence. It appeared as if he looked right at them.

"I've been here a few times, and not once have I seen one do that," Katarina said.

Jase chuckled. "Maybe he thinks another big cat has come to threaten his territory. I wonder what he'll do if I growl back at him."

Before Katarina could say anything in response to that, Jase let loose with a cat growl that almost put the tiger to shame. The big cat went completely still, then took off the way it'd come.

"Not so tough, after all," Jase said with a laugh. "I guess I'm the head cat around this place."

She looked at him. "That's quite a talent you've got there. I don't think I've met anyone who could perfectly sound like a big cat as you do."

Jase stepped closer, bent his head, and nuzzled the crook of her neck. "I can also do this."

He purred, the sound vibrating along her skin. He continued to do so just like a real cat as he dragged his lips down the column of her throat. Katarina shivered, and her pussy clenched as a surge of pure desire shot through her. She became instantly turned-on. She put her hands on Jase's waist and leaned into him. She couldn't help herself.

Jase didn't seem to mind. He cupped her cheek and turned her head toward him before he brought his mouth down to hers. The kiss started out as just a simple meeting of lips, but that quickly changed. Katarina clutched him tighter and sighed as it became far from chaste.

She tried to push closer, even though she was basically as close as she could get to him. Jase licked the seam of her mouth, seeking entrance. Katarina opened and sucked his tongue inside. Arousal pulsed through her. A throbbing ache deep inside her pussy demanded her attention. It increased as he purred once more.

The sound of a child's laughter instantly brought Katarina out of the haze of pleasure that had surrounded her. She jerked back from Jase and looked around him to see a little girl no more than six or seven years of age watching them. The girl's mother grabbed her hand, then led her from the exhibit.

Katarina took a few steps away from Jase and turned to face the tiger's enclosure. She'd completely forgotten where they were. Being caught necking in such a public place wasn't something she was prone to. She wasn't one for putting on displays. The way he'd kissed her, she hadn't thought of anything else but how good it was to have his mouth moving over hers. If not for a child breaking the mood, she had a feeling that kiss would have lasted a lot longer.

CHAPTER THREE

Jase looked at Katarina as she turned her back to him. Had he gone too fast for her? He hadn't intended to kiss her quite that soon on their date, but having her so close to him, and the scent of her skin filling his nose, he hadn't been able to resist.

"Did I do something wrong?" he asked as he came to stand beside her.

"No. The problem is me."

"How so? I have nothing to complain about with that kiss."

Katarina turned her gaze his way and gave him a small smile. "Neither do I. The problem is I liked it too much and forgot where I was."

Jase grinned, put his arm around her shoulders, and kissed the top of her head. "There's nothing wrong with that. It shows you're into me just as much as I'm into you."

"Come on. Let's see the snow leopards, and then we can get something to eat if you're hungry."

He turned them away from the tiger's enclosure and

got them walking toward the walkway that would take them to the snow leopards. "The question is — when am I not hungry? You put food in front of me, I'll eat it."

"If I ate like that, I'd be the size of a house. It's already bad enough I'm so short."

Jase pulled slightly away and looked her up and down. "I can honestly say you're perfect the way you are. If we weren't in such a public place, I would show you exactly what the sight of you does to me."

He dragged in a deep breath, detecting Katarina's arousal in her scent. He'd first smelled it while he'd kissed her. He was getting to her, which was fine with him. She did the same to him. His cock was semi-hard, and it wouldn't take much for it to become a full-blown erection. That one little taste of her had him longing for more. Jase had no idea what else was on the agenda for their date, but he hoped at some point he could get her alone somewhere so he could continue where their kiss had abruptly ended.

At the snow leopard's enclosure, one of the large cats came up to the fence to investigate them. Jase knew full well it had to do with his scent. He didn't smell like a human. The snow leopard, as well as the tiger, could detect the cougar in him. At least this large cat wasn't trying to intimidate him. It was a female, whereas the tiger had been male, which would have had him trying to stake his territory.

They finished looking at the rest of the animals, which took an hour, then headed to the parking lot. Jase had never been to the zoo before. He found he didn't mind it as much as he'd thought he would. Being a cougar shifter, he hated to see animals that were meant to be in the wild locked up. The enclosures, though, had been made specifically for each species, trying to mimic as much of their natural territory as possible. So they weren't as terrible as he'd thought they'd be.

Once Jase and Katarina reached the cars, he asked,

"Where to now?"

"Time to eat. You can follow me."

"You're not going to tell me where we're going beforehand?"

"No. That way if you don't like it, you won't have the chance to try to change my mind about going there."

Jase shook his head. "I wouldn't since I said you could plan our date, but lead on."

They got into their cars. Katarina backed up, then waited for Jase to pull behind her before she drove to the lot's exit.

On their way to their next destination, he had no problem following her. He saw her checking her rearview mirror every once in a while to make sure he was still there.

So far, Jase had no complaints about the date. If Katarina thought the zoo would be enough to scare him off, she was mistaken. It would take a lot more than that. He had to laugh when he saw her pull into the parking lot of a place that from the outside looked like a dive. He couldn't help thinking she'd picked that restaurant as a test to see if he would say something about her choices. If he did, he was more than sure she would use that as an opportunity to get rid of him. For some reason, he didn't think she trusted him.

After parking, Jase met Katarina at her car. She looked at him as they headed toward the entrance. "Have you ever been here before?"

"No, but I'm always willing to try new things."

They stepped through the door, and Jase's assumption of it being a dive was proven correct by the interior. It was kind of dark and dingy. The bar took up a lot of the open space. All the seats there were taken. The TV hanging on the wall above it played a sports channel. No hostess or host came to greet them, and there was no sign saying for them to wait to be seated.

Katarina had obviously been there before. She headed for one of the tables near the back. Once she selected the one she wanted, she took a seat. Jase sat across from her. She seemed to be watching him closely, as if judging his reaction.

He looked around. "I bet this is one of those places that doesn't look like much, but the food is really good."

Katarina nodded. "That about sums it up. I've been coming here for a while now." She shrugged out of her jacket, and Jase did the same with his.

A waitress came and gave them menus. Before she left, she took their drink order. Jase was mildly surprised when Katarina ordered a beer just like him. In his experience, women generally stuck with wine.

Jase looked over the menu, liking a lot of what he saw. For a dive, it had quite a few main dishes he wouldn't have expected. He'd finally decided on what he wanted to eat when a heavy hand landed on top of his shoulder. He looked up to find the last person he expected to see there.

"Dacian," Jase said. "What a surprise."

The large cougar shifter smiled as he pulled out one of the empty chairs between Jase and Katarina, then sat. "Jase. I've never seen you here before."

"That's because this is my first time. Katarina" — Jase glanced toward her — "brought me to try the food."

Dacian nodded at her. "Nice to meet you, Katarina. You don't mind if I join you two. I hate eating alone in a restaurant. I'd planned to get some takeout, but since you're here, I can stay." He slid Jase's menu toward himself, then looked it over.

"Sure, go right ahead," Jase said dryly.

He looked at Katarina to see what her reaction was to Dacian inviting himself to eat with them. She looked at him and nodded. Obviously, she didn't mind. Jase sighed inwardly. He wasn't too thrilled with it, but he couldn't very well be rude and tell the other cougar shifter to get lost. For one thing, Jase wasn't sure Dacian wouldn't pound the crap out of him if he did. That wasn't something he wanted Katarina to be witness to on their first date. It wouldn't go over well. It was bad enough she'd already seen him kick in Caleb's apartment door.

The waitress returned with Jase's and Katarina's drinks. She brought another table setting for Dacian, then finished taking all their orders. She returned only long enough to bring Dacian his beer before leaving them alone once more.

All three of them sat in silence, sipping their drinks. If Dacian noticed he was the third wheel, he showed no sign of it. Especially when he started up a conversation that Jase would have preferred Katarina didn't hear.

"So, Jase, did you manage to track down that asshole Caleb?"

Jase glanced at Katarina to see her closely watching him and Dacian. "Ah, yeah, I did. He gave me the slip, though."

"That's a start. If you do need any help capturing him, let me know. I consider Blaise one of my good friends. I wouldn't mind getting my claws into Caleb for what he tried to do to Blaise's father."

"Thanks for the offer. I'll be sure to give you a call if I can't handle it on my own."

Dacian nodded. "Good." He turned his gaze toward Katarina. "So, where did you and Katarina meet? Was it at one of the bars where you go to check out all the women? You said you'd take me with you and Grady the next time you went. I guess you forgot to give me a call. If the ladies were as pretty as Katarina, I missed out on something good."

Jase couldn't hold back the warning growl that rumbled out of him. He thought he was bad for saying what was on his mind, but Dacian was worse. From the way Katarina now scowled at Jase, he had a feeling his new friend hadn't done him any favors.

"No," Jase said in a tight voice. "I didn't meet Katarina at a bar."

"He met me when he tracked Caleb down at the apartment building I'm superintendent at and kicked in his door," she said, her expression guarded.

Dacian laughed. "I guess that's one way to pick up a woman."

"Let's change the subject," Jase said, wondering how much damage control he'd have to do once he and Katarina found a way to lose Dacian.

Katarina looked from Jase to Dacian and back to him again. "You both have the same cougar-head pendants."

Now that was a bit awkward. Jase had no idea how he'd explain that one, but he soon had that chance taken away when Dacian did it for him.

"It's a popular item among the circle of people we know. The men wear it with the hopes that one day a woman, who ends up being his to keep, will take it from him and put it around her own neck. Think of it as her showing him how much she loves him and is willing to commit to him." Dacian winked. "Would you like to try mine on and see what happens?"

Katarina looked at Dacian as if she didn't know if she should take him seriously or not. "No, that's quite okay. If it came down to whose necklace I would take, sorry, I'd choose Jase's over yours. You're not exactly my type."

Jase had to hold back a smile. Katarina had quickly put Dacian in his place. The other cougar shifter took it in stride.

Dacian shook his head and chuckled. "It would seem I've been told. It would stand to reason you'd pick Jase over me since you went out with him, after all."

Their food showed up at that point, and everyone focused on that for a short while. Dacian started the conversation rolling again, talking about some of the computer projects he worked on. Luckily, he didn't say anything more that would put Jase in an awkward situation with Katarina.

Jase was surprised to learn Dacian actually ran his own business of repairing computers and building new ones out of his house. He'd thought the other man mostly worked on programs that could be questionable at best.

Once they finished eating, Dacian reached into his pocket, then threw some money onto the table. "Thanks for letting me eat with you. I'll leave the two of you alone." He stood before he continued. "Jase, I hope to hear from you soon about the Caleb situation. Tell your brother, Grady, that I'm free whenever he is to go to the bar. I have a feeling you won't be joining us anytime soon."

With that, Dacian gave Katarina a smile and walked away. Jase watched him go through the restaurant's door, then faced the other way to find Katarina staring at him.

"Thanks for putting up with Dacian," Jase said. "I really don't know him all that well. We just met yesterday."

"I find that hard to believe. Didn't Dacian say the men in the circle you're both a part of wear those cougar-head pendants? That gave me the impression you knew him quite well."

"I knew *of* him but hadn't had any interaction with him until now."

"Oh."

"So, what's next on the agenda?"

"I'm not so sure if I want to suggest it."

Jase cursed to himself. Obviously, Dacian had done some damage. "Why? Is it because of something Dacian said?"

Katarina met his gaze. "Partially."

"Was it his comment about me going to bars to check out women? If that's what's bugging you, I wouldn't do that as long as you and I continue to see each other. You have my word on it."

She swirled the last of her beer in her glass. "Okay, I guess I believe that. The entire time we've been out, you haven't had a wandering eye."

Jase reached across the table and captured Katarina's free hand in his, then smiled. "I don't need to look at other women when I have one I'm very attracted to right here with me. How about you get all your concerns out on the table and I'll do my best to lay them to rest."

Katarina smiled back. "I think you're a bit of a sweet talker. All right. I'll be blunt with you. I don't have a good track record with men. I usually attract the bad boys and losers. They take advantage of me, get whatever they can, then dump me for someone else. To be honest, I've pretty much given up looking for someone I want to settle down with."

Now Jase understood why Katarina hadn't wanted to go out with him at first. She sounded an awful lot like him, but in his case, it was females of his kind who had lost their appeal. The last one he'd dated for a month had only been with him because she was going through all the single males she knew to find her mate. She really hadn't had any true feelings for him. All she'd cared about was whether or not the magic had been set off in his pendant.

"I can understand where you're coming from," he said. "I've had my fair share of women who have used me, then turned to another when I didn't turn out to be what they'd hoped. So, are you willing to give me a chance?"

She appeared to think over what he'd said, then nodded. "Okay. Why don't you come to my apartment for a drink?" Katarina smiled. "Plus, that way you can reimburse me for the repairs done to Caleb's door."

"I'd love to have a drink with you, and I'll gladly pay up."

Jase took care of the rest of the bill, then walked outside to the parking lot with Katarina. He followed her to her apartment building. Same as the last time he was there, he found the neighborhood not so nice. He would have loved to tell Katarina to move, but at this stage in their relationship it wasn't his place.

This time he parked in the visitors parking instead of on the street. Jase doubted Caleb was back. It was too soon. He met Katarina at her car as she got out, and then they walked to the building's entrance.

Inside her apartment, Katarina motioned for Jase to go into her living room. "Take a seat and I'll bring us each a beer."

He did as instructed. As he sat on the couch, Jase noticed the bill for the door's repairs sitting on the coffee table. He took some money out of his pocket to cover it, then placed the cash on the piece of paper.

Katarina returned and handed Jase a bottle of beer before she sat next to him. "You didn't have to give the money now."

"I don't mind. That way I won't forget." He took a sip of his beer. "Since you didn't say anything, I take it Caleb hasn't come back."

"No, he hasn't. You never said exactly how he tried to kill your uncle."

"He poisoned him. My uncle had been sick for over half a year before we found out it wasn't an illness causing it. His sons confronted Caleb about it, but he managed to run by using my cousin's wife as a shield. I've been trying to locate him ever since."

"I still think you should be leaving that to the police. It's their job, after all."

Jase needed something to distract Katarina from the topic of having the police involved in Caleb's capture. He leaned toward her and took her lips in a kiss. Remembering how good the other one they'd shared at the zoo had been, he slanted his mouth more firmly over hers and pushed his tongue inside. Hers twined with his, stroking and tasting. A surge of intense desire shot through him. His cock grew hard. Purrs rose out of him that he couldn't hold back. As if someone had set a match to gasoline, he burned for her.

*

Katarina hungrily kissed Jase back. All it took to bring her to almost full arousal was his lips against hers. She wanted him. Her pussy grew wet as desire flooded her. A year was a very long time to go without sex, and her body craved it, especially now that he held her in his arms. The hours she'd spent with him, she'd caught herself more than once imagining what he'd look like naked. How his skin would feel under her hands, and all those hard muscles under her lips.

Jase purred as he'd done back at the zoo. That just ramped up Katarina's desire even more. With her eyes closed to better experience the sensations shooting through her, she blindly reached out with her beer bottle to put it on the coffee table. He took it from her. Without letting her go, he accomplished what she'd tried to do. His soon followed.

Now that she had both hands free, Katarina reached up and wrapped her arms around Jase's neck. He held her along her waist, then lifted her and settled her on his lap, facing him. The meeting of her pussy and his cock through their clothes had both of them moaning. She sucked on his tongue as she buried her fingers into his hair to hold him exactly where she wanted him.

Jase ran his hands up and down her back before he shoved one under her shirt and deftly undid the hooks on her bra. He reached around to her front and pushed the garment out of the way. He cupped one breast and brushed a thumb back and forth across her taut nipple. Katarina pushed closer, needing more of his touch. No longer able to remain still, she rocked against his erection.

Jase broke contact with her mouth and held her gaze as he slowly lifted her shirt, giving her the chance to stop him. She didn't. She wouldn't. He'd more than passed her tests. It was time she took another chance on a man. Right now, he was the one she wanted to do that with.

Katarina took hold of her top and finished pulling it over her head, taking her bra with it. After tossing them to the floor, she reached for Jase's shirt and stripped him of it.

She ran her gaze along his broad, muscular shoulders, then his defined chest and abs. From what she'd bared of his body so far, she definitely liked what she saw. Katarina trailed a finger from the hollow of Jase's throat, down the center of his pecs to his pendant. She brushed a finger against the cougar head. It felt warm to the touch from the heat of his body, though it seemed a little warmer.

With her bottom lip caught between her teeth, Katarina continued her downward journey. Jase's abs tightened, showing off more of his six-pack once she reached it. At the waistband of his jeans, she ran her finger under it before she traced the outline of his hard cock. It jerked beneath her touch.

Jase grabbed her finger and brought it to his mouth. He kissed the very tip before he released it and leaned forward. He ran his cheek over her nipple as he purred like a big cat. He did it twice more before he circled the peak with his tongue. Katarina held on to his shoulders and arched her back in invitation.

"You smell so damn good," Jase said in a husky voice. "I'm going to make love to you." He looked up and met her gaze. "Unless you want to stop."

"Hell no."

Katarina ground her pussy against the very large bulge in Jase's jeans. She sucked in a sharp breath as he leaned forward again, and this time took her nipple into his mouth. She couldn't hold back the loud moan of pleasure that pushed out of her. Wetness leaked into her panties, and her heart beat faster in anticipation of what was to come.

Jase continued to suck at her breast as he dropped his hands to the button on her pants and quickly undid it. The zipper was pulled down next. His knuckles brushed against the front of her panties as he parted the material of her jeans. Katarina stilled her movements and waited to see what he'd do.

She didn't have to wait long to find out. He caressed her lower stomach before he took hold of her hips and lifted her off him, placing her to stand in front of him between the couch and the coffee table. He tugged her jeans down until they reached her ankles. She stepped out of them and kicked them away.

Jase spread his legs and hooked the front of her panties with his finger, using it to tug her forward to stand between them. His hot gaze swept her body. He purred. "Cats are partial to cream. I know where I can lick some up."

Katarina couldn't tear her gaze off Jase as he pushed down her panties and waited for her to step out of them before he tossed them away. He ran his hands up the insides of her thighs and gently nudged them farther apart. She held on to his shoulders, then gasped as he dipped one of his fingers into her pussy. He brought it to his mouth and sucked it clean.

"Oh, there's definitely cream there," he said.

Her legs just about gave out on her. She was so turned-on her body shook with the need to come. She wanted his mouth on her, licking and sucking her to orgasm. She was already at a fever pitch, it wouldn't take much to achieve that.

Jase lifted her again. This time he maneuvered them so she lay on her back on the couch with her legs hanging off it while he kneeled on the floor in front of her. He yanked her bottom to the very edge of the seat cushion, then licked her pussy with the flat of his tongue.

Katarina gasped and lifted her hips as he lapped at her like a cat would cream. All the while Jase continued to purr, sending shock waves of pleasure through her. Her body coiled tight. She reached down and held him to her as she rocked against his mouth.

He sucked on her clit and pushed one finger into her pussy, then stroked it in and out. A second soon joined it, scissoring, stretching her. That, added to what he did to the small bundle of nerves that was the center of her pleasure, was enough to send her over the precipice and into release. Katarina let out a keening moan as her inner muscles clutched and released the digits buried inside her.

Once the last sensation hit her and she went limp, Jase held on to her bottom, and with his free hand, undid his jeans. He pushed them down past his hips and sprang his cock. Katarina lifted her head and got her first look at it. It was thick and long, and she couldn't wait to have it in her pussy.

He fisted himself at the base of his shaft and led it to the wet opening to her body. Jase dipped the head into her juices, then rubbed her clit with it. Katarina lifted her legs and wrapped them around his waist.

Jase aligned his cock with her pussy and pushed forward until she'd taken the tip of him. He pulled back before he thrust deeper. He continued to work his length into her a little bit at a time. Once he was seated to the hilt, he grabbed her hips and took her in long, hard strokes.

Katarina matched the pace he set. She squeezed around his plunging cock, increasing the pleasure she felt. Jase groaned. He kept hold of her and bent his upper body over her as he thrust faster. She lifted her hands behind her and braced them on the cushion to stop her head from knocking into it. His shaft grew even harder, stretching her even more. The sounds of their heavy breathing and bodies meeting filled the room.

She sucked in a breath as something warm landed on her chest. Katarina looked to find Jase's cougar-head pendant resting against her. She soon forgot about it when he angled his hips in just the right way for his cock to stroke her G-spot. Another release quickly built. She locked her ankles at his waist and thrust up to meet him.

Jase pistoned into her, purring and groaning at the same time. "I can't hold back anymore."

"Come," she said on a moan. "I'll be right there with you."

He dug his fingers into her hips as he pumped once, twice, then held her to him as his cock pulsed deep inside her pussy. Katarina's sounds of pleasure joined his as she too climaxed. This one lasted longer than when she'd come against his mouth and was more intense. By the time it ended, she was completely wrung out and didn't think she could move to save her life.

CHAPTER FOUR

Jase had to be squishing Katarina, but the thought of lifting himself off her seemed beyond his capabilities at that moment. He'd come so hard he felt as if all his bones had turned to jelly. He tried to catch his breath. Their mingled scents filled his nose, causing little aftershocks through him. Making love to her was like nothing he'd experienced in another woman's arms.

He finally managed to brace his weight on his forearms and lightly kissed Katarina. She put her arms around his neck and played with the ends of his hair. Jase took satisfaction in seeing the satiated look she wore.

"Want to do it again?" he asked with a crooked grin.

Katarina smiled. "Give me a few minutes to catch my breath. The couch was fine, but for round two, I'm going to suggest we move to my bed. I don't think my back will stand another go here."

Jase put his arms around Katarina's waist, then lifted her as he sat on the floor. He held her to him to keep his softening cock inside her as she straddled his hips. "This better?"

"Much," she said and brushed his lips with hers. She glanced down his body. "How come I'm naked and you still have your jeans mostly on?"

"That's your fault. You made me so worked up I got impatient and couldn't wait to have you. I didn't feel like waiting to remove them all the way."

"I guess I can overlook it, then."

"Well, thank you." He kept hold of her and stood. One-handed, he hiked his jeans up enough for him to walk unimpeded before he carried her toward her bedroom. "Rest time is over. Let's get back to the fun."

* * * *

Jase came awake to the pleasurable sensation of having his cock sucked. He groaned and lifted the sheets to see Katarina under them with him buried in her mouth. Her head bobbed up and down as she slid him in and out. He flipped the covers off her and watched until his point of no return edged close.

He took hold of her by her arm and gently urged her up his body. She made a trail of kisses as she went and stopped with her lips hovering above his.

"Good morning," she said.

"Good morning. I have to say you really know how to wake up a man."

"I couldn't resist. You were lying there all naked. I didn't think you'd mind."

Jase reached between their bodies until he encountered her pussy. She was wet and ready for him. "I can see you didn't mind either." He dipped a finger inside her. She moaned.

Katarina shook her head. "No, I don't. In fact, I want more. It seems I can't stop craving you."

"Then take what you want."

She didn't hesitate to do exactly that. Katarina positioned herself over his fully engorged cock, then slowly impaled herself. Purrs he couldn't hold back rumbled out. He'd made love to her most of the night, but he hadn't come anywhere near slaking his need for her. Each time he took her, he only wanted to possess her more.

Katarina put her hands on his chest, sliding him in and out of her pussy. Her strong inner walls gripped him, wringing more purrs out of him. He could get lost inside her and never want to come out.

She sat up, then raised and lowered herself on him. Jase looked at her to see she had her eyes closed and her bottom lip between her teeth. He shifted his gaze to where their bodies were joined. The sight of her pussy taking his cock was the most erotic thing he'd seen. He lifted his hips and surged up into her as she rode him.

Jase's balls rose closer to his body as his climax edged ever nearer to the surface. To make sure Katarina came with him, he reached between them and found her clit with the tip of his finger. He rubbed it as she rode him faster, her breath coming in pants.

The first flutter along his cock heralded her release. She moaned his name, her movements growing jerky. As her pussy milked his shaft in a tight fist, he could no longer hold off his orgasm. He thrust up into her one final time, lifting her knees off the mattress, and emptied himself inside her. She collapsed on top of him once there was nothing left for him to give.

"If we keep this up, I don't think we'll be leaving the bed anytime soon," Jase said.

Katarina slid off him and then propped herself on her bent arm as she lay on her side to look down at him. "I think you're right. As for myself, I blame it on the year of celibacy I forced on myself."

"A whole year? That does deserve a marathon of sex, but if I don't get up and go home, I have a feeling my brother, Grady, will come looking for me."

"You two live together?"

"Yes, and with my parents as well."

Katarina gave him a stare that said she wasn't sure what she thought about that. "Really? Your parents?"

"It's not what you're thinking. I haven't moved out because I can't stand living away from Mommy and Daddy. It's a tradition of my family. I'll be blunt here. We're rich, very rich. I live in what you'd call a mansion, I suppose. My bedroom is more like an apartment, maybe a little bigger than yours." He reached up and tucked some of her brown hair behind her ear. "I'll take you there and show you."

"If you're that rich, I take it you don't have a job."

"No, I don't. I have a lot of investments that have done very well. One of them being the software company my uncle started." Jase said the name and saw by Katarina's expression she recognized it.

"If you own stock in that corporation, then you can't be hurting."

A loud knock sounded on the door, breaking into their conversation. Katarina shifted as if to get off the bed. Jase grabbed her hand and pressed it to his chest before she could.

"Leave it. Maybe the person will go away," he said.

Katarina pulled out of his grasp. "Unlike you, I have to work for a living. I'm the superintendent, remember? I have tenants knocking on my door all the time or calling me about something. It's my job to take care of it."

She got off the bed, then headed for her closet as the knock came again. Katarina took out a thick bathrobe and pulled it on. She tied the belt around her waist as she walked toward the bedroom door that stood open.

"You're not answering the door like that," Jase said as he sat up.

Katarina rolled her eyes. "I'm completely covered. I'm

not getting dressed until after I've had a shower. It wouldn't be the first time I've done this."

She continued on her way. Jase remained in bed and listened to Katarina open the apartment door. With his sensitive cougar shifter hearing, he was able to hear as if he stood next to her. At the sound of the voice that answered when she asked what she could do for the person outside in the hall, he quickly climbed off the mattress and yanked on his jeans. He was almost out of the bedroom when Katarina came to get him.

"Grady is here. You won't have to worry about him calling you, after all."

"I'll try to get rid of him."

Jase gave Katarina a quick kiss before he walked around her. Once he stepped into the living room, he saw his brother standing near the closed apartment door. Jase came to stand in front of him.

"What are you doing here, Grady?"

"When you didn't come home last night and didn't answer any of the text messages I sent, I wondered if you'd had a run-in with Caleb."

"So you came here to make sure I was still with Katarina," Jase said as a statement rather than a question.

"Give me a break. Caleb's apartment is across the hall. He could have gotten the jump on you."

Jase held out his arms to either side of himself and did a quick turn. "As you can see, I'm perfectly fine. You can leave now."

"I was thinking while I'm here, the two of us can check out Caleb's place and see if he left any clues behind. Your new girlfriend will be able to let us in since she's the superintendent of the building."

"I'll ask Katarina, but if she won't do it, I'm not going to push. I don't want her to think I'm trying to take advantage of her."

Grady smiled. "By how thick her scent is all over you,

and how you smell like sex, I'd say you already did. You're a lucky bastard. She's gorgeous."

Jase decided to ignore what his brother had said. "I'll ask. Wait right here."

He left Grady by the door and headed back to the bedroom. He found Katarina sitting on the bed, waiting for him. She gave him a questioning look.

Jase shook his head. "No, I didn't get rid of him yet." He paused as he came to stand in front of her. "Would you be against letting us into Caleb's apartment to have a look around? Grady thinks there's a chance Caleb would have left a clue behind as to where he could have gone."

"I don't think I really should do it, but considering what he tried to do to your uncle, I'll bend the rule just this one time. Whatever you do, don't break anything, and be quiet. The tenant one door down is an older lady, and she knows everything about everyone who lives here. I'm sure she'll set up a fuss if she learns I let you in. She's gone over my head a few times and brought issues up with the owner, who in turn came down hard on me because of it."

"You have my word we'll be as stealthy as cats." Which wouldn't be hard for him and Grady. His kind could move without making a sound when they wanted to.

"Just see that you do. You two can look around while I'm in the shower. I'll let you in now."

Jase followed Katarina out to the living room. She stopped only long enough to get a ring of keys from the kitchen. He and Grady fell into step behind her as she walked across the hall to Caleb's place. She unlocked it and then stepped aside for them.

"I'll lock the place up after you're done," Katarina said. "I'll be in the shower." She turned and walked back inside her apartment.

Jase opened Caleb's door, then stepped through it with Grady before quietly shutting it behind them. A quick glance showed the window that Caleb had escaped through had been shut. Other than that, the place was the same as it'd been the day before.

"You want to start in here and I'll take the bedroom?" Grady asked.

"All right. Try not to disturb anything. We don't need Caleb to come back and find out we've been snooping around his things. He might really run then. As for our scents, I doubt he'll be back soon enough to be able to smell them. After all, scent trails don't last that long."

"Gotcha. I'll be careful."

Once Grady disappeared into the bedroom, Jase started his own search in the main part of the apartment. After a closer inspection of the furniture, he had a feeling Caleb had rented the place furnished. His prey wouldn't have had the time to pack all that stuff and move it there in such a short period of time. And then there was the fact everything was mismatched and on the old side. They didn't match the Caleb he knew.

A thorough search of the living room didn't turn up anything. Not that there were many things there to hide something. Jase went to the kitchen. He looked through the cupboards, which were mostly empty. There was only a plate, bowl, and cutlery for one person with a couple of glasses. The inside of the fridge didn't hold anything but a few bottles of water. Obviously, Caleb hadn't been eating there. The freezer was bare, and there were no canned goods anywhere.

Jase was about to head for the bathroom when Grady called his name. He hurried into the bedroom to see what his brother had found.

"Did you find something?" he asked as he closed the distance between himself and Grady.

"Well, I have a feeling Caleb will be coming back soon. If anything, he'll want to get this." Grady held up a clear plastic zippered bag that had a thick wad of cash in it.

"Where did you find it?"

Grady snorted. "Under the mattress. What a bonehead."

"I have to agree with that, considering the neighborhood. Put it back. You're right. He won't leave that amount of cash behind."

"I'd suggest you find a way to stay with Katarina so you can be here when Caleb does return, but your scent will give away your presence. If he were human, that would be another story."

Jase blew out a breath. "I still don't think it'll be within the next couple of days. I scared him off, but I have to agree about not having my scent hanging around. I better not stay at Katarina's place again. The fresh scent will tip him off."

"Then where will you take her to do the nasty?" Grady asked with a laugh.

"I'll bring her home."

His brother instantly sobered. "You would take her to our house? Where Mom and Dad are?"

"Well, yeah."

"Aren't you worried about what their reaction will be to you bringing a human into our home?"

"No. I doubt they'll be too upset by it. Their nephews are mated to humans, and our leader has accepted them into the family group. Our uncle has had a complete reversal in opinion about them."

"That does help. I do have to say our parents are more open about them than others." Grady chuckled. "At least you'll be the first one to bring a human home and not me. If I happen to one day, they'll have adjusted to it by that point."

"I'm so glad I can be your guinea pig. Anyway, did you find anything else?"

"No. There's hardly anything in here. Just a few articles of clothing hanging in the closet and stored in the dresser. What about you?"

"Nothing. There's not even food in the kitchen. I have a feeling this was only a temporary place for him to stay. We won't find any clue here to where Caleb can be. I'm going back to Katarina's place. I'll see you later."

Grady smiled. "I guess you won't be going out to the bars with me for a while now that you're with Katarina. It won't be as much fun if I'm alone."

Jase fished his cell phone out of his front jeans pocket, then brought his contacts list up. "I know the perfect person who would go out with you. Remember Blaise's friend, Dacian?"

"Yeah. Isn't he the computer nerd, though?"

He grinned. "He is, but he in no way looks like one. The guy is as big as a werewolf. Give him a call." Jase rattled off Dacian's number as Grady put it into his contacts in his cell phone.

"I'll do that," Grady said. "If anything, it should be an interesting night."

Once his brother left, Jase headed across the hall. Inside Katarina's apartment, there was no sound of the shower running. He went to the bedroom and arrived in time to watch her drop her towel, then start to get dressed. He leaned against the doorframe, admiring the sight she made.

Even though he hadn't said anything to Grady, Jase already had strong feelings for Katarina. She was everything he liked in a woman. She could stand up for herself and had no qualms about saying what was on her mind. She wasn't afraid to show him exactly what she wanted from him in bed, or take it, either.

Jase followed the line of her back as Katarina picked up a comb and ran it through her long, damp hair. At that moment, as he stood there taking her all in, he realized he wanted her to set off the magic in his cougar-head pendant. He wanted to see it grace her slim neck and rest just above her more-than-a-handful breasts. He wanted to tell her what he was, but with her baseball bat somewhere close at hand, he didn't think shifting to his cougar form in front of her right then would be a good idea.

"Are you going to only stand there and stare?" Katarina asked as she met his gaze in the dresser mirror.

Jase pushed away from where he leaned and closed the distance between them. He slipped the comb from her hand and took over the job of getting the snarls out of her hair. "I finally got rid of Grady."

"Did you find anything useful?"

"Only a big wad of cash that was hidden under Caleb's mattress."

"So he'll be back."

"I'm ninety-ninety-point-nine percent sure he will. I can't see him wanting to leave that amount of money behind."

Jase reached around Katarina and put the comb onto the dresser before he wrapped his arms around her waist and pulled her back against his chest. The top of her head just reached it. He met her gaze in the mirror once more.

"How about you spending tonight at my place?" he asked.

"Don't you have to get your parents' permission first?" A small smile tugged at Katarina's lips.

"That was so funny I forgot to laugh. No, I don't. I'm all grown up at age twenty-seven. I can invite whomever I want over."

"That's how old I am."

"Oh, really now? When's your birthday? Mine is on May 10th."

Katarina turned in his arms to face him. "So is mine."

Jase laughed. "We're twins."

"Hardly. You won't ever have to worry about me forgetting your birthday."

"Nor me yours. So, will you spend the night at my house?"

"All right." Katarina went on tiptoe and kissed his chin. "I'm really interested in seeing this massive bedroom of yours."

"I hope that isn't the only thing of mine that you'll find massive."

She rolled her eyes. "Oh, baby, you're so well-hung I can't think of anything else but your enormous cock."

The way Katarina said it in such a monotone voice, she had Jase laughing. "Okay, you got me back for that one."

"I'll make us some breakfast. Then I have to get to work."

Jase tugged her closer and kissed her until she moaned into his mouth. He lifted his head. "Are you sure you have to work today? Wouldn't you rather spend the day with me instead?"

Katarina reached up and fingered his pendant as she looked him in the eyes. "I would, but I can't. The owner is coming by late this afternoon to collect the rent checks. I have to have this place clean or he'll come down hard on me."

"I could help you."

She arched a brow. "Have you ever cleaned before?"

"Well, not really."

"I figured that much. If you live in a mansion, then I would expect you have hired help to do that for you. Thanks for the offer, but I'll get it done faster by myself. I have a whole system worked out."

"Then I won't suggest I help with breakfast either since I don't know how to cook."

Katarina laughed and shook her head. "Good idea. Let's get something to eat, and then you have to hit the road."

Jase released Katarina. She walked out of the bedroom. He gathered up the rest of his clothes and then pulled them on before he joined her in the kitchen. As she went about making breakfast for them, he decided he'd gear their evening all for her. He'd wine and dine her, after which he'd take her to bed and make her come until she begged him to stop. *If* she begged him to stop. Though he had no problem with the idea of taking her as many times as it took to have her calling for mercy.

CHAPTER FIVE

Caleb watched Grady walk out of the apartment building before he headed for the parking lot at the side from his hiding place across the street. He lifted his upper lip in a snarl as the other cougar shifter got into his car, then drove away.

He remained where he was, though. Jase was still inside there somewhere. Caleb had recognized the brothers' cars in the lot as he'd driven his beater by them. He'd come to retrieve the last few things he'd left in the crappy apartment he'd been forced to rent. With Jase and Grady already there, he couldn't take the chance of either one of them encountering him.

How Jase had known where to find him in the first place, Caleb hadn't a clue. He'd purposely picked the worst part of the city, an area where none of his family would think to look for him. Obviously, that hadn't worked as well as he'd thought it would.

He should have left Anchorage, but Caleb wasn't going to just walk away from the life he'd built for himself and leave it behind. He'd worked too hard for it all. He needed to liquidate all his assets before he could start over again, in another country perhaps.

If only his uncle had died as Caleb had planned, then none of this would have happened to him. For over half a year, no one had been wise to what he'd been doing. They'd all accepted his word that his uncle suffered from some kind of new illness. He'd been so close to reaching his goal. He'd had it all worked out too. Since his cousin, Blaise, didn't want the leadership role in their family group, and Taylor had been exiled, Caleb would have easily stepped into it. No one would have stopped him. He would have been there for his aunt, and little by little, he would have taken the reins.

Then his uncle had done the unthinkable and brought Taylor back into the family fold and reinstated him as his heir. All Caleb's plans had fallen apart the day Taylor had returned. Caleb once again was relegated to the orphan whom his uncle took pity on.

After waiting ten more minutes without Jase appearing, Caleb made the decision to come back another day. What the other cougar shifter was doing inside the building, he had no idea, and didn't intend to stick around to find out. He'd wait until the coast was clear before he attempted to get what belonged to him.

* * * *

Katarina worked like a dog to get the apartment building up to the owner's standards. She thought there was nothing wrong with how she normally cleaned it, but he'd made it perfectly clear that wasn't acceptable to him. To be honest, the man was an asshole, but since she didn't have any other job options available, she put up with his shit.

She'd finally gotten to sit down when a loud knock on

her door heralded the arrival of the owner. Katarina got up and answered it. She stepped back to let Fred in. He was a balding, overweight sixty-year-old man who thought he had a way with the ladies, even though she highly doubted he even had it when he was younger.

"Hi, Fred. I have the rent checks all ready for you."

"Are there any late ones?" he asked as he walked in, looking around.

"A couple, but they've assured me they'll have the rent to me in the next couple of weeks. They were a little short."

Fred came to stand in the middle of the living room, appearing to give it a close inspection. "I've told you before not to allow that. I'm sure it's the same tenants every month."

Katarina bit back a caustic remark. The ones who she gave leeway to were the tenants who'd lost their jobs and had young families or who were seniors. They always managed to make up their rent. It just took them longer.

"I know. I've told them how you feel about it."

Fred crossed to the coffee table and picked up the manila envelope she'd put the rent checks in. He came to stand in front of her.

"As I've said, this has happened one too many times. That being the case, let this be your two-week notice. I need you out of the apartment by then." He paused to look around again. "I have to have this place painted before my daughter takes over as superintendent."

At first, Katarina didn't know what to say. She'd worked there for the last three years. "You're letting me go? Shouldn't I at least have a month's notice like any other tenant?"

He snorted. "You aren't a tenant. You've lived here rent free. Two weeks is sufficient for letting a person go when it pertains to a job. I'll be around for the keys at the end of that time period. Make sure you've taken all your belongings. Anything left behind will be disposed of."

Katarina could only stare at Fred as he walked out of the apartment. She counted to three, but that didn't do a thing to cool her temper. The big, fat asshole had let her go. She knew it had nothing to do with the late rent checks or her work performance. It had to do with the fact his daughter must be out of a job. In her early thirties, the woman was as spoiled as it came. Fred gave her whatever she wanted. Obviously, she had wanted Katarina's position as superintendent.

She looked around her apartment. There was no way she could find a new place in that short amount of time. If she were lucky, she could get another job in two weeks, but she'd have no place to stay. Well, if Fred thought she'd be kissing his ass and going out of her way to do anything that wasn't in her job description, he was out of luck. To be honest, Katarina felt as if she shouldn't do anything. It wasn't as if he'd show up until the weeks were up. She would have the major job of packing her whole place. It would take all her time to do it. She'd accumulated too much stuff over the years.

The more she thought about it, the madder Katarina got. She needed to get out of her apartment. Thank goodness Jase had invited her to spend the night at his place. She really needed to get away. Plus, there was the fact he might be able to help her. She considered him her boyfriend now, and she thought he felt the same way about her.

Katarina grabbed her purse, keys, the overnight bag she'd packed, and the piece of paper Jase had written his address on before she stalked out of the apartment. She left the building and then headed for her car. Hopefully, Jase would have some suggestions. She really didn't want to go home to her parents. They didn't live in Anchorage. She'd come from Butte, which only had a population of a little over thirty-two hundred. There was no way she could live there again. She was too used to the large city of Anchorage.

She followed the directions Jase had given her along with his address. The area became increasingly more affluent the closer she came to his house. This was definitely an area where all the rich people lived. When she'd first moved to Anchorage, she'd driven through the neighborhoods like this, wondering what the insides of the houses looked like.

Katarina pulled onto the long drive and then drove her car off to the side where some parking spaces were close to the four-car garage. She looked up at the large brick home. It was indeed a mansion.

She got out of the car and then grabbed her bag and purse from the backseat before she walked to the front door. Katarina rang the doorbell. It seemed to take a while before she heard footsteps coming toward the door. It was opened by a woman who appeared to be in her middle thirties. She wore dress pants and a blouse that looked to be silk. Her tawny hair, the same shade as Jase's, was pulled back in a ponytail. Her light brown eyes that verged on gold were also the same color.

The woman smiled and opened the door wider. "You must be Katarina. Jase told me you were coming. Come on in."

Katarina smiled. "Thanks. Jase didn't tell me he had a sister. I thought he only had a brother."

The woman laughed. "I'm not his sister. I'm his mother. My name is Olivia, and I'll take you upstairs. He's in his room."

Katarina followed Olivia across the large, open foyer to the oak staircase that curved upward. Olivia didn't look old enough to have a twenty-seven-year-old son. Katarina would have sworn the other woman was only a few years older than she.

At the top of the stairs, Olivia led her halfway down the

long hallway and then stopped at a closed door. She knocked on it. "Jase, honey? Katarina is here."

Jase opened the door and motioned for Katarina to come inside his bedroom. "Thanks, Mom. I take it you introduced yourself."

Olivia smiled. "Of course. Will the two of you be eating downstairs with us, or are you going to stay up in your room?"

"I figured we'd stay here."

"All right. I'll let the cook know. She can make a tray for you to bring up." Jase's mom looked at Katarina. "I hope to get to know you better, Katarina."

Once Olivia left, Katarina walked farther into Jase's bedroom and looked around. He hadn't been kidding. It was huge. There was a full sitting area complete with a couch and glass coffee table. There were even glass sliding doors that opened onto the wraparound balcony she'd seen on the outside of the house. It really was like having his own apartment.

Jase came to stand beside her and took her overnight bag. "You're early. I thought it would be closer to dinner before you could get away. Did the owner show up sooner than you expected?"

Katarina turned to face him. "He did." Some of her anger returned at the mention of Fred.

"You look pissed off. What happened?"

"The asshole let me go. I now have two weeks to clear out my apartment. He didn't leave me enough time to find another place. I highly doubt I can get a new job in that short amount of time. Being jobless will make it even harder to get another apartment."

"You're kidding me."

"No. I wish I were." Katarina met Jase's gaze. "I know we still have to get to know each other better, but I have no idea what to do. Is there any place you know of that I could rent? Even if you could help me find one, I'd appreciate it."

Jase pulled her close and kissed her. "I can do even better than that. You can move in here with me."

Katarina shook her head. "I can't do that. We've only known each other a couple of days. It's too soon to be talking about moving in together. Don't you have a guesthouse or something?"

"No, we don't. How about this? You move in, and I'll pay to put what you won't need in storage. If you feel it isn't going to work out, you can stay here for as long as you want until you find another place. At least you don't have to feel as if you'll have to live on the street." Jase kissed her again and gave her a crooked smile. "I don't mind sharing my space with you. There's plenty of room."

"Your parents? What would they think?"

Jase chuckled. "You're always so worried about what they'll think. You met my mom. Did she look upset with the idea of you staying overnight?"

"No."

"Did she act unfriendly toward you?"

"No."

"Then stop worrying. Think of it this way. You'll have a better place to live, all your meals will be cooked for you, and you won't have to clean anything that you don't want to."

Katarina smiled. "I could get used to that and won't ever want to leave. Can I look around?"

Jase released her. "Be my guest." He placed her bag on the floor, walked to the sitting area, and sat on the couch. "I'll stay out of your way."

She made a show of sitting on the king-sized bed and bouncing as if she were checking out the mattress. Katarina had to practically climb up on it to accomplish that since it had one of those high-profile box springs and the mattress had a thick pillow top. At her height, she'd have found a step stool handy.

Next, she walked through the sitting area and looked out the sliding door. It had a nice view of the perfectly landscaped backyard. Katarina felt Jase's gaze following her as she left there and headed for the en suite.

It turned out to be a little larger than her bedroom at her apartment. There was a glass-enclosed shower stall and a big whirlpool bathtub. Katarina walked to it. It would definitely hold two adults, even if one was as large as Jase.

"So, what do you think?"

Katarina turned to find Jase leaning against the granite countertop on the long vanity. She hadn't heard him come into the bathroom.

She nodded. "I like it. There's just one thing I want to try first before I give you my final answer."

Jase stepped closer. "What would that be?"

"I want to test the whirlpool bathtub. After all that cleaning I did earlier today, a good soak is what I need."

"That's doable. Since I'm the one who owns this, and handling the viewing, it would only be the right thing for me to join you. To show you the other benefits you'll receive if you take up my offer to cohabitate."

Katarina closed the distance between them, then ran her hands up his muscular chest. "I'll have to add that to the pro column."

"I should hope so. If I may ask, is there anything in the con column so far?"

"Not a one, but I still want that whirlpool before I give you an answer."

"Then I shall run the lady a bath."

Jase stepped around Katarina and headed to the bathtub. He turned on the faucet and adjusted the water temperature to the way he wanted. Once he finished that and the tub was filling, he turned toward her and crooked his finger for her to come closer.

Katarina stripped off her clothes before she joined Jase

by the bathtub. She reached up and touched his pendant, something she found herself wanting to do more than she probably should. At least he didn't seem to mind.

"I saw your mom wore the exact same necklace as yours. I guess Dacian was right about people in your circle giving it to their wife or girlfriend."

Jase yanked his shirt off over his head. "She actually took it from my dad. That's generally what happens. It's a way of showing she wants him all to herself."

Katarina took a deep breath as Jase undid his jeans and then pushed them down his legs to step out of. "I'll have to remember that."

Her heart really got pumping after he took off his underwear. His cock was fully erect, jutting from his body, tempting her to wrap her hand around it and stroke. She had to definitely add that as another item in her pro column.

*

Katarina licked her lips as she stared intently at his cock. It jerked, and he bit back a purr. Showing someone around his bedroom had never been such a turn-on as it was with her. What she'd said about having to remember it was his mother who had taken his father's cougar-head pendant just added fuel to his already raging fire. She had no idea what it meant when a female claimed a male's necklace, but she apparently liked the idea of it.

Katarina took the step needed to bring her toe-to-toe with him. She slowly went onto her knees in front of him, his erection now eye level to her. She dragged a finger through the drop of pre-cum that had leaked from the very tip, then brought it to her mouth to lick clean. There was no holding back his purrs any longer after that.

As if she had all the time in the world, Katarina wrapped her hand around his cock and slowly pumped it up and down. She did that a few more times until he was about ready to beg her to take him into her mouth. As if she'd read his mind, she did just that.

Jase looked down to watch Katarina pleasure him. She dragged the flat of her tongue up his length, then ran it around the head before she opened and took him between her lips. She sucked him almost to the back of her throat before sliding him out until only the tip remained in her mouth.

He purred and growled, no longer able to hide his cat side. Katarina drove him wild, almost literally. She kept up a steady suction as she took him in and out, keeping a tight grip on him at the base of his cock. She brought up her other hand and fondled his balls. She gave them a gentle tug, and Jase purred with pleasure.

The sound of the overflow drain on the tub gurgling broke through enough of the fog of arousal to have Jase carefully pulling away from Katarina. He quickly turned and shut off the faucet. He let some of the water out before he faced her once more to find her already on her feet.

Jase cupped her face and kissed her thoroughly until she moaned into his mouth. He lifted his head, scooping her up into his arms. He stepped into the tub. The water was the perfect temperature. He sat, positioning Katarina so she was between his legs, facing him. He pushed the button on the side of the tub to start the jets.

"Mmm, this is nice," Katarina said. "But I think this will make it even nicer."

She shifted until her legs were on the outside of his, then leaned over him, straddling his hips. Katarina rubbed her pussy along his cock. Jase lifted his hips, and her, out of the water. She held on to the sides of the tub and slowly worked his length deep inside her.

As she rode him, their movements stirred up the water, even more than the water jets already were. He rested his head against the back of the bathtub and reached around to her shapely bottom. He held on to it as she raised and lowered herself on his shaft. Being buried deep inside her pussy was better than anything. It felt right, as if she belonged to him and he'd only been waiting to find her.

He thrust up, sloshing some of the bathwater onto the floor. Jase grew even harder, loud purrs rumbling out of him each time she took him to the hilt and gripped his cock with her inner walls.

Katarina rode him faster, moans pushing out of her, a look of pleasure written on her face. She had to be close to her release. Jase's point of no return was steadily edging nearer.

He leaned his head forward and captured one of her nipples in his mouth. Jase sucked on the tight bud before he gently nipped it. Katarina's moans increased in volume. He played with her other breast as he continued to suck.

Katarina whimpered his name as her pussy milked his cock in a tight fist, her orgasm taking hold of her. Jase surged up into her and held still until the last spasm passed. He thrust into her over and over again. As he found his release, he let loose with a cat's growl.

The water continued to bubble around them. Katarina grew relaxed on top of him and kissed his lips. "I'm ready to give you my answer now," she said through panted breaths.

"That would be?"

"I'll move in with you."

Jase skimmed his hand down her back to her bottom and squeezed. "When?"

She chuckled. "I have to stick it out until the end of the two weeks. Plus, I'll need that time to pack everything up."

"Can I help with that?"

"I wish you could, but it's better I do it myself. I'll more than likely get rid of some of it. I've kept things I really shouldn't have."

"Well, I'll rent that storage unit for you, and when you're ready, we'll get you moved."

Katarina met his gaze. "Thanks."

"For what?"

"For helping me like this. If Fred had pulled this crap a month ago, I wouldn't have had anyone to turn to. I probably would have had to move home with my parents in Butte."

"Then we never would have met. I'm glad I can be here for you." Jase pushed the button to turn off the jets. "Now that you've made your decision to live with me, I think it's time to celebrate. We'll need the bed to do it properly."

Once he got them both out of the bathtub and then dried off, Jase took Katarina to bed. He'd had no idea how much it would mean to him to have her agree to live with him. Given the fact she had agreed, it was time he told her about his being a cougar shifter. She deserved to know the truth, especially since she'd be living with some. All it would take to blow their secret was to have one of his family members shift in front of her. Having Katarina find out that way wouldn't be ideal.

Jase pulled Katarina to him and kissed her passionately, ready for another round of intense lovemaking. Telling her what he was would have to wait, though. He didn't want to ruin their celebration.

CHAPTER SIX

Katarina came awake and turned her head to see Jase was still sound asleep. She smiled. He had to be all worn out. They'd had another night of marathon sex. She could have slept longer as well, but the thought of all the packing she had to do didn't allow for it. She felt stressed over it, which had her wanting to return to her apartment to get to work.

She rolled onto her side and looked at Jase. He still hadn't moved. Quiet snores rumbled out of him. Katarina poked him, but they didn't lessen, nor did he awaken. She had a feeling he was one of those people who once in a deep sleep was hard to wake up. A smile spread across her lips as she remembered one way that had done the trick the morning before.

Katarina wouldn't be doing that, though. For one thing, she wouldn't be leaving anytime soon if she woke Jase up with a blowjob. She ran her gaze over his handsome face and down to his chest, which wasn't covered by the blankets. She was brought up short once she reached his pendant.

She leaned closer to make sure her eyes weren't playing tricks on her. The cougar's ruby ones looked to be glowing. How, she had no idea. There was no light on in the room, and the thick curtains on the sliding glass doors had been pulled closed, which blocked out most of the sunlight, but the rubies continued to glow. There had to be something inside the pendant to cause it. That was the only answer.

Katarina picked it off Jase's chest and flipped it over. The back was smooth, solid gold. The sides didn't reveal any seam to show there could be something in the middle. It didn't make any sense.

The longer she held the cougar-head pendant, the stronger the urge to take it from Jase became. It snuck up on her at first but increased until it was almost a compulsion. She wanted it. To be fair, Katarina had agreed to live with him. According to what the pendant seemed to be used for, she should be wearing it around her neck to show Jase her commitment to him. The more she thought about it, the more justified she felt in taking his necklace.

She touched the pendant and found it warm, warmer than Jase's skin. Before she could talk herself out of doing it, Katarina closed piece of gold in her hand and carefully lifted. At Jase's head, she slowly tugged the chain over and off. He continued to sleep, none the wiser of what she'd done. She slipped off the bed, still holding the necklace by the pendant, then headed for the en suite. She grabbed her overnight bag on the way.

With the door closed behind her, Katarina put her bag down before she placed the necklace on the granite countertop. She had it, now did she really want to put it around her neck without Jase being aware of it? She decided to make that decision after she brushed her teeth and got dressed.

After accomplishing all that, she looked at the pendant. The ruby eyes still glowed, and not from the lights inside the bathroom. Should she or shouldn't she? Katarina scooped it up and held it flat on her palm. She really wanted to put it on. Jase wouldn't mind—at least, she didn't think he would. He'd been the one to suggest she move in with him, after all.

Katarina stepped back into the bedroom, the pendant closed in her hand. Her stomach growled, reminding her it'd been hours since the last time she'd eaten. Jase had told her the cook usually set up breakfast in the dining room with food the family could come and eat whenever they wanted.

After one last look at Jase, Katarina quietly stepped out of the room and closed the door behind her, thinking she'd find the dining room and get them something to have in bed.

"I see Jase finally let you out of his room."

Katarina just about jumped out of her skin. She turned around to find Grady standing at the closed door directly across the hall. "You scared the crap out of me. I didn't see you there."

"Sorry. Didn't mean to do that."

She put her closed fist over her chest. "That's okay. I just have to tell my heart that."

Grady came to stand in front of her with a curious look as his gaze landed on the gold chain that hung from her hand. "What have you got there?"

Katarina felt her face heat at getting caught. "Before I show you, you should know Jase asked me to move in with him and I said yes."

"Really? I had no idea you two were getting that close, and what about your job as superintendent?"

"I have two weeks before I no longer have that position. That's part of the reason Jase asked me to move in. I don't have any other place to go."

"I see. So, what are you holding?"

Slowly Katarina held out her hand, then turned it palm

up and opened her fist. Grady's expression went from curious to surprised. He looked from the pendant and its glowing ruby eyes to her face, then back down at the pendant.

"Does Jase know you have that?"

She shook her head. "No. He's dead asleep in there. I just took it." Katarina sighed. "I know all about the circle of people you're part of and how you guys give your necklace to the woman you get serious with."

"Okay, that's sort of what happens. What are you going to do with it now that you have it?"

"This."

Katarina lifted the chain and pulled it on over her head. The instant the cougar-head pendant came to rest on the center of her chest, she felt as if something snapped into place. As if she were invisibly connected to something, or someone. It took her breath away, and she stumbled back against the closed bedroom door. Through it, she heard Jase suddenly call out her name.

Grady took hold of her arm to steady her before he opened the door at her back. He gave her a kiss on the cheek. "Welcome to the family." He walked her inside the room and toward where Jase sat up on the bed, his gaze locked on the pendant. "Time for some explanations, bro," Grady said to him. "I'll leave you to it."

Katarina turned her head and watched Grady walk out of the room, then close her and his brother inside. She looked back at Jase. "You're awake."

His gaze didn't seem to leave the pendant as he flipped back the covers before crossing the distance to where she stood. "You took my pendant."

She gave him a sheepish smile. "Sorry. I should have asked. I really don't know what came over me. I couldn't help myself. The ruby eyes glowed, and I had the biggest urge to wear it. I didn't actually put it around my neck until a few seconds ago when Grady caught me with it in my hand. Are you mad?"

Jase captured her face in his hands and kissed her hungrily. It was unlike any kiss they'd shared before. It was almost as if he worshipped her at the same time, as if she were something he wanted to hold on to and never let go.

Once he released her lips, Katarina gave Jase a small smile. "I'll take that as a no."

"I'm not mad. Far from it." He met her gaze. "I love you."

Katarina sucked in a sharp breath. "What?"

"You heard me. I love you."

"Are you only saying that because I agreed to move in with you?"

"No. I mean it with all my heart." He said softly, "You felt it, didn't you? When you put my pendant around your neck, you felt the bond form."

"Yes," she whispered.

"That proves my words are true. Just as I know you love me too because of it."

"All because I took your pendant and put it on?"

"Yes. I'd hoped you'd be the one, but I couldn't be sure until you set the magic off in it."

Katarina shook her head. "I think you're getting a little ahead of yourself. Magic and invisible bonds caused by necklaces are not part of my everyday world."

Jase dropped his hands and nodded. "I'd decided to have this conversation with you before this happened. I think I'd better put some pants on first."

She followed him with her gaze and sighed to herself at the gorgeous figure he made with no clothes on. A smile played across her lips as the knowledge that he loved her settled in. She loved him too and had come to that conclusion sometime during the night while he'd held her in his arms. She'd tell him, but she wanted to hear what he said first about what had just happened between them.

After pulling on a pair of jeans and a T-shirt, Jase crossed to Katarina. "Let's sit on the couch."

She walked with him to the sitting area and took a seat where he'd suggested. She turned on the cushion so she could face him. "Okay, what is it you want to tell me?"

Jase stared at her for a few seconds as if he tried to figure out what to say. Finally, he said, "Okay. Before I start, I want you to remember I do love you and that you don't have to be afraid of anything, especially not when you're with me."

"All right," she said as her brows drew together.

"I've been keeping a secret from you, about me. I'm not exactly like you."

Katarina smiled and reached between them to run her fingertips along the front of Jase's jeans. "I know you're not, and I do like your differentness—a lot."

He captured her hand and linked his fingers with hers. "No touching or I'll never get through this. You can do as much as you want after, if you'll still want to."

"I doubt there's anything you can say that'll change that."

"We'll see. Anyway, I'm different. I think it'll be best if I just get this all out at once." Jase took a deep breath. "I'm a cougar shifter. When a male finds his mate and has subconsciously accepted that she could be the one, she'll set off the magic inside his pendant and the cougar's ruby eyes will glow. Each male is given one once he reaches adolescence. It's the female's choice to claim it, and him, as hers by taking it from him and placing it around her neck, thus causing the mating bond to form between them.

"You set mine off. Once that happened, I was supposed to get a surge of testosterone. It would have me able to only think about sex, with you. I wouldn't be able to eat or sleep until you claimed me. I would try to make love to you until you did, but I skipped all that since you took my pendant and put it on while I wasn't aware of it. There, I said it."

"The eyes did glow. That explains why I had such a desperate urge to take your necklace. A cougar shifter. I never knew you even existed."

Jase gave her a perplexed look. "Aren't you feeling a little freaked out? My two cousins have humans as mates. When Aspen and Harley found out what Taylor and Blaise were, they lost it and had a hard time accepting them as cougar shifters."

Katarina grinned. "Shift for me, baby. Your mate wants to see her cat."

"You're sure? The way you're acting about all this, it's confusing the hell out of me."

She leaned forward and gave him a kiss. "Shift and I'll explain."

Jase's body blurred and shimmered, and then a large cougar took his place. Katarina inched closer and stroked the top of his head before she ran her hands down his back and sides.

"You're gorgeous, cat of mine. I'm going to tell you my family's secret. My uncle, who married my mother's older sister, is different just like you, except he's a werewolf. He's a lone wolf since his pack's numbers had dwindled to a handful and they all decided to go their separate ways. Uncle Mack ended up in Butte, where he met Aunt Julie. Their first meeting, and his first whiff of her scent, he'd known she was his mate. Within a week, he'd gotten her to accept his being a werewolf, and they were married at the justice of the peace. That was something my aunt had demanded. They have two kids, my cousins, Dawn and Mitchell, who inherited their dad's wolfy genes.

"They're close in age to me, so I grew up with them. I've seen them and my uncle shift to their wolf forms countless times. I've lost count how many times I wrestled with Mitchell after he'd shifted when we were kids. The whole family knows what they are and has kept it a secret.

So, my mate, you being a cougar shifter would never cause me to freak out. If anything, it makes me love you even more. If our mating bond is as strong as a werewolf's, then you are exactly what I've been waiting for."

Jase shifted once more, then took Katarina into his arms. "It is, though we don't have to worry about suffering separation anxiety. Here I was worried you'd run from me."

Katarina nipped his chin. "Never. Even though I didn't understand the significance of your pendant, I'm glad I took it from you. I now know what Dacian meant by 'your circle.' He's a cougar shifter too."

"Yes, but from another family group. We don't have packs like werewolves. We've even kept our presence a secret from them as well."

She brushed her lips across his. "Enough talking. Take me to bed. I want to make my cougar purr."

Jase gathered her close and carried her across the room to the large bed. He then proceeded to make love to her, purring out his pleasure.

* * * *

Katarina straightened, then stretched out the kink in her back. She was at her apartment, packing, and had been doing so for the last three hours. She'd made headway into it, but there was still a lot to go.

At least she didn't have to worry about moving her stuff into a storage unit. Now that she was mated to Jase, she'd never be moving out of his family home. It'd been four days since she'd claimed his pendant as hers. His parents and brother had immediately accepted her, and when she'd been introduced to the family group's leader, Jase's uncle had officially welcomed her into it.

She looked at the clock on her living room wall and wondered if she should try giving Jase a call. He'd been helping her pack and had been the one to drive them to the apartment. He'd brought his tablet with the program Dacian had given him to track Caleb through his cell phone. His prey, as Jase liked to call Caleb, had used it, and Jase had gone off to see if he could catch him.

Katarina now understood why the police hadn't been called in, even though Caleb had tried to kill Jase's uncle. To the rest of the world, cougar shifters didn't exist, and they wanted to keep it that way. Their numbers were smaller than the werewolf population, and the anonymity they'd worked so hard to build over time helped to protect them. No, Caleb wouldn't be facing human law, but he would cougar shifter law.

She didn't know what would be done to him once he was caught and didn't really care. He deserved whatever the consequences were. Katarina liked Jase's uncle. They'd hit it off right from their first meeting. She still found it hard to believe it was only recently he'd looked down his nose at humans. The way he treated his sons' mates, especially Harley, who'd been the one to find out what Caleb had been doing, she swore they were his daughters by blood.

Katarina heard the sound of heavy footfalls just outside in the hallway. Thinking it could be Jase coming back, she hurried to open the door for him. It didn't turn out to be him, though.

"Caleb," she said, doing her best to act as if she didn't know anything different about him. "You're back."

He kept his back to her as he put his key into the lock on his door. "Did something happen here? There appears to be new wood on the frame."

"Yeah. There was an incident. I got it fixed right away, though."

Caleb turned to face her without opening his door. "What kind of incident?"

Before Katarina could answer, Caleb's eyes narrowed,

and his gaze dropped to her chest. Too late, she remembered the cougar-head pendant. Being a cougar shifter, he knew exactly what it meant for her to be wearing it.

He shot across the hallway faster than a human could and had her by the shoulders before she had a chance to step into her apartment and slam the door. Caleb sniffed the air around her, and a low cat growl rumbled out of his chest.

"You stink of Jase, which means that's his pendant you have around your neck. Another male in my family group has taken a human for a mate. How disgusting. Since he isn't here, I'm going to assume he'll be back. So you're going to stay with me until I get everything I want out of my apartment, and he won't be able to stop me from leaving unless he wants something to happen to you."

He grabbed a fistful of her hair at the back of her head and force-walked her across the hall. Caleb opened his apartment door and left it open as he took her inside. With his free hand, he pulled a plastic bag out of his pants pocket, then pushed her toward the bathroom.

"Take off the lid of the tank on the toilet," he said. Once Katarina did as he ordered, he continued. "Remove the packet in the plastic zippered bag and put it inside this one."

She reached inside the tank and took out the item. There was a thick wad of cash in it. Katarina stifled a cry of pain as Caleb yanked her out of the room by her hair and tugged her into the bedroom.

She already knew there was another large amount of money under the mattress, so she wasn't surprised when Caleb asked her to get that one as well and put it inside the bag he carried. That completed, he steered her out to the living room.

The sound of a loud growl had Caleb painfully pulling Katarina up short by her hair. Jase stood in the open doorway, his upper lip snarled as he glared at Caleb.

"Release Katarina," Jase said, a menacing growl threading through the words.

Caleb shook his head. "Not unless you allow me to walk out of here without trying to stop me."

"You know I won't do that. You have to stand before our uncle and answer for what you tried to do to him."

"That isn't going to happen."

Caleb dragged Katarina to the window. He jerked the curtain and rod down from in front of it, then roughly slid it open. He pushed the screen out to land in the alley below. He positioned the both of them in front of the open space.

"To show I'm not all bad," Caleb said with a smile that didn't reach his eyes, "I'll let you keep your mate."

Caleb fell back with her but gave her a shove toward Jase at the last minute as he went through the open window. Only he'd waited a second too long, and Katarina found herself on the verge of falling backward instead of forward.

With a shriek, she made a grab for the window frame. Her fingers slipped, but a strong hand wrapped around her wrist and hauled her back into the room. Katarina whimpered as she threw herself into Jase's arms and clutched him tightly. He held her firmly to the point she almost had a hard time taking a deep breath. She didn't care and refused to let him go.

Jase kissed the top of her head. "Are you okay? He didn't hurt you, did he?"

"No, he didn't. I'm fine. I think he was more interested in using me to make sure you didn't try to stop him from running again. He got me to get all the money out of the apartment that he had stashed. Sorry."

"Why are you sorry?" Jase loosened his hold on her and leaned back so she could look at him. "You didn't do anything wrong."

"I heard someone in the hallway and thought it was you coming back. When I saw it was Caleb, I thought to start a conversation with him to keep him here as long as I could in case you were on your way to the apartment. I completely forgot I wore the pendant. Once he saw it, I knew he'd be able to put two and two together and figure out it had been yours."

Jase kissed her. "If I'd figured he'd come here when I couldn't find him at the location where he'd last used his cell phone, I never would have left you alone. I really thought he wouldn't return so soon."

"He's gone, isn't he?"

"Long gone."

"Sorry. If it wasn't for me, you could have chased after him and maybe caught up to him."

"Stop apologizing. We'll catch him. It won't be today, but we will. Grady has already decided he'll take over the hunt. Now that I'm mated, I'm not willing to put you in jeopardy."

Katarina stroked Jase's cheek. "You know I love you, right?"

Jase smiled. "Yeah. I love you just as much." He put his arm around her shoulders and walked her out of Caleb's apartment. "Let's go home. That's enough packing for today. Plus, I need to let Grady know what happened here so he can cross this off the list of possible places Caleb will show up."

Katarina allowed her mate to walk her into what was soon to be her former residence. Who would have known what she thought was someone trying to break into her apartment would turn out to be the best thing that ever happened to her. She'd found the love of her life and had the commitment she'd always wanted from a man. She now had years to look forward to spending with her cougar mate. There was nothing better than that.

MARISA CHENERY

The End

FATED TO A COUGAR

Out on the hunt for the fairer sex, cougar shifter Grady never thought he'd run across his other prey. As he follows Caleb on a mad dash through Anchorage's dark streets, Grady ends up on the receiving end of a metal pipe to the head. When a police cruiser arrives on the scene, Caleb takes off, leaving Grady in the dirt.

As a cop, Sage's job is to protect and serve, but she doesn't expect to be kissed senseless by the sexy man she's trying to help. She can't resist his charm—or his touch—and agrees to see him again.

A relationship started on passion changes quickly when tragedy slams into Sage's life. With Grady by her side, Sage finds the one thing she's been missing.

CHAPTER ONE

Grady took a swig from his beer, then nodded in the direction of a group of women who'd just taken a table close to where he and his friend sat. "What do you think about any of them?"

Dacian turned his head for a look before focusing back on Grady. "Not bad, but I think I'll pass. They aren't exactly what I'm looking for."

"I have to say the same thing." Grady watched one of the women put a plastic tiara on the head of another that had "Bride" on it. "It looks as if it's a stagette, which means they wouldn't be interested in a guy trying to pick them up, anyway."

Dacian chuckled. "True. They're here for a good time that involves lots of alcohol. Don't be surprised if their table gets noisy after they have a couple of drinks."

There was a loud outburst of laughter from that direction. "It's already started," Grady said with a smile.

He and Dacian were single cougar shifters who had no interest in dating the females of their kind. Human women held more appeal, especially now that his cousins, Taylor and Blaise, along with his brother, Jase, had ended up mated to humans and were extremely happy. Grady wanted that.

"I think this night is going to be another bust," Dacian said after he finished his bottle of beer, then signaled their waitress that he wanted another.

Grady first met Dacian three months ago, after Jase had introduced them. Dacian was Blaise's go-to guy for anything to do with computers and the Internet. When Jase had needed a way to track Caleb, Blaise's cousin who'd tried to poison Blaise's father, Dacian had been the logical choice. He'd given Jase a computer program to track Caleb's location every time the other shifter used his cell phone. It'd worked for a little while, but Caleb now appeared to have gone deep into hiding. It was Dacian's project to see if he could find any clues as to where Caleb had gone.

"Maybe the bar scene is getting old," Grady said. "We should try the mall or something like that instead. After all, that's where Blaise met his mate, Harley."

Dacian nodded. "I guess we could give that a shot. There definitely would be a lot of women there, but a grocery store can be just as good."

"You're welcome to try that, but you'll be on your own. That's not exactly my ideal spot to pick up a woman. I can just picture getting slapped if I went up to one and asked if I could compare her melons to the ones the store has for sale."

His friend barked with laughter. "That's what I like about you, Grady. You probably would do something that stupid just because you can."

"Damn right."

Another loud burst of laughter came from the women who were having the stagette. There was a tray of shots in the center of their table, and they pounded them back pretty fast. One looked at Grady and winked while she pursed her lips in a kiss. He smiled but made no move to go over there.

The waitress brought Dacian a fresh beer. She asked Grady if he wanted another, but he shook his head. She left to wait on another table. "So, any progress on finding where Caleb has slunk off to?" Grady asked.

"Nothing yet. The asshole has done a better job of keeping his tracks hidden than he did a few months ago. I think Caleb smartened up after his last encounter with Jase, which isn't working in our favor."

Jase had managed to track Caleb to an older apartment in the low-income section of Anchorage, a place none of them would have expected him to go. His brother had come close to capturing their prey, but Caleb had used Katarina, Jase's mate, to make good his escape. She'd been the superintendent of the building at the time. That had been the last time they'd seen Caleb.

Now it was Grady's job to bring him in. As a cat shifter, Caleb wouldn't be facing human law enforcement. No, his fate would be decided by Taylor and Blaise's father, Nate, the leader of their family group. Even though Caleb wasn't Grady's cousin, he was cousin to Taylor and Blaise. Their father was the older brother of Caleb's father.

"Well, let's hope he didn't smarten up too much," Grady said. "I need to find him."

"Don't worry. I'm not giving up yet. He's bound to make a mistake. It's only a matter of time."

Grady hoped so. He was afraid that as time went by, the chances were Caleb was no longer in Anchorage. If that happened to be the case, it was more than likely that Caleb would never be found.

After Grady downed the rest of his beer, he said, "Since nothing is happening here, I'm going to head home."

"All right. I'm going to finish my drink, then I'll go home as well. I have a new game that's calling my name.

I'll probably stay up all night playing it."

Grady shook his head with a grin. Dacian was a huge computer geek, but he didn't look like one. He was the largest cougar shifter Grady had ever seen. At six foot seven, with a body thickly padded with muscles, Dacian had the build of a werewolf.

"You're going to fry your brain if you do that too often."

Dacian chuckled. "Not a chance."

"I guess I'll have to take your word for it. I'll give you a call in a couple of days to get together again."

"Sounds good."

Grady stood, pulled on his jacket and headed for the bar's entrance. As he passed the stagette's table, the same woman who'd blown him a kiss let out an appreciative whistle. He smiled and shook his head as he kept walking. There was no way he was going to get involved with that. A group of women who'd been drinking large amounts of alcohol usually spelled trouble.

He zipped up his winter jacket once he stepped outside. A fresh layer of snow had fallen while he'd been in the bar. Now that it was mid-winter, the white stuff was piled high on the sides of the streets from the plows. Grady shivered as a gust of cold wind blew his way. He shoved his hands deep into his pockets and hunched his shoulders. He wished he could shift to his cougar form. His thick fur did a better job of keeping him warm than the jacket he wore.

Another gust of wind hit him, bringing the scent of another. Grady let out a low growl as he jerked his head in the direction the scent had come from. He took a quick look around to make sure no one was around, then put on a burst of speed no human would be capable of.

Grady followed the scent to the end of the street, which was a parking lot. He saw two men standing in the deepest shadows. He recognized one immediately. It was Caleb. The man with him was human.

Not caring who saw him, Grady put on another burst of preternatural speed and ran toward his quarry. He'd be damned if he let Caleb slip through his fingers after having no leads on his whereabouts for months.

The wind suddenly changed direction and blew from Grady's back and toward Caleb, who jerked around. Grady caught a flash of teeth as Caleb snarled and made a run for it. Grady didn't give it a second thought as he gave chase.

His prey led him through backs of buildings and down alleyways. After turning onto one of the latter and coming out on a street that was lined with industrial buildings, Grady swore under his breath as he slowed to a fast walk. Caleb was nowhere to be seen. His prey had gotten a little ahead of him, but he hadn't thought he'd manage to get away.

Grady came to a stop and looked around. Caleb hadn't gotten that much distance between them. He had to be around there somewhere. A cougar shifter didn't have the ability to just disappear into thin air. They had magic inside them, but not to that extent.

Something slammed into the back of Grady's head, knocking him to the ground. A second hit came before he had a chance to gather his wits about him enough to roll out of the way. The blow made him see stars, and darkness hovered around the edges of his consciousness. It felt as if his head had almost cracked in two.

The sound of a police siren coming saved Grady from another blow. Dazed, he vaguely heard a metal pipe being dropped to the ground near him and then footsteps running away. A car came to a screeching stop a few feet from where he lay at the side of the road. The door opened, and another set of feet hurried toward him.

Grady reached up and felt the back of his head. Wetness came away with his fingers, and the smell of blood filled his nose. He groaned. Caleb had done a number on him. He knew it was his prey who'd gotten the jump on him from his scent.

"Don't move," said the person who crouched beside him. The voice was female. "Let me check you to see where you're hurt."

"I already know where I am. It's my head."

"Let me have a look."

Grady turned his face in the woman's direction and had a split second to see she wore a cop's uniform, and how beautiful she was, before she clicked on a flashlight and aimed it at him. He closed his eyes as the light hit them and sent a surge of pain through his skull.

Fingers gently touched the spot where Caleb had beaned him. Grady sucked in a sharp breath when she hit a particularly sore area. At least his head had to still be in once piece. The woman cop surely would have said something by now if it wasn't.

"Sorry," she said. "I just want to see how bad this is. I think I should call an ambulance. You'll more than likely need stitches."

That had Grady surging to his feet. He moaned and clutched his head. The quick movement made it feel as if it would fall off. "No hospital. I'll be fine," he said with his eyes closed as he concentrated on stopping the world from spinning.

She grabbed his arm to steady him as he swayed a trifle in place. "I'm pretty sure you have a concussion. The doctor will want to keep you in the hospital for observation. I'm going to make the call."

Grady snapped his eyes open and took hold of the cop's hand that held her radio. "Please don't do that. It might look bad, but it really isn't that serious."

It probably was as bad as she thought, but as a cat shifter, Grady healed a lot faster than a human. By tomorrow the wound would be almost a hundred percent gone, and because of what he was, there was no way he could go to a hospital. One little blood test and the doctor would know there was something different about him.

"I have to disagree with that," she said.

He focused fully on her face. Able to see in the dark as well as if it were daylight, Grady had no problem seeing her. She wasn't just beautiful, she was very, very beautiful. Her eyes were an unusual light blue. What he could see of her hair that wasn't tucked under her uniform's hat was auburn. Plus, she was tall. He guessed her to be around five foot nine. Being six foot three, he liked his women not to be too short.

He looked at the nametag pinned to the front of her jacket. "Well, Officer Sage Moran, we're going to have to agree to disagree. There's no need for an ambulance."

"What's your name?"

"Grady."

"Grady, I have first-aid training." She lifted her flashlight and shone it into his eyes, which caused him to groan. "From the looks of you, my assumption of you having a concussion has to be correct. You really need to see a doctor." She jerked her hand with the radio out of Grady's grip. "I'm calling an amb—"

Grady took hold of Sage's hand again and tugged her to his chest before he brought his lips down to hers. He couldn't think of anything else to distract her, and the thought of kissing her had come to mind more than once since he'd seen her face. He kissed her deeply, pushing his tongue between her lips to get a good taste of her. Not sure if he could get arrested for coming on to a cop, he decided to get as much as he could.

He licked and sucked and couldn't hold back from purring like the big cat he was as Sage's fingers gripped his arm tighter and she kissed him back. Grady's cock grew hard. The scent and taste of her filled his head, pushing some of the pain away. She sighed into his mouth, and it took everything in him not to take her to the ground and see how far she'd let him go.

The scent of Sage's arousal wafted around them. From the way she continued to kiss him as if she were going to crawl inside him, Grady had the feeling she wasn't going to put an end to this any time soon. He wanted nothing more than to let their kiss go on, but the pounding in his head reminded him all too well where they were.

He lifted and looked at Sage. Her eyes were closed, and she breathed at a fast rate. Her lips were puffy from his kisses. Damn, even wearing her cop's uniform she looked delicious enough to eat. He definitely had to see her again.

"See? I'm okay," he said. "Will you go out with me?"

*

Sage blinked open her eyes, suddenly aware of where she was and what she'd been doing. Talk about totally unprofessional. She'd been so completely involved in sucking face with Grady that anyone could have snuck up on them—like the guy who'd hit Grady with the metal pipe—and she wouldn't have cared. This was the first time since becoming a cop she'd let her guard down while on duty.

She looked at Grady and had to admit his gorgeous looks were mostly to blame for her bad behavior, as well as the toe-curling kiss he'd laid on her. Even when he'd been down on the ground, Sage had to have been blind not to see he was a hunk. He had features a male model would kill for. His tawny-blond hair was on the long side, perfect for a woman to bury her fingers into and hold on as she kissed him for all she was worth. His eyes. They were such a light brown they were damn close to gold. She'd never seen anything like them, and right now, they appeared to be eating her up. Plus, he was tall. She had nothing against shorter men, but at her height, she wanted to be able to wear heels and not feel as if she towered over the guy she was with.

It dawned on her what Grady had asked. "You mean like a date?"

He gave her a sexy crooked grin that made her pussy clench with unfulfilled desire. "Yeah. A date. Then we can continue where that kiss ended."

At first, Sage didn't know how to answer Grady. Since she'd started her career as a police officer, she really hadn't taken the time to date. She worked long hours, and her being a cop wasn't something a lot of men could handle. Sometimes she had a hard time shutting off that side of her when she wasn't on the job. She had to have a tough personality to do it.

"I...ah..." Now she sounded like an unsure teenager being asked out on her first date. It'd been a long time since she'd had sex, but she hadn't thought a mind-blowing kiss would strip her of the confidence she usually had in spades.

Grady put his arm around her waist and tugged her even closer. There was no missing how hard his cock was as it pressed against her stomach. Sage quickly swallowed back a moan before it pushed past her lips.

"Just say yes," he said.

Sage heard herself agree to the date before her brain could catch up with her mouth. Grady took her lips in a hard, fast kiss, then let her go. She vaguely heard him ask for her address, which she gave him. He also asked her when would be a good time for them to go out. She mumbled that tomorrow night she was off work. He said he'd see her around seven and then turned and ran toward the alley closest to them.

She shook her head, coming out of the haze of arousal that'd taken her over after Grady had kissed her again. What was the matter with her? She didn't normally act so ditzy around a guy. She realized Grady had left before she could call an ambulance for him.

Sage took off at run in the direction he'd gone, but once she reached the alley there was no sign of him. For someone with a head wound, he sure could move fast. Deciding there was no point in trying to chase after him, she returned to her cruiser and got inside. She turned off the flashing lights before she put it into Drive and drove away.

She really couldn't believe she'd so quickly agreed to go out with Grady or that she'd allowed him to distract her enough to slip away without making sure he went to the hospital. Tomorrow night she'd get to see if he'd had someone look at his wound or not.

For the rest of her shift, Sage went from looking forward to seeing Grady again to dreading it. With no way of contacting him, it wasn't as if she could call and cancel. Then there was the fact she'd given him her home address without knowing anything about him. At least being a cop, she would know how to handle him if things got out of hand. The big question was, who would handle her if she got out of hand with him and jumped his bones?

CHAPTER TWO

"**O**w. Would you take it easy?" Grady asked.

He sat at the kitchen table at his home that he shared with his parents, his brother, and his brother's mate. Katarina, who'd become mated to Jase three months before, tended to Grady's wound.

"Stop being such a baby," Katarina said. "I thought all you cougar shifters were tough guys."

"We are, but that freaking burns."

"It needs to be disinfected with rubbing alcohol. I know it'll be healed by tomorrow, but it'll help to have it cleaned out."

"Yeah, Grady, stop being a crybaby," Jase said with a chuckle. He sat across from Grady as he watched his mate work.

"Bite me," he said with a growl. "I still can't believe Caleb managed to get the drop on me. I guess he did me a favor."

Jase gave him a confused look. "How can getting your skull almost cracked in two by a metal pipe do you a favor?"

Grady smiled. "I ended up with a date for tomorrow night."

His brother snorted. "With who? An imaginary woman? Caleb must have hit you harder than I thought. You're seeing things."

"No, Sage was very much real. She's the reason Caleb stopped hitting me and took off."

"He was afraid of a human woman? I'm assuming this Sage is human."

"She is, and she's a little more than just a human woman. She's a cop. She saw Caleb with the metal pipe and turned on her flashing lights and siren."

Katarina stopped poking at Grady's head and leaned around to look at him. "You have a date with a police officer?"

"Yeah. I asked her out after I kissed her, and she said yes."

His brother's mate whistled. "You kissed an on-duty cop? You're lucky she didn't try to arrest you."

"I thought she might, but it was the best thing I could think of to distract her from calling an ambulance for me. She insisted I go to the hospital. I don't think she would have taken no for an answer if I hadn't laid one on her."

"So, you only kissed her and asked her out for that reason?"

"No. Sage is gorgeous. I would want to date her even if I hadn't been trying to stop her from getting me to go to the hospital."

Katarina went back to cleaning Grady's head wound, and he sucked in a sharp breath. He had to be thankful his mother wasn't at home. She would have been fussing over him too much. His parents had gone away for the week. They'd flown to the Gulf Islands, which was off the eastern coastline of Vancouver Island in British Columbia. They owned a cottage on their own tiny private island. It was big enough—and had enough trees for coverage—for them to shift to their cougar forms and go for runs. Grady figured his parents mostly went there to have some alone time without him and Jase hanging around.

"At least we now know Caleb is still in Anchorage," Jase said, changing the subject.

"Yeah, but he got away," he added. "The male human he'd been talking to when I first spotted him was gone when I went back to see if I could pick up his trail. He must have had a car in that parking lot because I lost it there."

Jase shook his head. "That's too bad. It makes me wonder what Caleb was up to. It couldn't be anything legal if he had that meeting in a dark parking lot in the middle of the night."

Katarina gave Grady a tap on the shoulder. "All done. I have to agree with that, Jase. Who knows what he was up to, but it couldn't have been anything good."

"I was thinking he has to be running out of money," Grady said. "The amount he had stashed in that apartment that he took before he went into deeper hiding won't last him forever. As far as Dacian has been able to find out, Caleb still owns his house. There's a lot of capital tied up in it. If it suddenly burns to the ground, we'll know what that meeting was about."

"Actually," Jase said with a nod, "that makes a lot of sense. That way Caleb won't have to go through the hassle of having to sell it. He'd only have to collect the insurance money from it. That's a quick way to turn it into cash."

The more Grady thought about it, the more likely a scenario it could be. They'd have to watch Caleb's house for anything suspicious taking place around it. If Caleb did decide to do away with it like that, there was always a chance he'd risk returning there to take what he wanted from it beforehand.

Grady stood and walked to the fridge, where he took

out a bottle of beer. "I think I should tell Uncle Nate. As the leader of our family group, he could get others to watch Caleb's house when we can't."

"Good idea." Jase stood, went to his mate, and put his arm around her shoulders. "Now that your head is taken care of, Katarina and I are heading upstairs."

They walked out of the kitchen. Grady wouldn't be seeing those two for the rest of the night. With his room directly across from theirs, at times his damn sensitive cougar hearing allowed him to hear more than he wanted to. That was the only part that sucked about living with his family.

Grady went upstairs to his room. As he neared Katarina and Jase's, the sound of feminine giggles came through the door. He continued into his bedroom and closed himself inside. He put the bottle on his bedside table and then yanked his long-sleeved T-shirt over his head. The collar of it was stained with blood. Katarina had already put his winter jacket in the washer since it'd gotten the worst of it. Head wounds always bled like a bugger.

After putting his shirt into the dirty laundry hamper, Grady settled on the king-sized bed and turned on the large LED television that hung on the wall across from it. He sipped his beer and a small smile played on his lips as he thought about Sage. He wondered if he asked nicely if she'd cuff him, then have her way with him.

* * * *

Since Sage had worked the night shift, she slept until early afternoon the following day. Usually, she would have slept longer, but having two days off and then going back into work on day shift, she had to get her sleeping times adjusted.

After she showered, she returned to her bedroom to get dressed. Seeing the almost overflowing dirty laundry basket, she could no longer put off doing the washing. Luckily enough, she had something to wear. She tugged on her last pair of clean jeans and a sweatshirt.

She lugged her laundry downstairs before she put the first load into the washer in the main-floor laundry room. That'd been one of the big selling points for her when she'd put in an offer for the two-story semi almost a year ago.

That task done, Sage went to the kitchen and put the kettle on to make a pot of tea. She grabbed a muffin from the package she'd bought the day before and then sat at the table to eat it while she waited for the water to boil.

Before going to bed she'd come to the conclusion it wouldn't be a great idea to go out with Grady. She hadn't been thinking when she'd agreed to see him in the first place, and she wasn't looking for a steady boyfriend. Her work kept her too busy, especially now that she strived to become a detective. As for having a short fling, she couldn't separate her feelings enough to have one.

A knock on her front door brought Sage out of her musings. She went to answer it, having an idea who it could be. She pulled open the door and smiled at the woman who stood on the other side.

"I had a feeling it was you," Sage said as she stepped back to let her older sister, Macy, walk through the entrance. She carried an infant car seat with her six-month-old son, Josh, inside, almost buried under all the blankets on top of him.

"Well, you did tell me you weren't working today and that you'd be switching to day shift," Macy said as she set the car seat on the floor, and then took off her winter boots and jacket.

"Very true. I'll take Josh."

Sage picked up the car seat by its handle and carried her nephew into the living room. She pulled the blankets off him and unbuckled the straps. She laid him on the couch while she took off his snowsuit. The poor thing looked as if he couldn't move in it.

Macy sat on the couch once Sage picked up Josh. "So, how goes the police business?"

"Not bad. I'm still working my way to becoming a detective. The hard part is finding the time to study to take the test."

"You work too much. You don't even have time to date. I know you feel your career has to come first and that you're still young, but you won't be twenty-four forever." Macy nodded toward her son. "Wouldn't you like to have a rugrat of your own someday?"

"Of course." Sage gave Josh a kiss on his little pouty lips. She loved him as if he were hers. "It'll just be something I do when I'm in my thirties. Unlike you, I won't be ready at twenty-six to be married and already starting a family."

"You know why I wanted those things sooner rather than later."

Sage did. They'd lost their parents when Sage had been eighteen and Macy twenty. Their father had never been a great father or husband. Even though their mom had tried to hide it, there had been times when Sage and Macy had seen marks on their mother after their father had lost his temper with her. Once Sage turned sixteen, their mom finally kicked him out and told them the truth about her marriage. Then two years later, while Macy and Sage were away for a week with their grandparents, their dad had forced his way into the apartment their mom had rented and killed her. He took his life afterward.

So Sage understood why Macy had wanted to have a family of her own. As for herself, Sage had made the decision she'd become a cop. She wanted to be able to help protect women who were in the same situation her mother had been in. Something she hadn't been able to do for her mom.

"I know," Sage said.

"This is a change in subject, but since you're off tonight, do you think you could do me a favor?"

"What would that be?"

"Hank and I haven't gone out alone since Josh was born. I wondered if you'd agree to babysit so we can go out for dinner. I'd have Josh all bathed and ready for bed. We'll bring the playpen for him to sleep in. He's usually asleep for the night around seven thirty or eight at the latest."

Sage thought it over, but quickly decided it would be the perfect way to get out of her date with Grady. She'd just tell him she'd forgotten she had to babysit. With Josh already at her place when Grady arrived, it wasn't as if he could do anything about it.

She nodded. "Sure. I don't mind babysitting. In fact, why don't you go out for dinner and see a movie. If you want, you can even leave Josh here overnight."

"Really? I only thought to ask you to watch him for a few hours."

"Seriously, I'm okay with him staying over. I don't get to see him as often as I'd like, and he's growing so fast. It'll give you a break."

"If you're really sure you want to have him all night, I'm not going to turn you down. You might have to put up with me calling more than a few times to see how Josh is doing, though."

Sage smiled. "You can call as much as you want."

"All right. Then he'll be all yours tonight. That being the case, I shouldn't visit for too long. I'll have to get everything you'll need for Josh ready. Nowadays, I swear I can't leave the house with him without taking half of it with me."

"Do you have time to stay for some tea? I put the kettle on. I just have to make it."

"That would be great."

Sage passed Josh to his mother and then stood and headed for the kitchen. She took two mugs from the cupboard and smiled. Sage was actually looking forward to having Josh to herself all night, even if he'd be sleeping most of the time. For now, he was the closest thing to her having kids of her own.

* * * *

Grady pulled onto Sage's street and kept track of the house numbers until he arrived at her place. He turned into the two-car driveway and parked next to the vehicle already there. He got out of the car and then headed to the front door. Before he rang the doorbell, he ran his fingers through his hair to straighten it. The wind had blown it into his face. He touched the spot where his head wound had been. It was completely healed. He didn't even have a headache anymore.

It didn't take long for Sage to answer the door. He ran his gaze over her, thinking she was more beautiful than he'd remembered. Even in jeans and a sweatshirt she looked sexy. Her auburn hair was down and fell around her shoulders, which made his fingers itch to touch the silky strands.

"Hi," he said with a smile. "I hope you remembered we have a date."

"I do."

He frowned a bit when she made no move to invite him in or get her jacket. "Are you ready to go?"

"Actually, no. I have to cancel. I forgot I'd promised my sister I'd babysit her son. I'm looking after him overnight."

"That's okay. Have you eaten supper yet?"

"No."

"Then why don't I come in and we can order something for delivery."

Sage hesitated before she answered. "I don't know if

that's such a good idea."

"You have my word I'm not some nutcase. Besides, you're a cop. I'd be stupid to try something. I can help you babysit. I like kids."

Grady did, but he hadn't been around too many of them. Since cougar shifters lived to be around two hundred years old, they tended not to have too many kids. Family groups were mostly made up of extended family and others from outside of it who'd become mated to a member of the group.

She took a little longer answering that time. "Look, I'm going to be straight with you. I don't think I have time to have a steady boyfriend. I hate to say it, but my career as a cop comes first. I don't think it'll work out. And I don't date casually."

Grady wasn't about to let Sage push him away that easily. The kiss they'd shared the night before told him she wasn't unaffected by him. He had to say it'd ranked up there as his all-time best. She was the first human woman he'd ever kissed. He definitely wanted to see where their attraction for each other led.

He took a step closer. "I can understand that it would, but I'm willing to put up with that. At least take the time to get to know me better before you shoot me down."

The sound of a baby crying reached his ears. Sage turned her head to look into the house, then back at him. She seemed to search for something while she gazed at him before she nodded as the baby's cries grew louder.

"Fine," she said. "You can come in, and we'll get something delivered to eat. I have to get my nephew."

Grady stepped inside as Sage turned and walked farther into the house. He took off his boots and winter jacket before he followed her into the living room. A thick blanket was spread out on the middle of the floor, where he presumed the baby she held had been lying.

Once Sage noticed him, she walked toward him, then

passed the baby. "I have to warm up a bottle for Josh," she said. "You said you wanted to help, so you can hold him while I do that. After he's done, I'll put him to bed, then we can order some food."

Grady looked at the little person he held, not sure what to do. This was his first time holding a baby. Josh smiled and proceeded to try to stick his drooly hand inside Grady's mouth.

"Enough of that, you," he said as he pulled Josh's hand away. "You might like to suck on your hand, but I don't." Josh tried again, and Grady let out a quiet cat growl, which the baby thought was funny and giggled. "You like that, huh?"

He really was a cute little thing. Grady purred as he nuzzled the side of Josh's neck, causing Josh to giggle again. The baby managed to grab hold of Grady's cougar-head pendant as he lifted his head. He held it in a tight fist and refused to let go.

"Don't even think about putting that into your mouth," Grady said with a chuckle. "You might like it because it's shiny and has rubies for eyes, but I don't need baby slobber all over it."

"Here, let me help before he pulls too hard and breaks the chain on you," Sage said as she came to stand beside Grady.

"I doubt he'd be able to do that. It's pretty strong."

Sage gently pried the pendant out of Josh's hand. "Nice cougar. I'll take Josh now and give him his bottle."

"Thanks. All right."

Grady couldn't resist giving the baby a quick kiss on his soft cheek before he passed him to his aunt. She settled on the couch with Josh, propped him into the crook of her arm, and put the nipple of the bottle into his mouth. Josh greedily took it.

"I guess he was hungry," he said as he sat next to Sage.

"My sister has started him on solid food, but Josh still

loves his bottle. She said he'll fall asleep while he takes it, and that'll be it for the night. He usually sleeps through."

Already, Josh's eyes fluttered closed. "In that case, we should decide what we'll want to eat. I can order it while you finish feeding him."

"Okay. I don't think it'll take very long."

"Then what would you like to have?"

"It'll probably be easier to order pizza. I like almost anything on it, except for onions and anchovies."

"That makes it easy. Do you have a usual place you get it from?"

Sage told him of a pizza place not too far from her house. So as not to disturb the baby, who'd fallen asleep, Grady stood and went to stand near the entrance of the living room. He used his cell phone to find the restaurant's phone number, then made the call.

CHAPTER THREE

Sage set her gaze on Grady as he turned his back to make the call to order pizza. She had a great view of his ass, which was encased in black denim. His jeans were tight enough to show it off. His wide back tapered to a narrow waist. She had to admit he had a great body.

She sighed to herself as she fixed her attention back on Josh, who was asleep and still sucking on his bottle. It was already half gone. Sage had thought the baby would be a great excuse to cancel her date with Grady. What she hadn't counted on was him asking to help babysit and then wanting to order in food. For some damn reason, she couldn't bring herself to tell him no, be it going out on a date or inviting him inside her house.

Seeing him again brought how attractive she found him to the forefront of her mind. She wanted him, there were no ifs, ands, or buts about it. What she wanted to do with that knowledge was something entirely different.

Usually able to pick up a vibe off people who she thought she'd have to watch out for, Sage didn't get any of that from Grady. He seemed like a genuinely nice guy and seeing him hold Josh and hearing him make her nephew giggle had almost melted her insides.

Grady came and sat once again on the couch next to her. He spoke in a quiet tone. "I ordered a large pizza with just about everything they had, except for the two toppings you didn't want. It should be here in twenty minutes."

Sage looked down at Josh. He'd finished the bottle and had pushed the nipple out of his mouth. "It looks as if Josh is all done. I'll put him upstairs."

After leaving the living room, she took the stairs to the upper level and headed for her bedroom. Even though she had two guestrooms, Sage wanted Josh in her room in case he did happen to wake up in the middle of the night. She tended to be a deep sleeper, especially when she was trying to make the changeover to another shift.

Inside her room, she carefully placed Josh into the playpen and covered him with blankets. Before she headed downstairs, she turned on the baby monitor that sat on her dresser, and then picked up the receiver to take with her.

Sage returned to find Grady sitting on the couch exactly where she'd left him. He smiled as she closed the distance and took a seat next to him. She placed the receiver for the baby monitor on the end table.

"Did Josh stay asleep?" Grady asked.

"Yeah. He was out like a light."

"Good." Silence stretched between them for a few seconds before Grady said, "I'm glad you didn't cancel our date." He turned on the cushion toward her. "I was looking forward to seeing you again."

"I guess you could say I was as well." That was mostly true. Even though Sage had wanted to come up with a way to cancel their date, she really had thought about seeing Grady again. Now that they were together once more, she didn't mind having him around.

"So, what do cops do on their days off?" Grady asked with a grin.

"Well, this one, besides babysitting for her older sister, usually hangs around at home and relaxes. I get caught up on laundry, house cleaning, and grocery shopping that I tend to neglect during a workweek."

"Sounds exciting."

Sage chuckled. "No, it's not, and you know it."

"Okay, that's true. How long have you been a police officer?"

"A couple of years now. It can be a stressful job, but I wouldn't want to do anything else. How about yourself? What do you do for a living?"

Grady smiled. "Live. Seriously though, I don't work. I don't have to. I own stocks in my uncle's multinational software company, which is the biggest here in Anchorage." He said the corporation's name.

Sage instantly recognized it. "Yeah, you must do well for yourself."

The doorbell rang, and Grady pushed to his feet. "That has to be the pizza. I'll get it since I'm paying for it."

He left the room. She heard him talking to the delivery guy. It didn't take long for Grady to return, holding a pizza box. The smell of it made her stomach growl once it hit her nose. Sage hadn't realized how hungry she actually was until then.

"I'll get some paper towels," she said as she quickly headed for the kitchen.

She handed Grady a sheet once she returned. He opened the pizza box, and they dug in. A quiet moan pushed out of Sage after she took the first bite, chewed, and swallowed. It was exactly what she needed. She looked at Grady to see him watching her eat. He stared at her as if he wanted to taste her along with the food. A surge of arousal shot through her. To hide it from him in case she showed any outward sign of it, she took another big bite of pizza.

"Enjoying it?" Grady asked.

Sage nodded and swallowed. "This place always has the best pizza. I'd hate to tell you how often I order it. Cooking is another thing I find hard to do while working."

"You must work long hours."

"I do, and a lot of them can be during the night shift."

They didn't talk too much after that and concentrated on finishing their meal. Once they were done, Sage got rid of the pizza box in the kitchen and then returned with a beer for each of them.

Now that they were no longer eating, Sage decided to bring up the subject of how she'd met Grady. So far, she hadn't seen any sign of the nasty head wound he'd received. He seemed to have recovered rather quickly.

"How's your head?" she asked.

"Fine."

"Did you end up going to the ER?"

"Actually, no. It wasn't as bad as you thought it was. Even though it bled like a bugger, it was only a scratch."

Sage frowned. Having taken a metal pipe to his head, Grady would have been pretty lucky to only end up with a mere scratch. The light from her flashlight hadn't been the best, but what she'd seen when she'd checked his head the night before was a lot more than that. Yes, head wounds bled a lot, but the amount of bleeding he'd done, it hadn't been something as minor as that.

"Really?" she asked. "Then you won't mind if I look at it. I never did get a chance to ask if you knew who your assailant was before you took off."

"I thought you were off duty today," Grady said with a short laugh.

"I am, but that doesn't mean I stop being a cop. I take my job very seriously. Some of the guys I've dated in the past have said I'm too uptight about it, but that's the way I am. So, are you going to let me look?"

"There's nothing wrong with that, and I'm fine. As for the guy who hit me, it was dark and I didn't see his face very well."

"Do you normally walk around that area alone late at night? The buildings are mostly industrial. I thought it was kind of strange."

Grady looked at her, not showing anything on his face. He said, "You ask too many questions."

Sage didn't get a chance to say anything else before Grady closed the gap between them and took her mouth in a heated kiss. A small voice inside her said he used it to distract her from what they'd been discussing, but the rest of her didn't give a shit. She quickly lost herself to the sensations coursing through her as his lips moved over hers. It became more so once he pushed his tongue inside and stroked hers, tasting her.

Things quickly heated up after that. Sage basically said the hell with it, wrapped her arms around Grady's neck, and tugged him even closer. She wanted him. She didn't know if what they started would last, but right now her body craved his touch—bad. She'd just feel and enjoy what he could give her.

Grady reached between them and palmed one of her breasts. His thumb stroked back and forth across Sage's taut nipple. It immediately tightened even more. She kept hold around his neck, shifted, and fell back flat onto the couch cushions, taking him with her. His heavier weight stretched full on top of her with his hips wedged between her spread thighs, which had her moaning. His erection landed right on her pussy, rubbing against it, driving her arousal higher.

Soon Grady stepped things up a notch. He lifted his upper body off her, breaking contact with her mouth, and pushed her sweatshirt to her chin. He stared down at her bra-covered breasts, his gaze filled with hunger. With one finger, he traced an invisible line from the hollow of her throat to her cleavage. He hooked into one of her bra cups and tugged it to the side, exposing her nipple.

"Beautiful," Grady said on a sigh.

A noise that sounded like a true cat's purr pushed out of Grady as he bent his head and kissed the tight bud. Sage arched her back, pushing herself closer. Her heart beat faster and an ache built inside her pussy. She panted in anticipation, silently begging him to touch more of her. Once again in a man's arms, she now realized how much she'd missed it, how much she craved it.

Grady rubbed her nipple along his cheek and then opened his mouth and took it inside. He rested his weight on a bent arm as he used his free hand to caress Sage's side. He thrust his hard cock against her pussy, making her wish there weren't layers of clothing separating them. Wetness pooled between her legs, and she lifted her hips to meet his.

Their breathing became harsh as they strained against each other. Grady tugged the cup aside that covered her other breast and took the nipple between his lips, sucking, making her even wetter.

Sage reached down and pushed her hands under the back of Grady's shirt. She ran them up the muscles along his spine, scraping her nails against his skin. He groaned and released her breast.

He lifted his head and met her gaze. "I need to see and feel more of this gorgeous body of yours."

"I won't stop you," Sage said in a low voice. "I intend to do the same to you."

Grady gave her a sexy grin. "I get to go first."

He shifted to his side, wedging himself between her and the back of the couch. Sage turned to lie on her side as well, facing Grady. There was just barely enough room for both of them. She was about to suggest they move to the floor, or any flat surface that was a lot bigger than the piece of furniture they were on now, but the words died in her throat as he undid her jeans and then shoved a hand down the front of them and her panties.

Sage moaned as a finger stroked her pussy, playing in her wetness. It pushed inside her, pumping in and out. It wasn't until a second joined it that she could no longer lie still and rocked against him. She squeezed her inner muscles around the plunging digits while pleasurable sensations shot through her. Sadly, it wouldn't take much more of that to make her come. She was already strung tight.

She panted and ran her hand down Grady's chest, encountering his cougar-head pendant. It felt warm to the touch, and Sage couldn't resist wrapping her fingers around it. She used it to anchor herself to him as he skillfully worked her body.

Grady took her lips in a carnal kiss, his tongue thrusting inside her mouth, mimicking the movement of his fingers. Sage clutched his pendant tighter as her orgasm slammed into her, almost taking her breath away. She moaned against his lips, riding his fingers while wave after wave of pleasure swamped her. He continued to thrust into her pussy, pushing every last bit of her release out of her until there was nothing left.

He removed his fingers and nibbled her lips. "God, I love the way you look when you come," he said, his voice husky with arousal. "I want to see you do it again, but with my cock buried deep inside you."

"Yes." Sage reached for the button on Grady's jeans and undid it. With a quick tug, she had his zipper down as well.

She'd been about to get her hand around his erection when the doorbell rang. Sage stiffened and turned her head in its direction.

"Don't answer it." Grady grabbed her leg, draped it over his hip, and nuzzled the side of her neck.

"I have to," she said reluctantly. "It could be my sister.

This is the first time she's let me keep Josh overnight. She might be regretting that decision."

Grady sighed and slowly let Sage go. "You're right. You have to get it in case it's her."

Sage rolled off the couch and stood. She quickly did up her jeans and fixed her shirt before she headed for the front door. She smiled as she pulled it open, all prepared to see Macy standing on the other side, looking anxious. Her smile died when her gaze landed on the police officer who stood on her porch. She knew him well since she worked with him almost on a daily basis.

"Hey, David. What brings you to my house? I'm off duty today."

He nodded and took a deep breath as if he really didn't want to be there. "I'm not here about you being off. It's a personal matter."

Sage frowned. "I don't understand. What could that possibly be? As far as I know, I haven't unconsciously broken any laws, because that's about the only way I'd do something like that."

David looked at his feet, then back at her. "Damn, this is a lot harder to do when you know the person."

"Now you have me feeling a little nervous."

"Sage, I'm sorry." He paused, then continued in a businesslike voice. "There was an accident almost an hour ago. A drunk driver slammed into a car and pushed it into the oncoming traffic where it was hit head-on. The driver of the car the drunk hit was killed instantly. The passenger was rushed to the ER barely alive and not expected to make it." He paused again, a look of pity on his face. "It was Macy and her husband. You need to go to the hospital to be with her. I know she had a baby. He wasn't in the car. Do you know where he is?"

"He's asleep upstairs in my room," Sage said softly, not wanting to accept what David had told her. "Are you sure it was Macy and Hank?"

"I'm positive. I was first to arrive on the scene. I recognized them from the family picnics the department has in the summer. Plus, we found ID on them, which confirmed who they are. I'm so sorry. Would you like me to drive you to the hospital? As I said, your sister isn't going to make it. When I left the ER, they were doing their best to keep her alive."

Sage swallowed back the tears that threatened to rise to the surface. "Is she conscious?"

"No, and the doctor doesn't think she'll wake up. You need to see her before…" David's words trailed away.

She knew what he'd been about to say. Before Macy died. "I'll drive myself. I don't want to take Josh with me, though."

"Then don't take him," Grady said as he came up behind her. "I'll stay with Josh. You go to the hospital."

Sage turned and looked at him. "Are you sure?"

"Positive. He's asleep, and you said he'd more than likely stay sleeping for the rest of the night. I can handle that."

"Is there anyone you need me to contact?" David asked, drawing Sage's attention.

She shook her head. "No. I can call Hank's parents. They live in Fairbanks. As for my family, it's just Macy and I. We don't have anyone else. I'm legally Josh's guardian. Macy made sure of that right after he was born." Sage's voice cracked a little.

Grady put his arm around her shoulders and tucked her against his side. "Are you going to be okay to drive?"

"Yes," she said after she cleared her throat. "I'll get ready and leave in a minute."

"I'll follow you," David said.

Sage stepped away from Grady, feeling about ready to break down, but she wouldn't. At least not yet. She had to be strong, be there for Macy. She wouldn't let her sister be alone.

* * * *

Grady stood in the open door and as Sage pulled away in her SUV. The police cruiser parked at the front of the house fell in behind her. Once they disappeared from sight, he shut the door and let out a deep breath.

The night had gone from being perfect to a disaster. After Sage had answered the door, Grady had easily been able to hear the conversation that took place there. He'd wanted to go to her, but he couldn't since he wasn't supposed to know what was going on. Once she'd said she didn't want to take Josh to the hospital with her, there was no way he could remain in the living room. He'd had to tell her he would look after the baby. It would be one fewer thing she had to worry about. She already had enough on her plate with her sister not expected to live.

He returned to the living room and sat on the couch. Grady was prepared to stay with Sage for however long she needed him. Hearing she had no other family besides her sister, he wouldn't let her go through this alone. Yes, they'd just met, but he liked her a lot. He would be strong for her, help her through this difficult time in her life. He'd be a huge asshole if he left now. Plus, it went against everything he'd been taught. Cougar shifter family groups were tightknit. Each member could be counted on to be there for another when they were in need. Since she didn't have anyone to fall back on, Grady would step in and fill that role for her.

Right then the baby sighed over the monitor. Grady turned and looked at it. If Sage's sister didn't pull through as expected, Sage would become an instant mother. Even though Josh wouldn't remember his parents, he at least wouldn't have to suffer through watching them being buried or know what was going on.

CHAPTER FOUR

Sage sat in one of the hard-plastic chairs in a hospital waiting room. She'd been there for hours. She figured it had to be pushing close to dawn, though she really hadn't been paying close attention to the time. At least not until after Macy had passed away.

Sage had made it to the hospital to be with her sister before she'd succumbed to her injuries. Macy had had massive internal injuries and head trauma, and there had been nothing the doctors could do to save her. The damage had been too severe. Sage had been able to hold Macy's hand, kiss her one last time, and tell her that she didn't have to worry about Josh. That she would look after him and would always be there for him. As if her sister had only been waiting to hear those reassurances, her heart had stopped beating and didn't start again, no matter how hard the doctor and nurses had tried to bring her back.

Now Sage sat, numb to the world around her, waiting to sign the paperwork to arrange to have her sister's body moved to the funeral home of her choosing. She also waited to talk to Hank's parents. They'd only arrived a short while ago, having taken the forty-minute flight from Fairbanks to Anchorage. There was no question of Hank and Macy not being buried side by side.

The older couple stepped into the room. They seemed to have aged ten years. Hank had been their only child. At least a piece of him would live on in Josh. The baby was the spitting image of his father but with his mother's eyes and hair color.

"Sage," Hank's mother, Kate, said as she held open her arms.

Sage hugged Kate and then Hank's father, Max. "How are you both holding up?" she asked.

"About as well as you, I'd imagine," Kate said as she wiped tears out of her eyes. "I just thank god Josh wasn't in the car."

That would have been even more devastating. "So do I. He's still at my place. My boyfriend, Grady, is there watching Josh." Sage figured it would sound better to have Grady as her boyfriend than tell them she'd just met him.

"A boyfriend?" Kate asked with a small smile. "Last time I talked to Macy she said you didn't have one, and that you were too busy with your police work to date."

"We haven't been together that long."

"I'm glad you have someone you can lean on for support. Just to reassure you, we'll give you any help you need with Josh. We know he'll be better off with you. It would just be too much for us."

Sage had known she wouldn't have to worry about Hank's parents trying to take Josh from her. Max's health wasn't great, and he had been in and out of the hospital because of his heart a few times in the past year. Looking after a six-month-old baby would take its toll on Max and Kate.

"I know," Sage said. "Thanks for the offer. I'll be sure to call if I need anything. Once we get finished here, you're both more than welcome to stay at my place for however long you're in Anchorage."

"That won't be necessary," Max said. "We already booked a room at a hotel. It'll be less stressful for you."

Sage nodded. "Okay, but you're welcome to change your mind."

After that, the rest of the time Sage spent at the hospital passed in a blur. She filled out the necessary paperwork, barely paying attention to what she signed. Once she'd done all she could for now, she said goodbye to Hank's parents with a promise to talk to them in the afternoon to arrange a time to go to the funeral home.

Sage drove home. She was tired but didn't know if she'd be able to sleep. For one thing, Josh would be awake soon. On the way, she stopped off at a store to buy diapers and all the other things such as food and bottles she'd need for her nephew. She had a key to Macy's house, but she couldn't bring herself to go there to pick up what she'd need just yet. Though she'd have to do it very soon. Josh would need his crib and clothes. Plus, she had to decide what to do with the home.

She pulled into her two-car driveway and parked beside Grady's expensive sedan. After getting out of her SUV, Sage headed for the front door. She unlocked it and then stepped inside, placing the items she'd bought in the entranceway. The house was completely quiet. It was early enough for Josh to still be asleep. She figured Grady must be sleeping as well since he didn't come to see her.

After taking off her coat and boots, she went to the living room. The scene that greeted her had her smiling despite what the night had turned into. Grady lay on the couch, his feet dangling over the end. Josh was on his chest, his little head tucked under Grady's chin. The quilt from the playpen covered the baby and the sides were tucked under Grady, holding Josh in place. Grady had his arms wrapped around her nephew. The sight of them together pulled at her heartstrings.

Sage leaned against the wall next to the entrance to the room and slowly slid down it until she sat on the floor. She couldn't tear her gaze from them. Being sleep deprived and an emotional wreck on the inside, she crazily thought Grady would be the perfect replacement father for Josh. It was stupid to be thinking like that when she'd had one date with him that had lasted a few hours at the most, but at the moment, he was the only person in her world who she thought she could lean on.

She noticed Josh had his little hand wrapped around Grady's cougar-head pendant just as she'd done when she and Grady had been fooling around. It was the second time her nephew had taken hold of it. He obviously liked it, and Grady mustn't have minded.

Sage lifted her knees to her chest and rested her forehead against them. She closed her eyes. The image of her sister lying in a hospital bed, broken and bleeding, rose inside her mind. It would probably be something she'd never forget. She swallowed past the lump in her throat as she fought back her tears. She wanted to wail and scream about the injustice of it. Macy and Hank had been too young, and Josh should have been able to grow up with his parents. She wouldn't do any of that. There was too much to do to settle her sister's affairs.

"Sage."

At the sound of her whispered name, she looked up to find Grady awake and staring at her. Sage pushed to her feet and quietly walked to where he lay. Josh was still sleeping. She kneeled on the floor in front of the couch and softly caressed her nephew's cheek.

"Have you been home long?" Grady asked in a whisper.

"No," she replied just as quietly.

"Did your sister…"

"She didn't make it. Macy died about a half hour after I

arrived."

"I'm so sorry."

"Did Josh wake up for you?"

"Yeah. He wasn't too sure about me at first. The only way I could get him to sleep was on me like this. I tried to put him back into the playpen, but he started to cry again."

"At least you got some rest."

Grady ran his gaze over her face. "You need to sleep as well."

Sage shook her head. "I can't. Josh will be awake soon. You'll want to go home."

He stared into her eyes. "You have to sleep. I'm not going to leave you alone."

"You've been here all night. You'll want to change your clothes and shower. Plus, there isn't much to eat here. I need to go grocery shopping."

Grady reached over and cupped the side of her face. "Then you and Josh can come to my place. We have a personal chef who makes all our meals. You're more than welcome to sleep in my bed. I'll take care of the baby. My brother and his wife will be there as well to help. We all live together, along with my parents."

Normally, Sage would have been able to manage everything on her own, but not now. Having someone take care of her, make it so she didn't have to worry about anything, was something she couldn't turn down.

"Okay, I'll go to your place once Josh wakes up. I'll have to feed him and get him dressed, and then we can go."

As if he'd heard his name, the baby squirmed against Grady and opened his eyes. Grady sat up and shifted Josh until he had him cradled in his arms before disentangling the baby's fingers from his pendant.

"Hey there, buddy," Grady said. "Did you have a good sleep?" The baby smiled at him.

Sage stood and took Josh from Grady. "I'll get him

ready to go."

She grabbed some of the things she'd bought on the way up the stairs. Once again, she was glad Grady was there. For someone who'd asked her for a simple date, he sure as hell got a lot more than he bargained for.

* * * *

Grady took a quick look at Sage, who sat beside him in his car. The baby was in his infant car seat in the back. It'd taken about a half hour to get Josh fed, changed, and set to go.

Sage looked about ready to drop. There were dark circles under her eyes and she seemed to be staring at nothing. Grady focused his attention back on the road. No matter what she said, he was going to have her tucked into his bed as soon as they got to his house. She needed to get some rest before she faced what she had to do that day. It wasn't going to be easy on her, but he planned to stay with her every step of the way.

Once they arrived at his place, Grady hit the remote to open one of the doors of the four-car garage. He pulled in next to Jase's car and parked. After he shut the engine off, he closed them inside.

He carried Josh in his car seat and one of the bags Sage had brought, while she grabbed the other one. They walked to the entrance to the house. Grady stepped aside for her to go in ahead of him and motioned for her to keep walking up the short hallway.

They stepped out into the foyer. Grady was surprised to see a pile of luggage sitting near the front door. He saw his dad coming down the stairs from the upper level. His father smiled as he came to join them.

"I thought you and Mom were going to be away for a week," Grady said.

His dad shrugged. "Your mom decided she couldn't

afford to take an entire week away. We just arrived home about ten minutes ago." His father looked at Sage and then the infant car seat Grady carried. "Who do we have here?"

Grady put down the bag he held and wrapped his arm around Sage's waist. "This is Sage." He turned the car seat around so his dad could look inside. "This is her nephew, Josh. They're going to be spending some time here with me. Something happened last night while I was at Sage's place on a date and she was babysitting. Her older sister and husband, the parents to Josh, were hit by a drunk driver while they were out for dinner. They died. Sage has been at the hospital all night while I stayed at her place to watch the baby. She's Josh's godmother. She doesn't have any family to help her."

"I'm sorry for your loss," his dad said solemnly. "I'm Charles, Grady's dad."

"Thanks," Sage said quietly.

"I'm sorry as well," his mother said as she joined them from upstairs. "I heard what Grady said about your sister. You're more than welcome to stay here for as long as you need. You look about ready to drop."

"This is my mom, Olivia," Grady said. "I was going to put her to bed," he told his mother.

"Well, in that case, I'll look after the baby while you take care of Sage."

Before Grady could say anything, his mom took the car seat from him, then placed it on the floor so she could unbuckle Josh. She squatted and took the baby out and then managed to take off his snowsuit.

She stood and smiled. "He's gorgeous. How old is he?"

"Six months," Sage answered. "You don't mind looking after him?"

"Of course not. I love babies." His mom lifted Josh and gave him a kiss.

The baby's little hand came up and took hold of his mom's cougar-head pendant, which was identical to

Grady's. It'd once belonged to his father. All male cougar shifters were given one once they reached puberty. The pendant was made with a bit of magic inside. When a male met his mate, the cougar's ruby eyes glowed. It didn't necessarily happen right after the couple met. It could take days, weeks, even months. It was triggered once the male could accept the female as the one he loved and wanted as his, be it consciously or subconsciously.

Once that happened, he would only be able to think about her, being unable to eat and sleep. He wouldn't be able to stop thinking of making love to her, using sex to help convince her to claim him. It was the female who decided to claim the male as hers by taking his cougar-head pendant from him and putting it around her neck, thus having the mating bond form as their souls joined.

"You have the same pendant as Grady," Sage said. "Josh liked his, so I guess he likes yours as well. I'll take it from him."

His mom laughed. "It's okay. He can hold on to it if he wants. He can't damage it." She looked at Grady. "Sage looks about ready to fall over. Take her upstairs. I have everything under control here. I'm sure Jase and Katarina will be down soon as well. They'll want to meet Josh."

"All right," he said as he took the bag Sage carried from her and placed it with the other one. "We're going up now."

Grady guided Sage up the stairs and down the hallway to his bedroom. Once they were inside, he closed the door behind them. He walked her to his bed before he tugged down the covers, then stepped aside.

"In you go," he said. "I'll wake you up in a few hours."

"Stay."

He looked at her. "What?"

"I want you to stay with me." Sage closed the distance between them and put her hands on his waist.

"You need to sleep. If I stay I might get worked up, if

you know what I mean?"

She met his gaze. "I want you to make love to me. I need it. Right now, I feel as if my whole world has been knocked off its axis. I want the connection sex will give me. I'm about ready to break down, and I can't. Please. Stay with me. I promise I'll go to sleep after."

"Are you sure? You've been through so much."

In way of answer, Sage went on tiptoes and kissed him. She pushed her tongue past his lips and thoroughly tasted him. Her grip on his waist tightened as she tugged him closer so their bodies met. Some guys would have done their best to stop what was about to happen based on principle, but Grady wasn't even going to try. If it was something she needed from him, then he'd give it to her.

He wrapped his arms around Sage and took over their kiss. He licked and sucked, pushing inside her mouth. It didn't take much to have his cock fully engorged. What they'd shared at her house before she'd been informed about her sister... He remembered all too well what she'd looked like as she'd come apart in his embrace. He wanted to make her come again, but this time while his cock was buried deep inside her.

Grady slowly stripped away her clothes one at a time, learning her body with each inch of skin he exposed. Once he had Sage completely naked, she helped him undress. Now as naked as she, he pulled her close again. The feel of her skin-to-skin caused his cock to jerk between them. He sucked in a sharp breath as she reached down and put her hand around it. She pumped up and down, squeezing tight.

He let her stroke him a few more times before he gently pulled out of her grasp and lifted her onto the bed. He came down beside her, running his hand along her body until he reached her pussy.

Purrs rumbled out of him. "You're so wet."

"I don't want to wait anymore. I want you inside me.

Show me I'm not alone."

Grady gently kissed her as he shifted to lie between her thighs. "I'm right here for you."

He nudged the head of his erection into her pussy. He pulled back before he sank a little deeper until he'd worked his full length inside her. Sage moaned as he set a pace that was sure to bring them to release. She lifted her bent legs to either side of his hips and matched his strokes. Her inner walls tightly hugged his shaft as he surged in and out of her.

Grady purred again, unable to hold it back. Making love to Sage didn't compare to other women he'd been with. He was more in tune with her, wanting to make this good for her, to show her this was all for her.

He thrust into her faster, loving the feel of her taking him. She panted and moaned, clutching his biceps after he lifted his upper body off her. He sank deeper, his cock growing even harder.

As her pussy tightened around his plunging shaft, then clutched and released it as Sage climaxed, Grady's point of no return rushed to the surface. He growled like the cat he was and surged into her one final time before his orgasm overtook him.

Once he'd given her all he had, and she'd settled beneath him, Grady lowered himself on top of her, bracing on his elbows so she didn't have to take his full weight. He kissed her gently. He pulled out of her as he rolled onto his back, bringing Sage against his side with her head resting on his chest. He ran a caressing hand up and down her back. She slowly, by degrees, relaxed. She reached for his pendant and closed her fingers around it.

Grady kissed Sage's forehead. Her eyes were shut and her breathing had evened out. He'd lie there with her for a while to make sure she stayed asleep, and then he'd get up and see how Josh was doing.

CHAPTER FIVE

Grady gave Sage one last look before he headed out his bedroom door. She was sound asleep. He'd gently eased out from under her and gotten out of bed without waking her up. Now dressed, he went downstairs to see how his other guest was doing.

He found Josh being showered with attention from his mom and Katarina in the living room. They had a thick blanket on the floor, which the baby lay on as the women sat on either side of him, smiling and laughing at what he did. Jase and his father were on the couch, watching them.

"You two are going to spoil him if you're not careful," Grady said as he went to join Katarina and his mom.

His mother looked at him and smiled. "You can't pay too much attention to a baby. Is Sage asleep?"

"Yes, but I have to wake her up in a few hours. She has to go to the funeral home with her brother-in-law's parents to make arrangements for Macy and Hank."

"Will you go with her?" his dad asked.

"If she'll let me. I already know none of you will have a

problem looking after Josh for us."

"Of course we won't," his mom said. "Jase and Katarina were telling your father and me how you met Sage, and that she's a police officer."

"Yes, she's a cop. I suppose you also know Caleb got the jump on me."

His dad nodded. "Jase told me about your assumption of what he could have been doing meeting a human in the middle of the night in a parking lot. I have a feeling if we don't capture him soon, he's going to leave the country and we'll be lucky if we find him again."

"I know. Dacian is working on something that will hopefully help us find him. I don't know how he plans to do it, and quite frankly, I'm not going to ask since I'm sure it'll be illegal."

Josh whimpered, and Grady went and picked him up. The baby smiled and rubbed a hand wet with drool over Grady's face. He didn't care. During the night when he couldn't get Josh back to sleep right away, he'd had lots of time with him. He'd grown attached to him, as he had Josh's aunt.

His mother sighed. "What?" Grady asked.

"Seeing you holding a baby, it makes me want grandchildren." She grew serious. "You feel something for Sage, don't you? For only knowing her a short time, you've taken on a role of a mate for her by standing with her during a bad time in her life. And for someone who has never looked after a baby before, that didn't stop you from taking care of Josh all night. Plus, you brought them into our home so you can continue to look after them."

Grady kissed Josh's cheek. "I'll admit I'm falling for Sage. I have no trouble with Josh being a part of her life. I'm just not sure how she feels about me yet."

Jase chuckled. "Well, from your scent, which smells like sex and Sage, she has to have some feelings for you if she slept with you, especially considering the state of mind she's in."

"Jase," Katarina said as a rebuke.

"It's okay," Grady reassured her. "She at first wanted to cancel our date, but she reluctantly invited me into her place. Now, losing her sister who was her only relative, I think she feels as if she's alone. I'll do everything I can to show her she isn't, that I'll be here for her."

"Don't be surprised if she sets off your pendant," his dad said. "It already sounds as if you're falling in love with her."

Grady didn't dislike the idea of that. The few short hours he'd been with her and then helping her through her loss, he had to agree with his dad that he truly was falling for Sage.

His brother chuckled. "If that happens, Grady will be an instant father and Mom will be a grandmother like she wants."

"True," he said. He softly laughed as he pried his cougar-head pendant out of Josh's grasp before the baby put it into his mouth. "He's always trying to put drool all over my pendant or tugging on it. Sage is the same, minus the drool. She fell asleep on me before I came downstairs. I had to get it out of her hand. She has a tendency to want to hold it too."

Katarina smiled. "I have a feeling she's your mate. Aspen, Harley, and me have been talking about what it's like being human and mated to a cougar shifter. All of us agreed about one thing—we were drawn to our mate's pendant, wanting to touch it, claim it, even before we set off the magic inside. We found it warm, warmer than it should be just from normal body temperature."

"Interesting," said his mother. "Cougar shifter females don't experience anything like that when we first meet our mates. I guess a human mate must affect the magic differently." She turned to Grady. "If what Katarina says is what's happening to Sage, how do you feel about that?"

"I would want her as my mate, and I would accept Josh as mine as well."

"Then you'll have to let her know what you are either before she sets off the pendant or after."

"I know. The only problem is when to do it. Right now, she already has too many emotional things to handle. Me telling her I'm a cougar shifter might just push her over the edge. She's barely hanging on as it is. She's fighting to stay strong and won't let herself mourn her sister yet."

"That will come," his mother said. "I think you're right about now not being the time to tell her. I'd wait until after the funeral, which I'm sure will be sometime this week."

"I would imagine so."

Grady kept hold of Josh and sat in the armchair kitty-corner to the couch. He could handle being a father. If what Katarina said was true about Sage possibly being his mate, he was all prepared to settle down with her and the baby. All that remained to see was if she did set off the magic in his pendant.

* * * *

Sage awoke from a bad dream, calling her sister's name. She snapped open her eyes and looked around. It took her a few seconds to remember where she was. She sat up and glanced at the clock on the bedside table next to her. According to it, she'd only been sleeping for an hour, and she seriously doubted she'd be able to go back to sleep.

She rubbed her eyes, remembering what she'd dreamed about. She'd been calling for Macy, searching for her, knowing she had to find her. When she did, her sister lay bloody and broken, her eyes staring sightlessly at Sage. Tears threatened to rise to the surface, but she pushed them back. There was too much to do. She had to call Hank's parents in an hour to arrange a time with them to go to the funeral home. She dreaded it.

Sage lay back on her side and clutched the other pillow to her chest. It smelled like Grady. She closed her eyes and took a deep breath. Without him, she didn't know how she would have been able to keep it together. Making love to him had her not wanting to lose him. For the first time in her life, she wanted to depend on a man.

Even though her emotions were in turmoil, Sage was falling for Grady. After having the kind of father she'd had, she'd never believed she would be able to fall in love with someone so quickly, or even at all. Macy had found it with Hank, but Sage hadn't thought she'd ever have it for herself. That was part of the reason she'd focused so much on a career that a relationship came last.

Now she didn't know how she was going to handle being a cop and raising Josh. There was no way she could continue working the night shift. He'd lost his parents. He didn't need her being absent most of the time. At least she'd be given time off because she'd lost a family member, and more after that since Josh was now hers. She could get maternity leave, she hoped. It wasn't something she paid too close attention to.

Giving up on sleep, Sage threw back the covers and got out of bed. She'd changed her clothes before leaving with Grady, but she hadn't had a chance to take a shower. She didn't think he would mind if she took one. It would help wake her up.

Sage took her first good look around Grady's room. It was huge. There was a small sitting area complete with a couch, side table, and brass floor lamp. She figured there would be an en suite bathroom since this was more like an apartment than a regular bedroom. The first closed door she tried opened up to a large walk-in closet. Grady's clothes took up half the space. The second door ended up being the bathroom.

Like the rest of the room, its proportions were huge. There was a two-person whirlpool tub at one end, two sinks set in a granite countertop, and a glassed-in shower stall that had been done in black-veined white marble.

Sage found some fluffy bath towels on a shelf near the shower along with shampoo, conditioner, and a bar of soap. Already naked, she stepped into the stall and closed the door behind her. Once she had the water at just the right temperature, she ducked her head under the spray. She didn't take very long to wash her hair and body. The water did help wake her up. She turned off the faucet, then stepped out before she dried herself.

As she walked out into the bedroom, Grady came in from the hall. She gave him a small smile. "I hope you don't mind. I took a shower."

He closed the distance between them and gave her a kiss. "Of course I don't. What's mine is yours while you're here. I was only coming to check on you. I figured I'd let you sleep for another hour."

"I couldn't sleep any more. Do you have a comb I can borrow?"

He took her hand, led her to the dresser, and handed her the one that sat on it. "Here."

"How's Josh?"

Grady smiled. "Fine and getting spoiled rotten by my mom and sister-in-law. They've pretty much claimed him as their own and won't let anyone else have him."

Sage nodded. "Would you mind watching him again while I go to the funeral home? I don't want to take him there."

"How about I have my mom and Katarina look after Josh and I go with you? You shouldn't deal with that alone."

"Hank's parents will be there."

"I know, but they have each other to lean on. I want you to feel you can do that with me."

She finished with her hair and put the comb on the dresser before she turned to face Grady. "I'd like that. I've always been strong but going through this shows I'm not all the time. I thought it was hard when my parents died. I was just a teenager then."

"What happened to them?"

"My dad killed my mother and then killed himself. He was abusive and didn't like the fact she'd left him."

"That would have been rough."

"It was, but it made me want to be a cop so I could protect other women from suffering the same fate as my mother. I just wish I could have done that for Macy."

Grady tugged Sage into his arms with the side of her face pressed against his chest. She reached up and held on to his cougar-head pendant. Holding it made her feel more connected to him for some reason. A part of her wanted to take it from him and put it around her neck so she'd have something of his on her all the time. The "old" her before her sister's death would have told her to smarten her ass up and not be so needy, but this "new" her didn't care if it made her appear weak.

"How about you get dressed and I'll take you downstairs for something to eat. The last thing you ate was the pizza we had last night."

Sage lifted her head and kissed Grady's chin. "All right, though I'm not very hungry. I'll force myself to eat. I can't be passing out from lack of food. Not when I have Josh to think about." She kissed him again when he angled his mouth in her direction.

"No, that wouldn't be good."

"Thanks for looking after us."

"You're welcome. I'm glad I can help."

With her free hand, Sage reached up and traced Grady's lips with her fingertip. "I probably shouldn't be saying anything right now, but having lost Macy, I've come to realize how quickly I can lose someone. I don't want it to happen before I get a chance to tell a person in my life how I really felt about them." She paused for a few seconds.

"Don't take this the wrong way, thinking I'm usually this quick when it comes to relationships, because I'm not. Grady, I want you to be a part of my life. For the first time, I have strong feelings for a man."

He cupped her face and smiled. "I feel the same way about you. When it's right, it's right."

"Really? I didn't think you would since I tried to get rid of you last night."

Grady chuckled. "I didn't let you, though. I think I started falling for you when you stopped me from getting my head bashed in and tried to take care of me."

Sage let go of his pendant and with both hands angled Grady's head down. She ran her fingers through his hair along the spot where he'd been hit. Much to her surprise, there was nothing there, not even a scabbed-over cut. It'd only been two days. There was no way it would have healed that quickly, even if it had been minor as he'd told her last night.

She pulled her hands away and met his gaze when he lifted his head. "There's nothing there. I can't feel where your wound was. That shouldn't be possible."

Grady ran the backs of his fingers along her cheek. "For me it is. It's something we can talk about, but not right now. Let's wait until after you've gone through what you have to do for your sister."

"Tonight. We'll talk about it tonight."

"I don't think you'll be in the right frame of mind for it."

"I'm going to be up front with you. I can't stand being lied to or have people keep secrets from me when it'll affect me. You do either of those things, we won't work out, and I don't want to regret accepting you into my life."

"Then tonight we'll talk. If you don't mind, I want my family there when we do."

"Okay."

"Now get dressed." Grady stepped away. "I'll wait for

you in the hall because if I stay in here, I can't promise I won't take you to bed again, and that wouldn't be good."

Sage smiled. "You'd make me late. I won't be long."

After Grady walked out of the room and closed the door behind him, Sage took off the towel she wore and then dressed. She was now intrigued as to what he'd tell her if he wanted his family present when he did so. She wasn't sure what he'd say to explain why his head had healed quicker than should have been possible.

Once she was ready, Sage stepped out into the hall, where Grady waited for her. He took her hand in his as he guided her to the stairs. They walked down the curved stairway to the foyer before entering a large living room. His parents were there along with another couple Sage assumed were his brother, Jase, and his wife, Katarina.

Grady's mom held Josh. She stood when she saw them. "There's Auntie Sage." She passed the baby to Sage and asked, "Couldn't sleep?"

She shook her head. "No. Thanks for helping to watch Josh."

"It was no hardship. I've already told Grady I'll look after the baby when you two go to the funeral home. I want you to invite Josh's grandparents over here for dinner when you're finished. They obviously haven't seen him since they arrived."

"Thanks. I'm sure they'd like that."

"Good. You and Josh are more than welcome to stay the night with Grady. You shouldn't be alone at a time like this. It's not as if we don't have the room."

Sage couldn't help noticing how young Grady's mom looked. Olivia didn't look old enough to have two adult children. If Sage had passed her on the street, she would have guessed her to be around thirty-five years old. Even his dad, Charles, looked the same age.

"I guess we can stay over," Sage said. She actually didn't like the idea of being alone. She'd have too much time on her hands and would think about Macy and how she was gone, which wouldn't be good.

"Great. You must be hungry. I'll have our chef whip you up something to eat."

Olivia hurried out of the living room. Sage looked at Josh, who smiled. She still thought it was a blessing he had no idea what was going on, but she wouldn't let him grow up not knowing about his parents. She would make sure he'd know them, and he wouldn't be calling her "Mom" either. She'd only be Auntie Sage.

CHAPTER SIX

Making the funeral arrangements for her sister was the toughest thing Sage had ever done. She was more than grateful Grady had decided to go with her. Him just being with her helped her get through some of the rougher moments.

Hank's parents had accepted Olivia's offer for dinner. Once they were done at the funeral home, they decided to return to the hotel before they went to Grady's house since there were more than a few hours to kill in between. Sage had Grady drove to her place to pick up Josh's playpen. On the way, she had him stop at a store to buy Josh some new clothes since there was no way she was going to her sister's house to get more.

At her place, Sage led Grady upstairs to her bedroom. She packed a bag with a change of clothes before she set to work closing up the playpen to take with them. After she had it collapsed and bundled, ready to go, she sat on the bed beside him and folded the blankets. She set them aside before she turned to him.

"Will your mom mind if we take a little longer getting back to the house?" Sage asked.

"I doubt it."

"Good."

Sage threw herself into Grady's arms, pushing him onto his back. She landed on top of him and kissed him hungrily. She needed to get as close to him as she could, have him make her feel alive.

Grady put his arms around her and kissed her back with the same fervor. He pushed his tongue into her mouth and thoroughly tasted her. Sage spread her legs and brought her pussy on top of his hard cock. She rocked against him, making them moan.

As arousal beat at her, Sage left Grady's mouth and kissed a trail down to the side of his jaw. She reached between them and dragged the bottom of his shirt up. He quickly pulled it the rest of the way off and then threw it over the side of the bed. He snaked his arm around her waist and held her to him as he positioned them in the center of the bed, giving them more room.

After they settled in place, Sage shifted lower on Grady's body, licking and kissing as she went. A cat-sounding purr rumbled out of him, something he seemed to do a lot during sex. She didn't mind — it turned her on just as much as his moans and groans. She figured he had a different way of showing how much he enjoyed what she did to him.

Sage paused at his cougar-head pendant and brushed it with her finger. It was warm to the touch, warmer than it should be from Grady's body heat. She couldn't explain her fascination with it. The thought of taking it from him once again flashed through her mind, but she pushed it aside. There was something else she wanted more.

Lower she went, taking the time to drag her tongue along his washboard abs. At the top of his jeans, she undid them and then parted the material. Sage ran a finger down the length of Grady's cock through his underwear. It jerked in response.

She met Grady's gaze as she took hold of the top of his pants and underwear and tugged them down past his hips. "Earlier I didn't get to explore as much as I wanted. I don't intend to miss out this time."

"By all means. Explore to your heart's content. It might kill me, but I'm giving you the control."

"If that's the case, then I want you completely naked."

Grady helped Sage as she pulled his jeans and underwear the rest of the way off before she tossed them aside. She feasted her eyes on him. He had a great body, muscular and cut but not overly bulky. What really made her mouth water was his cock. Fully engorged, it was thick and long. From their previous lovemaking, she already knew it filled her pussy all the way up. He definitely could use it to make her want to scream his name in pleasure.

She straddled his thighs and wrapped her fingers around his shaft. She pumped it a few times until a drop of pre-cum appeared on the tip. Grady groaned, his hips lifting off the mattress, thrusting his erection tighter into her hand.

Sage firmly grasped him at the base and circled the head of his cock with her tongue. Grady groaned louder, a purr mixing with the sound. She gave him one last lick before opening her mouth and taking the head inside. She sucked back more of his length, then slowly lifted her head until only the tip remained. His hands fisted the covers under him as she took him in and out, taking as much as she could handle.

His cock grew even harder. "Sage," he said with a moan. "I'm getting too close. I want to be inside you."

Sage sucked him almost to the back of her throat and then released his shaft. She sat up. "I want you there."

She watched Grady as she took off her shirt and bra. His gaze followed her every movement. Next came her pants. Her panties, she took her time removing. She was already wet for him, more than ready to take his cock into her pussy.

Once she was as naked as he, she straddled his hips, then lowered herself onto his erection. It stretched her as she worked it in and out until she completely impaled herself. Sage lifted to her knees, sliding him almost free of her body only to push back down until he was all the way inside.

Sage continued to ride Grady, clenching her inner muscles around his plunging cock. She set a slow and steady pace that had her climax inching toward the surface. He reached up and palmed her breasts, tugging on her taut nipples. She placed her hands over his to keep them there. It was just enough extra stimulation she needed to have her panting, straining for her release.

As Grady let out a strangled moan and his cock pulsed inside her, Sage fell into her own orgasm. Her pussy clutched and released his shaft, milking him as wave after wave of pleasure tore through her. Once it was over, she collapsed onto his chest, gasping for breath. She found his cougar-head pendant with her hand and held on to it.

"That was pretty intense," Grady said.

Lost in the moment, Sage blurted, "I love you."

Grady cupped her face and brought her lips to his. He kissed her slowly. "I love you too."

His pendant warmed even more. Sage opened her hand and looked at it. "Why are the cougar's ruby eyes glowing?"

"They are?" Grady asked with something akin to hope in his voice.

"Yeah. Look." She sat up and lifted the pendant for him to see. "Why do I have this almost overwhelming urge to put it around my neck?"

She couldn't see what made the rubies glow. The light was dim at best in the room since the curtains were closed and it was getting dark out. With it being the middle of January, the sun set around four thirty in the afternoon.

"Take it."

"What?"

"Take the pendant. You're meant to have it. I want to see you wearing it."

The way Grady spoke, it was as if the idea of her doing what he'd said was something that would mean a lot to him. Sage couldn't deny the fact she really, really wanted his necklace, and she wasn't even one for wearing jewelry.

"Take it," Grady whispered.

Sage gripped the pendant again and slowly pulled it over Grady's head. She turned it over and looked at the glowing eyes before she focused back on him. He lay there intently, watching her with a look of anticipation on his face. She took hold of it by its chain, turned it so the cougar head would face out, and slipped it over her head.

*

Grady held his breath as Sage lowered his pendant around her neck. Once it settled on her chest just above her cleavage, he sucked in a breath. The mating bond formed in an instant, joining their souls. From the look of surprise on her face, he guessed she felt it too.

Katarina had been right. Sage was the one. She was now his mate since she'd claimed him by taking his pendant as her own. Not that she knew that, but Grady did. Seeing her wear it, the love he had for her solidified. She was his. The moment the bond formed between them, he'd gained not only a mate but a nephew as well.

"What was that?" Sage asked as she searched his face. "I felt something—"

He cut her off by sitting up and taking her lips in a heated kiss. His cock went instantly rock hard inside her. He wanted her again. He needed to show her with his body how much he loved her and was glad she was his.

Grady held Sage close and took her down onto her

back. He pumped between her legs, glorying in the feel of her pussy taking his cock. She clutched his ass and pulled him in tighter as she lifted her hips to meet each thrust.

He wasn't going to last long. Grady hooked one of Sage's legs over his arm and spread her wider. He sank deeper. He angled his cock in just the right way so it hit her G-spot. She moaned, her fingers digging into the tops of his shoulders as she held on to him.

She panted his name as her inner muscles squeezed and released his shaft. As she came, his balls rose closer to his body and his point of no return tried to rush to the surface. He pushed it back. He wasn't ready to come just yet.

Grady waited until Sage settled under him after her climax ended. He pulled out of her, then shifted to her side. With gentle hands, he urged her over onto her stomach, then up onto her hands and knees. Once he had her in that position, he came up behind her and stroked his hands down her back to her hips.

He held her still as he probed her slick entrance with the head of his cock. Grady purred at the feel of her wetness bathing the tip of him. He stroked her pussy without entering her, rubbing her clit with each pass. Sage pushed back and moaned.

Grady kept hold of Sage as he pushed forward and seated himself to the hilt inside her with one stroke. He stilled as her pussy spasmed around his length. After it ceased, he stroked in and out of her. She took more of him in that position, and his balls slapped against her with each thrust.

He reached around her and found her clit. He rubbed it as he surged into her. It ended up being enough to send her into another orgasm. She moaned with her release, and that pushed him over the edge. Grady pumped his hips faster, and with a groan that bordered on a growl, he climaxed, filling her with his cum.

With no more left to give, Grady wrapped an arm

around Sage and took them to their sides. Both of them breathed as if they'd run a marathon. He was satiated and didn't know if he could move again. All he wanted to do was hold his mate in his arms.

After what had just happened, there would be no getting around telling Sage about him being a cougar shifter later that night. He should have had that conversation with her once the ruby eyes in his pendant had glowed, but he'd wanted to see if she would take it from him. Hopefully, she would accept him for what he was and not get too angry with him for not telling her before the mating bond formed between them.

* * * *

Sage and Grady arrived at his house twenty minutes after they'd made love at her place. She helped him haul all the things they'd brought inside. Olivia had greeted them and informed Sage that Josh had gone down for a nap and that she'd put him upstairs on the bed in the master bedroom with pillows around him so he wouldn't roll off. Olivia had then asked how everything had gone at the funeral home.

"Good," Sage answered as she set down the bag she carried.

"Will Josh's grandparents be coming for dinner?"

"Yes. They asked me to thank you for the invitation." Sage shrugged out of her winter jacket.

"Oh, my goodness," Olivia said as she looked at Sage, then at Grady, and back to Sage again.

"What?" Sage asked, not sure why Grady's mother looked awfully happy all of a sudden.

"You're wearing Grady's pendant." Olivia's smile grew even bigger. She gave her a hug.

Sage tentatively hugged the other woman back. "Ah, yeah, I am. I didn't realize it was that big a deal."

Olivia let go of Sage and looked at her son. "You didn't tell her, did you?"

Grady gave his mother a pained smile. "It happened really suddenly. I sort of didn't want to spoil the mood. I'd already decided we were going to have a talk with the rest of you. I figured it would be easier that way."

"Be sure you do, but I have to say I couldn't be happier. Now I get my wish." Olivia gave Grady a kiss. "I have to tell your father, Jase, and Katarina." She headed up the stairs to the upper level.

Sage turned to face Grady. "What was all that about? The way your mom talked, you'd think we'd just gotten engaged or something."

"I'm going to leave it at you taking my pendant is a bigger deal to my family than you know. The rest I'll tell you later tonight once Josh's grandparents leave."

"Okay, I think."

She wasn't sure what to make of what had passed between Grady and his mom. It was obvious they kept something from her for some reason. They didn't appear to think it was bad, since Olivia had been happy about Sage wearing Grady's pendant. That could stem from the fact the other women of the house wore the same necklaces as well. Maybe in their eyes Grady giving her his pendant was tantamount to him asking her to marry him, and she, not knowing the significance, had accepted while in the dark about the whole thing. She guessed she'd find out one way or the other later.

* * * *

Sage spent the rest of the afternoon taking care of Josh. Since they were eating dinner in the early evening shortly after the baby went to bed for the night, she made sure she had him bathed and in his pajamas before Hank's parents arrived.

Bathing a six-month-old was a new experience for Sage. She probably would have done a quicker job of it if Grady hadn't offered to help by getting into the whirlpool tub with Josh to hold him while she did the washing part. Her nephew had a ball splashing them, and he moved around so much Grady said it was like holding on to a slippery fish.

After Hank's parents arrived, they took turns passing Josh between them. It'd been a month since they'd last seen their grandson. Kate got a little teary over the fact Josh looked more and more like his father the older he got.

Once Sage put the baby upstairs to bed in Grady's room, the adults sat to dinner. They talked about the services for Macy and Hank that would take place in two days. Much to Sage's surprise, all of Grady's family said they would be attending. Even Jase and his dad stated they would be around to help with the heavy lifting when the time came for Sage, Kate, and Max to empty Macy and Hank's house.

That was something Sage still dreaded, but it had to be done and put on the market. There was no way she could keep her house and the other one. She couldn't afford to pay the mortgage for Macy's with only her income. Max and Kate had their own place in Fairbanks.

Hank's parents said their goodbyes once it grew late and promised Sage they'd talk to her the next day. After they left, everyone else headed back into the living room. She couldn't help noticing how nervous Grady looked all of a sudden.

They all sat, spreading out on the couch, loveseat, and armchairs. Sage and Grady ended up on the loveseat, which was across from the couch. At first, Sage wasn't sure anyone was going to start the conversation since the others all seemed to be waiting for something.

Grady cleared his throat. "I guess I'd better be the one to get the ball rolling." He cleared his throat again, took hold of Sage's hand and looked her right in the eyes. "What I'm about to tell you, I've never told anyone like you before."

She gave him a confused look over the "anyone like you" comment. Was he referring to her being a cop or was it something else entirely? "Okay."

"I've been told it's best if I just come right out and say it without easing into it too much. So here it goes." His face grew serious, not showing any emotion. "Sage, I'm a cougar shifter. You set off the magic in my pendant and made the cougar's ruby eyes glow, which means you're my mate. When you took it from me and put it around your neck, you claimed me as yours, and the mating bond formed, joining our souls."

CHAPTER SEVEN

Grady watched Sage's face carefully to see what her reaction would be to his confession of being a cougar shifter and what she was to him. At first, her expression remained blank, as if she really hadn't heard what he'd said. Then it switched to one that was guarded, almost as if she thought he wasn't all there in his mind.

"You're a cougar shifter?" Sage asked. She looked around the room before focusing back on him. "Your family already knows you think of yourself as being one?"

"We're all shifters."

"Except for me," Katarina said. "I'm just a regular human like you, Sage."

Sage shook her head. "I'm sorry, but do all of you think you're doing Grady any favors by playing along with his delusions? That's what it has to be."

Grady blew out a breath. "I really don't want to shift to my cougar form in front of you just yet. I need you to accept it a bit more or it'll freak you out. You can't deny you felt something pass between us when you put on my pendant. That feeling of an invisible bond forming, tying us together, was the mating bond. I felt it, and from the look on your face then, I know you had to have as well."

"I can admit I did feel something, but how can you be sure it was our souls joining? For all you know, it could have been us only caught up in the moment, if you know what I mean?"

"It wasn't that. It was the magic inside the pendant. Every male cougar shifter is given one once he reaches adolescence, and when we meet our mates, she sets off this bit of magic, which makes the rubies glow. To have the mate bond forming, the female has to be the one to take the male's pendant and put it around her neck."

Sage skipped her gaze over Olivia and Katarina. "So your mom and Katarina wearing cougar-head pendants means they claimed their males too."

"Yes."

"Look, Grady, I'm a cop. Do you have any idea of some of the weird stuff I see sometimes on a daily basis? I have to say this ranks right up there."

"You're going to have to shift," Jase said. He put his arm around his wife. "It's too bad Sage didn't grow up with an uncle who is a werewolf like Katarina. It would make this so much easier."

"Werewolf?" Sage asked, really thinking things couldn't get any stranger than they already were.

"The hell with it. I'm shifting," Grady said as he stood and stepped in front of her.

Sage watched, transfixed, as Grady's body blurred and shimmered. In a matter of a few seconds, a large cougar took his place. She opened and closed her mouth a few times and looked around at the other people in the room. They didn't at all seem surprised. Actually, Olivia appeared happy with it.

The cougar Grady had become took a step closer, which snapped Sage's attention back to him. He purred loudly and rubbed his furred cheek against her knee. She didn't know what to do. She felt frozen in place, her mind desperately trying to make sense of it all.

"It's okay, Sage," Katarina said as she crossed to her and took the spot where Grady had been sitting. "Touch him. It's still Grady inside there. He's able to think and react as he would in his other form. He just can't communicate with you."

Katarina took Sage's hand and led it to the top of the cougar's head and got her to stroke him. Maybe it was because the other people in the room weren't freaking out or acting afraid, or because Sage was already an emotional wreck from her sister dying, but whatever it was, she wasn't having an "Oh, my god, run for your life" moment.

She pulled her hand out of Katarina's grasp and petted Grady one more time. As she looked into the cougar's eyes, she said, "Okay, I believe you now." She looked at the others. "Do you mind if Grady and I talk alone?"

Olivia stood first and came to Sage. She bent and gave her a kiss on the top of her head. "Welcome to the family."

"Family?" Sage asked as the notion took her by surprise.

"Yes, family. You're no longer alone, my daughter. Being Grady's mate, you're now a part of our family group and are one of us, as is Josh. We'll take care of the both of you."

Sage lost it. Tears welled in her eyes and there was nothing she could do to stop them. Through a sheen of them she watched the others leave the room. Everything she'd kept bottled inside since losing her sister came out. Sobs racked her body as a strong pair of arms gathered her close. Grady had shifted back to his human form, but she hadn't noticed until he sat her on his lap with her head on his shoulder.

She had no idea how long it took for her to cry herself out, but he sat with her through it all, gently rubbing her back, telling her how much he loved her and that everything would be all right. Once her sobs subsided into hiccups, Sage felt as if she'd been through the wringer.

"Are you okay?" Grady asked.

"Yeah, I think so."

"Are you okay with what I am and what you are to me?"

Sage wiped her eyes with her sleeve as she sat up and looked at him. "Surprisingly, yes. It was what your mom said about me now being part of your family. It'd only been Macy and I since I was eighteen and she was twenty. Losing her, it was as if I'd lost everything. I know I have Josh, but he's so little and dependent upon me. Now I have you. I can lean on you and you're always going to be there."

"I will be. You're my mate, a part of my soul. I love you, and I'll love Josh as if he were my own child."

She cupped the back of Grady's head and kissed him, long and deep. After she lifted her head, she said, "I love you too." She gave him a small smile. "I guess you being a cougar shifter is the reason your head healed so fast, huh?"

"Yeah. We heal a lot faster than humans."

"I guess I have a lot to learn about what you are."

"Don't worry. No one is going to test you on it," Grady said with a crooked grin.

"Good."

"Now let's tell everyone that you're okay with us and that you're feeling better."

Grady stood and put Sage onto her feet. She placed her arm around his waist as he wrapped his along her shoulders, tucking her against his side. She was sure she'd have a ton of questions, but right at that moment, all she cared about was the fact he was hers and would never leave her. Facing a life with no family scared her more than him being able to shift into a cougar.

* * * *

It was three weeks after her sister had died and Grady had revealed what he was to Sage. She was back on the job, but only temporarily. She'd given her two-week notice and would no longer be a cop after that. Raising Josh was more important, and she wanted to be the kind of aunt slash mother Macy would have wanted for her son. Her sister had planned to be a stay-at-home mom, so Sage would be as well. It wasn't as if she needed to work. Her mate had more than enough money to support the three of them.

After going through her sister's belongings and getting the house on the market, Sage had focused on selling her own as well. She and Josh had moved into Grady's family home. The baby even had his own room right next to hers and Grady's. It'd been a guestroom, which Olivia had turned into a nursery. She'd even slipped in a few stuffed cougars instead of teddy bears.

This was the last day Sage would be on duty. It was an afternoon shift, but she didn't worry about Josh. The rest of her family was always there whenever she needed them to watch him. That was one thing she really liked about cougar shifter family groups. They always looked after one of their own.

Sage had learned about Caleb, the guy who'd jumped Grady the night she'd met him. Once back at work, she'd been using her police resources to see if she could get any leads on Caleb's whereabouts. Her methods were legal, unlike Dacian's. She'd turned a blind eye to whatever he did.

It was getting close to the end of her shift. Sage decided she'd do a drive-by of Caleb's house. Grady, Jase, and his cousins, Taylor and Blaise, took turns watching the place in case their suspicions about Caleb wanting to torch it turned out to be correct. So far, nothing had happened there.

She pulled the cruiser to the curb and scanned the front of the large house. There were no lights on anywhere inside or outside. With another pass, Sage caught something that looked like a person-shaped shadow darker than the rest heading around a corner toward the backyard. Not wanting to take any chances, she shut off the car's engine, then got out with her flashlight in hand. She headed in the direction she'd seen the shape go.

There was a full moon that night, and its light reflected off the snow. Sage turned on her flashlight once she neared the corner of the house. Since no one had shoveled in a while, the snow was deep. There were footprints in it that looked fresh. She followed them, keeping an eye out for the person who'd made them.

It didn't take her long to find him. He had his back to her, bent over, working on something. She heard the distinctive rasping sound of a lighter being used, but the wind must have blown it out. It didn't work in his favor either since it blew in their direction right into their faces.

"What are you doing?" she asked loudly.

The man shot around, and Sage aimed the light she held into his eyes. The first thing she noticed was that it was Caleb who stood a short distance in front of her. She'd seen pictures of him. The second, he held in one hand a glass bottle that had a rag hanging out of the top, which couldn't be anything but a Molotov cocktail, and in the other a lighter. It didn't take a genius to figure out what he was going to do with them.

"Everything is fine, officer," Caleb said. "This is my house. I locked my keys inside and was going to look for the spare one I have hidden in the yard."

"Really," she said. "You were going to use that homemade bomb to light the way for you?"

"It isn't what you think it is."

"Drop what you're holding and walk toward me,

keeping your hands in sight."

"You're overreacting. As I said before, this is my house. I'm not breaking any laws."

"You will do as I say, or I'll force you to comply."

Caleb walked toward her but made no move to drop what he held. "What's your name, officer? I'm going to go to your superior and tell him how you harassed me for no reason."

Once he was close enough, Sage said, "You can try, Caleb, but since this is my last night on the job, I don't think it matters."

He stopped and stiffened. "How do you know my name?"

Sage put one hand behind her back as she pulled out the cougar-head pendant she wore under her uniform shirt with the other after she pocketed her flashlight. Caleb's eyes widened, and he sniffed the air and a look of fury passed over his face.

"You're Grady's," he said with a snarl. "Did he send a woman after me?"

"No. I decided to come here by myself since I have more experience taking in scumbags like you."

"Do you think that you, a mere human, can best me enough to subdue me? I'm a cougar shifter. I'm faster and stronger than you."

As if to prove his words, Caleb let loose with a cat's growl and launched himself at her. Too bad for him, Sage had been all prepared for that. She pulled the hand she had at her back to her front and aimed her Taser gun right at him. She fired, and the two small electrodes hit him in the thigh. He went down like a ton of bricks, no longer able to move as his muscles involuntarily contracted.

Sage closed the distance between them and looked down at him. She kept the electricity flowing from the gun to Caleb. "Yeah, you might be faster and stronger, but you're no match for a Taser gun just like every other criminal out there. Now be a good boy and shift to your cougar form."

She turned off the juice and waited to see if Caleb would do as she'd ordered. Of course he didn't. Once he'd recovered enough to be able to move again, he growled threateningly and tried to have another go at her. Sage jolted him a second time, rendering him immobile.

"Go to hell, bitch," he said through clenched teeth.

"Wrong answer." She squatted in front of him. "If a human gets zapped too many times, it can kill them. As for a cougar shifter, who can heal a lot quicker, I'm not sure how many jolts you can take, but I'm willing to find out. Either you shift so I can put zip ties on you or you get the juice for however long it takes Grady and whoever else in his family wants to come collect you to bring you to face our family group leader. It's your choice."

To show she meant business, Sage turned off the electricity before she zapped Caleb again. It didn't take him long before he complied. It was then she found out a cougar shifter could take on his cat form while being tased. Obviously, the magic inside them wasn't affected.

After the change was complete, she quickly zip-tied his front legs together and then his back, and for good measure, she tied the front and back together as well. Satisfied he wouldn't be going anywhere, Sage turned off the juice and pulled the electrodes out of Caleb's leg. He snarled, showing off his sharp teeth. She chuckled.

Sage straightened and pulled her cell phone from the inside pocket of her uniform jacket and called Grady. After she explained the situation, he assured her that he, Jase, Taylor, and Blaise would be over to collect Caleb as quickly as possible.

Since Caleb's place wasn't in the same general area of her new home and Taylor and Blaise's, it took the men about twenty minutes to arrive. They came running toward her. Once Grady reached her, he tugged her close and kissed her almost senseless.

"I can't believe you caught Caleb after all the months we've been trying," Grady said once he released her.

"It was just a matter of being in the right place at the right time. Plus, I had some help from something none of you have." Sage help up her Taser gun. "It would seem cougar shifters aren't immune to being tased."

Taylor laughed. "Did you get him after he shifted?"

"No, I hit him before that."

"Then how did you get him to shift and lie still long enough for you to tie him up so well?"

"I told him he either shifted, allowing me to zip tie him, or I'd keep the juice going to him until you guys showed up. He chose the first option."

"Remind me never to piss your mate off, Grady," Blaise said with a laugh. "I think she's too friendly with that Taser gun of hers."

Sage chuckled. "You have nothing to worry about from me. Well, if you guys can take care of Caleb, I should get back on the road. My shift is almost finished, and I have to get to the station."

Grady pulled her to him again. "Are you still okay with giving up police work? You're giving up your chance to be a detective."

She smiled. "Raising Josh will be more rewarding, and he deserves to have me home. As do you."

"Well, if you're firm on it, I'm not going to complain." He grabbed her ass. "Though I'm going to miss seeing you wear your police officer uniform. It turns me on."

"I get to keep it," she said with a wink. "I can wear it anytime you want."

Jase cleared his throat. "You two do realize you aren't alone? I so didn't need to hear that."

Taylor and Blaise hefted Caleb out of the snow between them. "Time to go," Taylor said. "Dad will be happy to see what you caught him. I'm sure he'll want to see you tomorrow, Sage."

"Grady, Josh, and me will be by sometime."

After Taylor and Blaise left, carting Caleb with them, Jase said he'd meet his brother at home. Once Sage and Grady were alone, they slowly walked toward the front of the house. She was more than ready to turn in her badge and gun at her shift's end. In less than a month, her life had changed, some for the bad and a lot for the good. As she looked at the man she loved, she knew she'd never have to worry about being alone again. She owned her cougar shifter's soul as much as he owned hers.

The End

ABOUT THE AUTHOR

Marisa Chenery was always a lover of books, but after reading her first historical romance novel she found herself hooked. Having inherited a love for the written word, she soon started writing her own novels.

She now writes young adult books and erotic romances.

Marisa lives in Ontario, Canada, with her boyfriend, Steve, four children, four grandchildren (she's a young grandma in her fifties) and rabbit and dog.

www.marisachenery.com